THE BLANKING BRIDE

"Nicole?"

No response.

I touched her arm and again called her name.

She looked at me. Blankly.

"Are you okay?" I asked.

"Who are you?" she asked.

"Hank. Dr. Lawson. We met earlier."

She stared at me for a beat but said nothing.

"I'm your grandmother's doctor. Remember?"

No response. She glanced at Jill and then turned her eyes back toward me. "Why are you here?"

Now I was getting concerned. "Your party."

"Party?" Her gaze again rose to the night sky.

I grabbed her arm and gave it a shake. "Nicole?"

She looked at me, her face expressionless, her pupils slightly dilated but no more so than would be expected in the dim light that filtered down from the patio.

"Who are you?"

Other Books by D. P. Lyle

NONFICTION

Murder and Mayhem: A Doctor Answers Medical and Forensic Questions for Mystery Writers

Forensics for Dummies

Forensics and Fiction: Clever, Intriguing, and Downright Odd Questions from Crime Writers

Howdunnit: Forensics: A Guide for Writers

FICTION

Stress Fracture
(A Dub Walker Thriller)

Hot Lights, Cold Steel
(A Dub Walker Thriller)

Devil's Playground
(A Samantha Cody Thriller)

Double Blind
(A Samantha Cody Thriller)

RoyalPains

First,
Do No Harm

D. P. Lyle

AN OBSIDIAN MYSTERY

OBSIDIAN
Published by New American Library, a division of
Penguin Group (USA) Inc., 375 Hudson Street,
New York, New York 10014, USA
Penguin Group (Canada), 90 Eglinton Avenue East, Suite 700, Toronto,
Ontario M4P 2Y3, Canada (a division of Pearson Penguin Canada Inc.)
Penguin Books Ltd., 80 Strand, London WC2R 0RL, England
Penguin Ireland, 25 St. Stephen's Green, Dublin 2,
Ireland (a division of Penguin Books Ltd.)
Penguin Group (Australia), 250 Camberwell Road, Camberwell, Victoria 3124,
Australia (a division of Pearson Australia Group Pty. Ltd.)
Penguin Books India Pvt. Ltd., 11 Community Centre, Panchsheel Park,
New Delhi - 110 017, India
Penguin Group (NZ), 67 Apollo Drive, Rosedale, Auckland 0632,
New Zealand (a division of Pearson New Zealand Ltd.)
Penguin Books (South Africa) (Pty.) Ltd., 24 Sturdee Avenue,
Rosebank, Johannesburg 2196, South Africa

Penguin Books Ltd., Registered Offices:
80 Strand, London WC2R 0RL, England

First published by Obsidian, an imprint of New American Library,
a division of Penguin Group (USA) Inc.

First Printing, June 2011
10 9 8 7 6 5 4 3 2 1

ACKNOWLEDGMENTS

There are many people who made this book possible and I wish to thank each of them.

Lee Goldberg, who suggested me as the author for this series and introduced me to the world of tie-in novels.

Andrew Lenchewski and John P. Rogers for creating the *Royal Pains* TV show and the wonderful characters that populate the series.

My wonderful agent, Kimberley Cameron of Kimberley Cameron and Associates.

My equally wonderful editors, Sandra Harding and Elizabeth Bistrow, who offered needed advice and criticism.

All the great folks at Penguin, including the publisher of New American Library, Kara Welsh.

The Hamptons:
Exile or Refuge?

Life is funny. Just when you think you have it figured out, a curveball comes your way. For me, it came down to a single word: *triage*.

An odd word, for sure. But then we got it from the French, so what do you expect?

In a medical setting, it saves lives. Most of the time.

To the French, *triage* means "selecting," or "sorting." In medicine, it means to prioritize patients by need.

Every busy emergency department has a triage system. The one I had worked at did. A physician or nurse performs a quick cursory exam of each patient who comes through the door, and rather than rushing everyone into a treatment or trauma room on a first-come basis, the ones in the most precarious situations jump to the front of the line. Just common sense and good medicine.

Such a system becomes critical when the ER is overrun. Like when the Friday-night knife and gun club kicks into gear. You know, too much to drink, someone looks at someone the wrong way or hits on the wrong woman, and the weapons are hauled out. Soon the ER is smothered with the dead and the dying, the bleeding and the screaming, the angry and the frightened.

Seen it a hundred times.

So triage is your friend. Right up until it isn't.

That's what happened to me. Triage bit my butt.

I'm Hank Lawson. Dr. Hank Lawson. I now run a concierge practice in the Hamptons, but not long ago I ran an ER. A very busy ER.

One day we got hit. *Hard.* I was working on several patients at once, focusing on the most needy. Two in particular: a teenager who had suffered a cardiac arrest and an elderly man with an evolving heart attack—an acute MI to those of us in the profession. I moved both to the front of the line. The kid's CPR was successful and I managed to stabilize the MI patient.

So far, so good. Or so I thought.

In medical emergencies, stable is a relative thing. Often temporary. It can change in a heartbeat. Literally. A patient spiraling downhill toward death can be yanked back from the brink, while another that seemed to have weathered some crisis suddenly begins the death spiral.

The kid was the most fragile, the most likely to take a turn, the one that most needed my attention. He got it. His life was saved. While I was doing that, the MI guy wasn't so lucky. His condition headed south and ultimately he died. It happens. An MI kills someone every minute of every day. Even in hospitals.

The real problem? Mr. MI was Mr. Clayton Gardner. A very important man. A pillar of the hospital. A billion-dollar bank account and huge hospital donations will do that.

The next thing I knew, I was in front of a hospital review board, defending my "mistake." The board's take on it. To me it was a judgment call, and those can sometimes go wrong. I did it. I'd do it the same way again. The board thought differently and I was fired.

For the first time in my life I didn't have a job or school or somewhere to be or something to do.

Scary.

Things got worse from there.

No jobs opened. The word was out. I was blackballed from medicine in a way that only big money, huge money, could do. No ER work, no hospital privileges, and nothing on the horizon.

Even my fiancée decided I was a loser. She took off, leaving me a chair, a TV, and not much else.

Welcome to depression city. I slept. I brooded. I drank. I became addicted to the convenience and avoidance of social interaction supplied by frozen pizza. I sat in my one chair and watched reruns of, well, everything. Over and over. God, Lucy was funny.

My younger brother, Evan, a piece of work in the purest sense of the phrase, coerced me into a trip to the Hamptons for Memorial Day weekend. He said I needed to meet new people. I said Lucy and Ethel were enough. He said I needed a change of scenery. I said channel hopping and reruns were fine. He said I had no money and a pile of bills to pay. I didn't have a response to that. So I said okay, but just the weekend. No more.

Amazing how plans change.

During a party one night I saved a young woman's life. At the estate of a very wealthy middle-aged, mysterious dude named Boris. His full name, I later learned, was Boris Kuester von Jurgens-Ratenicz. A mouthful and a half, so everyone simply called him Boris.

Grateful for my help, and my discretion, Boris offered to pay me. I refused. He refused my refusal, so as Evan and I drove away from Boris's estate, Evan noticed a metallic briefcase in the backseat. Like a scene from *Pulp Fiction*, when he popped it open, a glittering gold bar stared back. Not coins or medallions or even pieces of eight, but a bar of pure gold. I never knew those actually existed except at Fort Knox and in movies. I remember James Bond's nemesis Auric Goldfinger being in love with them.

Ultimately, Boris fired his old concierge doc and I became his personal physician, and he my first true Hamptons patient. He even installed Evan and me in his guesthouse. Some guesthouse. In Middle America it would have gone for two hundred K easily and on the California coast ten times that. Here in the Hamptons? If you have to ask, move on up the road. Made the house Evan and I grew up in look shabby.

Soon, word spread, people began calling, and my concierge practice was born.

So here I was ensconced in the Hamptons. A place I never thought I'd be. A place I never wanted to be. But that old curveball changed everything.

Chapter 1

The Wentworth estate, a castle among castles, had three gray stone stories and too many rooms to count beneath its copper mansard roof, patinaed to a rich green by age and weather. It overlooked a tranquil cove and beyond to the Atlantic, today churned into whitecaps by a stiff breeze. Typical June in the Hamptons. Could be hot and sweltering or cold and drizzly. Today it was warm and breezy.

The estate, also known as Westwood Manor—seemed all the estates in the Hamptons had names—housed a dozen people: Mrs. Eleanor Louise Parker Wentworth and her staff of eleven. Mrs. Wentworth—or Ellie, as she demanded everyone, including me, call her—along with her husband, the late Walter Wentworth, had purchased the property some two decades earlier, when they hauled all their oil, land, and cattle money north from Texas. Walter died two years later, leaving Ellie the matriarch of the estate.

I wheeled my trusty aged green Saab convertible up the gentle S of Westwood Manor's treelined drive and parked in the circular parking area that fronted the humble abode of Ellie Wentworth.

As I was retrieving my portable EKG machine and medical bag from the trunk of my car, one of the two massive oak front doors swung open, revealing Sam, Ellie's butler. It was as if he had been standing by the door waiting. He probably had been since Ellie had called twenty minutes earlier.

Sam was maybe sixty, short, and round, with a trimmed collar of white hair circling his bald crown. He wore his usual pinstripe gray suit, crisp white shirt, navy vest, and red bow tie.

"Sam," I said as I approached.

Sam and I were on a first-name basis. At least I was. Sam was much too formal for that. I had been here dozens of times. Sometimes twice a week. Sam and I went way back. A year anyway.

"Dr. Lawson." He gave a half bow. "Thanks for coming."

"How's Ellie doing?" I asked.

"The usual, sir. Worried about everything. I made her tea, but it helped very little. So here you are." He smiled.

Though Ellie had legitimate medical problems, her typical complaints were stress, anxiety, and panic attacks, often more imagined than real.

"Where is she?"

"In the parlor." He held the door until I passed, and eased it closed soundlessly. "Would you care for coffee or tea?"

"No, thanks."

The parlor dwarfed most homes. Non-Hampton homes anyway. High ceilings, ankle-deep custom-sculpted carpets, and Louis-the-whatever furnishings. I wouldn't be surprised if one of the real Louises had actually planted his silk-covered butt in one or more of the chairs and sofas. The room also had a wall of glass that overlooked Ellie's prized garden and the gray Atlantic waters beyond.

"Hank," she said as I came in. "Please, sit." She patted the sofa next to her.

I placed my bag and the EKG machine on the floor and sat, wondering which Louis had rested there before me.

Ellie didn't look ill. Or stressed. Or even concerned. She wore a silk robe and slippers, and a gold necklace and bracelet gorged with stones worth more than my entire family had earned in a lifetime.

Here is the thing about a concierge practice: Your patients hire you to be available to them and to give them that personal service. That includes house calls, hand-holding, reassurance, and occasionally a real medical problem.

Ellie was one of my favorite patients. The fact that this visit would be more social than medical didn't bother me at all. Concierge medicine is filled with such visits.

"What's the problem?" I asked.

She sighed. "This wedding is going to do me in. I'll be glad when it's over."

Ellie's blood relatives were down to two. A daughter, Jackie, and a granddaughter, Nicole. I'd never met either but had seen pictures of them. Blond, blue-eyed, and gorgeous, they each resembled the photos I'd seen of Ellie when she was a young woman.

Ellie had told me a month or so ago that Nicole was getting married at the estate. Since that time, her stress had mounted and my visits had become more frequent. With the event now looming only two weeks away, she was having almost daily symptoms. Most I could handle with a reassuring phone call; others required that I visit. Like today.

Ellie never did anything halfway and the wedding promised to be one of her famous productions. I had nursed her through two other such events in the last year. One for her friends in the equestrian world and the other for one of the many international charities she supported. Both events were over-the-top.

Cracking the Hamptons' social nut was no easy task. Only old money, New York money, maybe Newport money, sometimes Connecticut or New Jersey money, need apply. Ellie and Walter had arrived with Texas money. Gazillions from what I heard. If the gazillions were big enough, the door could be pried open, but it was Ellie's theme parties that sealed the deal for the Wentworths. Always the talk of the town. A Renaissance Faire, a Texas

BBQ, a masquerade ball, and even Camelot had been themes. The latter required dismantling the elaborate gazebo that sat along one side of the garden so that a jousting track could be constructed. After the party, the track disappeared and the gazebo was reborn.

"You said your heart was acting up?" I asked.

"Those awful flutters. They've been rattling around in there all morning. Worse than last week when you were here."

I took her hand and felt for her pulse. Mostly regular and strong, a few skips.

"There," she said. "That was another one."

I smiled. "Probably PVCs from your mitral prolapse."

"That's what you always say." She had a mischievous twinkle in her eye.

"Because that's what it always is. I think you just want me to come over and hold your hand."

"That's true. At my age getting a handsome young man to pay attention is good medicine."

"That's what I'm here for." I lifted the EKG machine. "Let me get a tracing and see what's going on."

"Is that necessary?"

"No. But it'll make me feel better."

"I shouldn't take you away from your other patients, though. Not for my silly stuff."

"I told you, nothing is silly. If you're worried, I'm worried."

It took a couple of minutes to hook up and record Ellie's EKG.

"Looks good," I said. "Except for a few of those PVCs. You've been taking your beta-blockers every day, haven't you?"

Another mischievous twinkle. "I might have missed one. Maybe two."

"Didn't I tell you not to do that? That you'd have more symptoms?"

"Yes, dear, you did. I've just been so busy with all this." She waved a hand toward the wall of windows.

When I first came in, I hadn't noticed the half dozen workers shoveling dirt and pushing wheelbarrows around. One of them hugged a large shrub to his chest and moved out of sight to my left.

She saw my gaze. "They have to dig up part of the garden, I'm afraid. To put in a dance floor for the wedding." She sighed. "I'm sure it will rain and Nicole and her friends won't get to use it."

"Bet it doesn't." I smiled.

"The usual?" she asked.

"Sure."

We shook on it.

Ellie loved little bets, a dollar only. Laughed whether she won or lost. We'd wager on all kinds of things. The weather, whether the Dow Jones would be up or down the next day, the winner of some sporting event, college football with her beloved Longhorns being her favorite. I was never much of a gambler, never saw the fun in it, never had the money to lose, but this I considered part of the service. Laughter is good medicine, a great stress reducer, so making Ellie laugh was part of her care.

"Promise me you won't let this wedding drive you crazy," I said.

"It's not the wedding. The party part anyway."

"Then what?"

She sighed again. This one longer and deeper. "I wish she was marrying someone like you and not that . . . that . . . I can't even think of the proper word."

"I thought you were happy she was getting married."

"I am. Just not to him." She shook her head and her gaze dropped to her lap. I could see the stress lines in her face deepen. "I mean Robert's a decent enough fellow and he seems to adore Nicole."

"Then what's the problem?"

"Unfortunately he's a clone of my son-in-law, Mark. A Wall Street lizard. Robert even works for Mark. Both of them are too wrapped up in money and status."

"Hard not to be around here."

"Doesn't mean I have to like it." Her shoulders relaxed and she laid her head back on the sofa cushion. "This wedding is just too much."

"No, it's not. I know you. This is what you live for. Putting on better parties than anyone."

She raised her head and smiled. "I do, don't I?"

"Yes, you do, and I'm sure this one will be no different."

My cell buzzed. I checked the screen. Divya. I stood. "I need to take this."

Divya Katdare, my physician assistant, is pretty and smart. Too smart to be working for HankMed, the name my brother, Evan, gave to my practice. Divya had the smarts to do anything she wanted, but for some reason this seemed to be her passion. Not that her family agreed. They're old country. Think she should attend polo matches and charity events, not serve the huddled masses. Divya saw things differently, so she joined HankMed. Not that I had a choice. She didn't so much apply for the job as create it. When I said I didn't need a PA, she ignored me and jumped on board anyway. She doesn't accept no easily.

Before I could even say hello, Divya began talking. Rapidly. Not making much sense, but here's what I got: Ben Kleinman, the fourteen-year-old son of one of my patients, and three of his friends tangled with a swarm of jellyfish. Stung from "top to bottom," as she put it. Ben had called asking her what to do, so she drove to the beach to check him and his friends out.

The real problem? Evan came with her and now he wanted the boys to pee on one another. He was ranting about something he had seen on TV that suggested urine would take the sting out.

Did I mention that my brother is an idiot?

"Get down here and stop him," she said.

"Okay. I'm leaving right now. Tell Evan not to pee on anyone in the meantime."

I glanced at Ellie as I closed my phone. She raised an eyebrow.

"Your life is so exciting," she said.

"And with a brother like Evan it can be trying."

"Evan is sweet."

"Not exactly the word I would use about now."

Ellie laughed. "You run along. I'm fine."

I gathered up the EKG machine and medical bag. "Call me if you have any other problems."

As I started toward the door, she said, "My granddaughter and her best friend, Ashley, are driving out from the city today. They'll be staying here until the wedding. We're having a little welcoming party tonight. Nicole's invited some of her Hamptons friends over. I want you to come."

I hesitated. "I'll try."

"Don't just try. Be here. It'll be fun." She laid one hand over her chest. "Besides, with all the stress of entertaining I might have more palpitations. I'd feel better if you were here."

"Okay. What time?"

"Say seven. Bring Divya. I haven't seen her in a while."

"I'll ask her."

"And that beautiful young lady of yours. What's her name? The hospital administrator?"

"Jill."

"That's right. I don't know why I can never remember her name."

"I'll ask her, too." I started toward the door.

"And Evan and his girlfriend, of course." She shook her head. "I must be getting old. I can't remember her name either."

"Paige," I said. "I think she's leaving town today. Or maybe it's tomorrow. I'll ask Evan."

"Bring him regardless."

"I will."

Chapter 2

I found the boys on the beach, just below Panama Joe's Crab Shack, a local restaurant famous for its fresh seafood and Mexican beer. They were sitting on towels and seemed very uncomfortable. Jellyfish stings will do that. Evan was still extolling the benefits of urine.

"Yes, it does work," he said.

"No. According to *The New England Journal of Medicine*, there is no evidence that it has any benefits whatsoever," Divya said. "Except perhaps to humiliate the victim."

"You're a PA. That's with a little *p* for *physician*, and a big *A* for *assistant*."

"It would seem that in this case I know more than you." Her chin jutted toward him.

"You two knock it off," I said.

They both turned toward me, finally noticing I was there.

"Tell your brother that this is a medical issue and not a CFO problem," Divya said.

Evan is CFO of HankMed. A position he gave himself. I'm still not sure exactly what he does to earn the title, but it's better to let him have it than argue.

I raised a hand. She fell silent. Evan adopted a smug look. I turned to him.

"Are you crazy? Trying to get a group of fourteen-year-olds to urinate on each other?"

Divya stood with her arms crossed; the smug look had now migrated to her face.

"It works," Evan said. "Joey and Chandler said so."

"Who?" I asked.

"Joey and Chandler. *Friends.* Remember that show?"

"Of course I know the show, but what does that have to do with this?"

"In one episode Monica got stung and they said urine was the treatment. Joey'd seen it on the Discovery Channel, so it must be true."

"Let me see if I understand you correctly," Divya said. "You obtain your medical knowledge from a sitcom?"

"And the Discovery Channel."

Divya rolled her eyes. She can say more while saying nothing than anyone I've ever known. A look, a glance, a roll of her eyes, a fixing of her jaw, and it's impossible to miss her point.

"No more about this," I said. "No one is going to pee on anyone."

I knelt next to Ben. "Let's see what we've got."

I peeled away the towel he had wrapped around his leg, exposing an area of acute erythema—a bright red splotch—the size of my palm just above his left knee. Several equally erythematous streaks spiraled downward, around his calf, reaching his ankle. He had contacted the jellyfish's body and its tentacles had latched on. He had apparently managed to kick it free, but it left behind its angry red calling card.

I examined the other three boys. Each had similar splotches and streaks of angry flesh.

"Looks ugly," Evan said.

"And it stings like crazy," Ben said.

He started to scratch one of the streaks, but I grabbed his hand. "Don't do that. It'll get infected."

"But it itches and burns."

"I know. Just give me a minute and we'll take care of it."
I turned toward Evan. "Here's what I need. Some baking
soda, a knife, a small bowl, a bottle of water, and some
vinegar."

"Fresh out of all that. Got plenty of urine, though."

Stubborn. Aggravating. Exasperating. There are so many
words to describe my brother.

I nodded toward the restaurant. "Why don't you ask
them? I'd bet they have everything I need."

"You want me to go get that stuff?"

"I can't leave you here. You might pee on somebody.
Yes, go get it."

I looked at Divya. "Do you have any one percent hydrocortisone cream in your SUV?"

"I'll get it."

While waiting, I called Ben's dad, Mort, a big-time investment banker, and told him what had happened, assur-
ing him that Ben was okay, just uncomfortable. Mort was in
the city and said he'd deal with his son's stupidity later. He
thought it might do Ben some good to hurt for a while, but
he did give me permission to treat the poor kid. He also
said he knew the other fathers and that they would want
their boys treated as well. I hung up.

"What were you guys doing?" I asked.

"Racing out to the buoy and back," Ben said. "We've
done it before."

"Water's pretty cold."

"Not that bad."

"Who won?" I asked.

"Jerry." Ben nodded toward Jerry, a redhead with pale,
freckled skin. On such fair skin his welts appeared even
angrier than those on the other guys.

Evan and Divya returned and I went to work.

I mixed some baking soda with water in the bowl until it
made a white paste. I smeared this on Ben's wounds. I then
took the knife and gently scraped the paste away.

"What are you doing?" Divya asked.

"Jellyfish tentacles leave behind little venom-filled capsules called nematocysts. The paste locks in the ones that haven't yet released their toxin and the blade scrapes them away."

"Clever."

"Then we wash it with the vinegar and apply some of the hydrocortisone cream. All will be as good as new in a few days."

"Good," Ben said. "Because I want a rematch."

There is nothing more stupid than a fourteen-year-old boy. All that testosterone and no brakes. It's like having a Formula One car without a driver's license. I was sure Ben's father would tell him not to pull this stunt again. I was sure Ben would listen attentively, agree it was stupid, and swear he'd never do it again. I was also sure Ben and his buddies would indeed have a rematch. It's a guy thing. We simply can't walk away from a competition.

Testosterone is a dangerous drug.

Chapter 3

"The urine would've worked just as well," Evan said.

"No, it wouldn't have," I said. "It's mostly water."

After we returned the bowl and knife to the restaurant, we decided to stay for lunch. The manager, Will, a young man with tousled blond hair and a year-round tan, thanked us for helping the boys. Seemed that Ben's dad, Mort Kleinman, owned Panama Joe's. I'd been his doc for a year and I never knew that. But since Mort owned everything from strip malls to high-rise office buildings, I wasn't surprised.

Will gave us a prime umbrella-shaded table on a weathered, wooden deck that extended out over the beach and told us lunch was on the house. Not a bad deal.

Evan would not be deterred. "Chandler said the ammonia in it would kill the stinging."

I couldn't believe he was still on this. Wait a sec, of course I could. We're talking about Evan here. He gets something in his head and he won't let go. Been that way since we were kids.

"Somehow I don't see Joey Tribbiani and Chandler Bing as medical authorities," I said.

"Those TV guys research this stuff," Evan said. "They wouldn't put it on the air if it wasn't true."

"You actually believe that?" Divya asked. "Do you not see the flaws in that logic?"

"They have a staff that digs up all this stuff."

"Perhaps you should watch less TV and read a few medical texts," Divya said.

"Do you have any of those?"

"Of course. I'm a trained professional."

"Maybe I could borrow some of them."

Divya frowned. "I doubt you would understand them."

"Sure, I would."

Divya smiled. "Really? What is amyotrophic lateral sclerosis?"

"Something bad, I'm sure."

"It's Lou Gehrig's disease," I said.

Evan's brow furrowed and he hesitated a beat. "What did they call it before Lou Gehrig?"

Divya shook her head. "What do you think?"

"That amyo-thing."

"Like I said, you'd never understand them."

"Okay, Ms. PA," Evan said. "What's a P and L statement?"

"Profit and loss. It's a measure of a company's past performance and helps investors project future cash flow." She leaned back, crossed her arms over her chest, and aimed her chin at him. See what I mean? A gotcha without saying a word.

Evan stared at her, apparently at a loss for words. Finally he said, "That one was too easy."

"My father taught me finances at a very young age."

Evan was saved when our waitress appeared. She was blond and tanned. Could have been manager Will's twin sister except her eyes were bluer and her smile was brighter. She wore jeans and a brilliant yellow Panama Joe's T-shirt. Her name tag read: HELLO. I'M MIRANDA.

"Will said you're the guys who helped Ben and his friends," Miranda said.

"That's right," I said.

"He and his buddies hang out here all the time. I heard it was jellyfish."

I nodded.

She winced. "Been there. Hurts a lot."

"They'll be okay," I said.

Evan jumped in. "Miranda. That's a beautiful name."

"Thank you."

"Evan R. Lawson," he said. "CFO of HankMed."

"HankMed?" she asked.

"My brother's concierge practice." He nodded toward me. "This is my brother, Dr. Hank Lawson."

Miranda smiled at me.

"This is Divya. Our physician *assistant*," Evan said, accent on *assistant*.

Divya raised an eyebrow. "Our?"

"Our," Evan said. "HankMed's."

Miranda pulled a pad and pen from her hip pocket. "What can I get you?"

Evan and I ordered steamed clams, Divya a chopped salad.

Evan unzipped his backpack and pulled out his laptop. He cleared a spot on the table and booted it up.

"What are you doing?" Divya asked.

"ESM," Evan said.

"Emergency staff meeting? I thought this was lunch."

"It's called multitasking. You know, doing several things at once."

"I know what multitasking is," Divya said. "In your case it would consist of having lunch, conducting a quasi staff meeting, and suggesting dubious medical treatments."

"I was just trying to help Ben and his friends."

"I'm sure you were. The problem is that sitcom medicine doesn't work so well."

"Sitcom? Joey or Chandler, I forget which one, said they saw it on the Discovery Channel."

"Let me make sure I understand you. Two fictional characters talk about what was most likely a fictional documentary and you buy that as fact?"

Evan stared at her for a minute but apparently had no comeback.

The computer finished booting. Evan tapped a few keys and then turned the screen toward Divya and me. A picture of a gray building with two brightly colored vans angled nose to nose out front filled the screen. The sign that crowned the single-level structure indicated it was Fleming's Custom Shop. Evan tapped a key and we were now inside the showroom, where three more vans were on display. Each more colorful than the last. Each with fancy wheels that were worth more than my Saab.

We were being treated to one of Evan's slide shows. He loved PowerPoint. He loved productions.

"What is this?" I asked.

"The future of HankMed."

"A van?" Divya said.

"Not just a van," Evan said. "A mobile clinic. A chariot that brings health care right to your door."

"We already do that," Divya said.

"No, you bring yourself and a little black bag. Your SUV is too small. I'm talking about a full-service vehicle."

"What are we going to do?" I asked. "Open-heart surgery in the back?"

Evan hesitated as if considering that possibility, and then shook his head. "Not that full service."

Evan tapped the return key. Now a bright blue van, side doors open, appeared. A young attractive brunette stood next to it, smiling at the camera.

"Who's the girl?" I asked.

"Rachel Fleming. Her father owns the place. She does all the custom designs." Evan moved to the next slide. This one a view of the interior. "These guys can do anything. We can have one tricked out any way we want."

"Tricked out?" Divya asked. "Sounds like a rolling brothel. With mood lighting and a bar."

Evan raised his hands, palms toward her. "Okay, we can have it *suitably equipped* for our needs. Is that better?"

"What might our needs be?" I asked.

"A medical clinic on wheels. We can bring more equipment and meds to our clients. It can even have a workstation where you can type up your notes on the fly and not wait to get back home to do them."

"That would be nice," I said. Divya tossed a frown at me, indicating I shouldn't encourage him. Good thought. "But I don't think we need a ... how much does one of these cost?"

"Depends on how it's tricked ..." He glanced at Divya. "Equipped. Maybe a hundred and fifty."

"We don't have that."

"That's what banks are for."

"We just got out of debt. Why would we want to get back in the red?"

"It's an investment. And excellent advertising."

Evan scrolled through a few more pictures, finally stopping on an intricate graphic design. A black rectangle with "HankMed" in gold script. The script had so many loops and swirls it took a minute to decipher it. Beneath that, block lettering read: "Bringing health care to your door." Our phone number stretched across the bottom.

"My own design," Evan said.

"You propose this for the side of the van?" I asked.

"It'll be a rolling billboard."

"Don't you think our patients might find that inappropriate?" Divya asked.

Evan glanced at me and then back to Divya. "I don't see the problem."

"We offer health services," she said. "Private, discreet health services. I don't believe our clientele would appreciate the Hamptons grapevine knowing every time they had a doctor's appointment."

"She has a point," I said.

Evan persisted. "To build a successful business, you have to advertise."

"Which would be fine if we were plumbers," I said. "In case you haven't noticed, we aren't."

Miranda returned with our food. She glanced at the computer. "Cool. Did you do that?"

"Yeah."

"Very cool." After she distributed the plates, she asked, "You guys need anything else right now?"

We said no and she turned to leave, saying she'd check back in a few minutes. She suddenly stopped and wavered slightly, one hand clutching the back of the empty chair for support. Her knees seemed ready to buckle, so I jumped up and wrapped a supporting arm around her.

"What's the matter?" I asked.

She pressed a palm over her chest. "I'm fine."

Her face was flushed, not fine. "Sit down."

"I'm okay."

"Sit here." I pulled the empty chair away from the table.

"It'll pass. It always does."

"Do you have these episodes often?" I asked.

"Just recently." She offered a half smile. "I'm not pregnant, if that's what you're wondering."

"I wasn't."

"My friend Robin thinks I am."

I checked her wrist pulse. Fast. Regular, but fast.

"It's just something that happens," she said. "No big deal."

"What do you feel when it happens?"

"Warm and light-headed. And sometimes my heart does a little butterfly thing."

"You need to be examined and have some tests run."

"I don't have insurance."

"That's okay," I said. "We'll do it. No charge."

She looked at me suspiciously. "Why would you do that?"

"It's what we do." I looked around. The tables were fill-ing as the lunch crowd began to arrive. "Is there somewhere we can do a quick exam and draw some blood?"

"Not here."

"I didn't mean right here. Somewhere private. An office or a staff locker room?"

Worry gathered in her eyes. "I need this job. If my manager thinks there's something wrong with me, he'll fire me."

"He can't do that."

"Really? Tell the last girl he fired. Of course with her it was drugs and alcohol and not showing up, but still she had something wrong."

"Being a drug user isn't the same as being ill. You aren't using anything, are you?"

"No. Never."

"We can do this at your home. Later. After you get off work."

"I work until four."

"We'll come by after that."

She hesitated as if deciding what to do.

"Don't ignore this," I said. "It could be important."

"Or it could be nothing. Right?"

"Do you believe that?"

She sighed and shook her head. "Probably not." She opened her pad and scribbled her name, *Miranda Randall*, address, and phone number on it. She tore the page out and handed it to me. "See, I feel better now. It's probably just stress."

"Maybe, but we need to be sure."

She nodded and walked away.

"Any idea what she could have?" Divya asked.

"Anemia, stress, anxiety, hypoglycemia, thyroid. A ton of other things."

"I think she thought my idea was so cool that it gave her palpitations," Evan said.

"I imagine you do that to most people," Divya said. "Just not for the reasons you think."

"Still, she liked the idea."

"Then maybe Panama Joe's should buy the van," Divya said. "Not HankMed."

"Why not?"

"Because it's—what's the word?—cheesy."

"The word is *cool*," Evan countered. "Just like Miranda said. And you'll feel way cool when you pull up in the Hank-Med van."

Divya aimed her fork at him. "Only if *cool* means embarrassed."

We ate in silence, wonderful silence, for a moment. Only a moment, though.

"Just go by and take a look," Evan said. "Smell the leather. Check out the plasma screens they put in these things."

"Plasma TVs sound very practical," Divya said.

Evan paused a beat as if her tone took a minute to absorb. "Oh, sarcasm."

She looked at him, one eyebrow raised. "Surprised you caught it."

"Look," I said. "We can't afford a van and we don't need one."

"It's not far. Just over in Westhampton. I'll drive."

"We have two follow-up visits and two new patients to see this afternoon," Divya said. "You know, make money rather than spend it, Mr. CFO."

"You have to spend money to make money."

"Not that kind of money." I popped a clam in my mouth and spoke around it. "Who are the patients?"

Divya retrieved her notebook from her purse and shuffled through the pages. "The two follow-ups are up in Sag Harbor. The new patients are an elderly couple—Clifton and Lucy Lovell—in East Hampton." She closed the notebook. "Want me to do the follow-up visits?"

"That'll work. I'll visit Lucy and Clifton," I said. "Then we can meet at Miranda's."

"What should I do?" Evan asked.

"I'll lend you one of my medical books. One with pictures. Maybe you can learn something."

"Funny."

"Better than a sitcom."

"Maybe I'll go with you," Evan said.

"Me?" Divya asked.

"Sure. If you have to drive all the way up to Sag Harbor, wouldn't a little company be welcome?"

"Company, yes. You, no."

"It'll be fun."

"For whom?" Her eyes narrowed. "Wait a minute. Are you planning on tricking me into a detour by the van company?"

"I'm offended you'd think I'd be so devious." Evan laid a palm over his chest. "I'm just trying to be helpful."

Divya raised an eyebrow. "It must have slipped my mind that *helpful* is your middle name."

"You guys knock it off," I said as I stood. "Let's go get some work done."

Outside, Divya opened the rear door of her SUV. "I'll give you the charts I've started for the Lovells." She handed me the two folders.

"I almost forgot," I said. "We're invited to a party at Ellie Wentworth's tonight."

"Is this part of her granddaughter's wedding?" Divya asked.

I nodded and then to Evan said, "Is Paige still in town? She's invited, too."

Paige Collins. Evan's current girlfriend.

"I took her to the airport this morning. She'll be in California with her parents for the next two weeks."

"You can go with us," I said.

"Or we could hire a babysitter for you," Divya said. "Make sure you don't urinate on anyone."

Sarcasm again. By the look on Evan's face, he caught it right away this time.

Chapter 4

Clifton and Lucy Lovell proved to be a wonderful elderly couple whose private doc had recently retired. They were referred to me by Ms. Newberg, one of my more difficult but fiercely loyal patients.

The couple sat on a patterned silk sofa, holding hands throughout my history taking. Cute, but the anxiety I saw in their eyes revealed a dynamic I had seen all too often. Elderly couples who fear disease and death. Who fear a doctor, particularly a doctor new to them, discovering some awful medical problem. Who fear the possible loss of their life partner. What would the other one do if left alone?

The truth is that surviving spouses often don't live many years after losing a long-term companion. Depression is deadly. The survivor quits eating properly. Quits seeing friends. Quits visiting doctors and taking needed medications. Picks up bad habits like alcohol and drugs, usually of the prescription variety, given to help solve depression-induced symptoms such as insomnia.

I practically had to pry them apart to perform my examinations. Fortunately, both were fairly healthy, more so than most eighty-five-year-olds, and the few meds each of them took were appropriate and apparently working. Their previous doc had done a good job. I told them I'd schedule another appointment in two months but to call if anything changed or if they had any questions. When they walked me to the door, relief that all was well painted their faces.

When I arrived at Miranda Randall's apartment complex, Divya and Evan were already there, Divya sitting in her SUV talking on the phone, Evan leaning against the back obviously sending text messages. As Divya stepped out, she snapped her phone closed. I could see she wasn't happy.

"What is it?" I asked.

Divya parked a stray strand of hair behind her ear as she dropped her phone into her purse. "My mother. Sometimes . . ."

"Want to talk about it?"

"No." With Divya no meant no, so I let it go.

We climbed the stairs to Miranda's second-floor apartment. It was just before five. She greeted us in shorts and a tank top, barefoot, hair pulled back and bound into a ponytail by a red rubber band. Her apartment was small but not what I expected. Not the usual sterile white walls and secondhand furniture. It was stylish: walls a rich gray, doors and trim a bright white, floors polished hardwood, a pair of patterned area rugs, floor-to-ceiling drapes held open by braided tiebacks, and throw pillows everywhere. A deep-cushioned white sofa with a burgundy throw draped over its back and two matching wingback chairs cradled a glass-topped coffee table, where several interior design magazines were stacked near one corner.

She saw me looking at them. "I took night classes in design. A year ago. Can't afford them now. The Hamptons seem to get more expensive every day."

"That's true," I said.

"I love your apartment," Evan said. "It looks like a designer decorated it."

"A poor designer," Miranda laughed. "And just this room. You don't want to see my bedroom. Or for sure my closet. They're more Dresden nineteen forty-five."

"Even if they're messy, I'd bet they're classy," Evan said. My brother the charmer.

"So, where do we start?" Miranda asked.

"A few questions," Divya said.

"Sounds easy enough."

Miranda plopped down on the sofa. Divya and I sat in the wingback chairs. Divya pulled out her notepad.

Evan sat on a stool at the counter that divided the kitchen from the living room, and began fiddling with his cell phone. Probably checking e-mails. Or maybe following Paige's flight. He has an app for that.

"Tell us about these symptoms you've been experiencing," Divya asked.

"Fatigue mostly. Some soreness in my legs after exercise. And my heart racing from time to time."

"Any dizziness or passing out?"

"Dizzy a couple of times, but that's about it." She folded one leg beneath her. "And some sweats. Mostly at night. I thought I had a fever and took my temp. It was about ninety-nine or maybe a little more. Is that too high?"

"Do you feel warm when others don't?" I asked.

She nodded. "Sometimes. I've lost some weight, too. I'm eating like a pig, though, and not good stuff either. Mostly junk food."

Divya scribbled in her notebook and then looked up at Miranda. "You said you've had these symptoms for a month or more?"

"Maybe even two months. I forget."

"But you haven't seen a doctor?"

"I told you, I don't have insurance. I can't afford it." She leaned forward, resting one forearm on her knee. "Which makes me wonder . . . how come I don't have to pay you?"

"Because you can't afford it." I smiled.

"We have patients who pay us well," Evan said. "That lets us also see people in your situation."

"And you make house calls." She leaned back on the sofa. "Unbelievable."

"Any other symptoms?" I asked.

"A sore throat sometimes." She touched her neck. "Not like with a cold or the flu. More like when I turn my head or sometimes when I swallow."

Divya ran an EKG. It showed Miranda had sinus tachycardia, a rapid but normal rhythm. I then did a physical exam, finding nothing abnormal except that Miranda's thyroid was enlarged and tender.

"That's it," she said, as my fingers pressed over the front and sides of her neck. "That's the sore area."

I asked her to swallow. She did.

"That hurts."

I nodded and then glanced at Divya, who was making notes. "Thyroid diffusely enlarged and tender. No nodules or masses."

"What does all that mean?" Miranda asked.

"It means that your thyroid is acting up. Probably inflamed and putting out too much hormone. That would explain your symptoms."

Her eyes widened. "That sounds serious."

I smiled. "Probably not and probably easily fixed."

"You sure? It couldn't be cancer, could it? I had a friend in school whose mother died of thyroid cancer."

"No, I don't think it's cancer. It might be what we call thyroiditis."

"That sounds worse."

I laughed. "Not even close."

"Hmmm." She gave me a skeptical look. "I don't like big scary words I can't pronounce."

"Relax. We'll do some blood tests and get you started on a medicine. A beta-blocker. It'll slow your heart down while we get the labs done and see what we're dealing with."

"I'm not big on pills."

"You'll like this one."

"Will it fix this 'itis' thing?"

"Thyroiditis," I said.

"Yeah, that." She touched her neck.

"No. But it'll make your symptoms better while we decide what it is and what we need to do to correct it."

She nodded.

"Ready?" Divya said. She held a rubber tourniquet and a syringe in her gloved hands.

"I hate needles, too."

"It'll only take a minute."

While Divya drew blood, I wrote Miranda a prescription for fifty milligrams of metoprolol. I handed it to her.

"One each day," I said.

"Do I have to take this forever?"

"Just until we cool down your thyroid."

Divya placed the blood vials into a plastic bag and labeled it.

"I can work, can't I?" Miranda asked. "I have a double shift tomorrow."

I nodded. "You should be fine. Maybe a little tired."

"I'm tired already."

"Call us if anything changes. Otherwise we'll call when we get your labs back."

"Cool."

Chapter 5

Jill Casey is beautiful. Dark hair, dark yet bright eyes, brighter smile, and killer body. Everything I like. She's my on-again, off-again girlfriend. Right now we're on. I like that better than off.

Today, she appeared frazzled. She looked up from behind her desk as I came through her office door. She had the phone plastered to her ear. A strand of hair fell across her face. She raised a finger toward me and mouthed, "One minute."

I sat in the chair across from her.

After we left Miranda Randall's, Divya took Evan back to Shadow Pond and then headed home to prepare for Ellie's party. I drove over here to Hamptons Heritage Hospital to deliver the blood samples we had collected. Normally, I would've dropped them by the lab, but since one was a freebie, I brought them to Jill so she could smooth the path.

Besides, I wanted to invite her to the party.

"I understand," Jill said into the phone. "It isn't really that much." She hesitated, listening. "But if you look at the entire budget, a hundred and fifty thousand isn't that big. And the free clinic is important. It helps the community and our reputation. A win-win." Another pause. "Don't you think the community goodwill this program generates is worth the costs?"

Nearly a year ago, Jill had set up a clinic for the poor and uninsured. Yes, the Hamptons have regular folks, too. Not just the superwealthy. Jill's a fierce advocate of the clinic. Why wouldn't she be? It's her baby. Something that would never have happened had she not pried open a few sticky doors and butted down the many unforeseen obstacles that cropped up almost daily. Obstacles that were mostly ego-driven by several staff physicians protecting their individual turf—and wallets.

This one wants to manage the clinic and that one fears it will take patients from his practice. This one wants to interpret tests performed at the clinic, for a fee, and that one wants the testing done by a lab he wholly or partly owns. This one wants credit and power, and that one does, too. The politics of medicine can get ugly and that's why Jill often found herself in the political mosh pit.

Jill's passion for this project boiled down to her belief that the hospital should do things for those in need. Do things that weren't necessarily bottom-line driven. It put her at odds with the board, but she isn't one to back down. That's one of the many things I love about her.

"All I'm asking is for a chance to present this to the board," she said into the phone with a shake of her head. "At the meeting next week." Pause. "Okay, I'll wait to hear back from you."

She hung up the phone, parked the wayward strand behind her ear, and massaged one temple.

"Sounds like you're having a good day," I said.

"Money. Makes everyone get their hackles up." She sighed. "Please tell me you have some good news."

"I do." I placed four plastic bags on her desk, each with several vials of blood and a lab request sheet inside. "Three paying customers."

She nodded toward the bags. "Looks like four."

I smiled. "One isn't paying."

"You know I can't keep doing free lab work for you."

"Not for me. For Miranda Randall."

"Who's that?"

I told her Miranda's story as she tapped her pen on her desk.

"Three for one is better than your usual," she acknowledged. "I'll get these to the lab and cover the tracks on Ms. Randall's tests."

"Thanks."

"You owe me," she said. "Dinner tonight? I need wine."

"And maybe a little Hank?"

She laughed. "Don't go all piggish on me."

"Just offering."

"You're so generous."

"Just trying to ease your worried brow."

She laughed. "I need that about now."

"Actually I have something better than dinner. A party at Ellie Wentworth's place."

"Really? I love her. What's the occasion?"

"A prewedding party for Nicole, Ellie's granddaughter, and her friends."

Jill glanced at her watch and then opened her appointment calendar. "What time?"

"Seven."

"I have a meeting with a supplier at six. Then I'll have to go home and clean up. What's the attire for this party?"

"Ellie said casual."

"Her casual or my casual?"

"Hers, I would suspect." I smiled. "I don't think sweatpants and a T-shirt would be appropriate."

"I thought you liked my sweats."

"I do. But I'm not sure Ellie's other guests will be quite that casual."

She laughed again. "I'll be a little late, so I'll meet you there."

"That works for me."

*   *   *

By the time I got back home to the guesthouse on Boris's Shadow Pond estate, Evan was frantic. He had four pairs of pants, seven shirts, and no fewer than six sport jackets laid out on his bed. He was obviously having trouble deciding which ensemble worked best.

"What do you think?" he asked.

"I think you're an idiot."

"Not funny. Which combo looks the best?"

"On you? Any will do. The clothes aren't the problem."

"Still not funny. So really, which works best?"

"I'm not sure you want me for your fashion consultant."

"That's true."

"Why are you so wound up about what to wear?"

"A party at Ellie Wentworth's? A lot of Hamptons movers and shakers will be there. Future HankMed clients."

"You realize this is a party for Ellie's granddaughter? For her wedding? Right?"

"Business never sleeps."

"Maybe you could tuck it in just for tonight. Besides, I think this will mostly be Nicole's friends. You know, young and healthy."

"But they have parents who might need our services. That's why I need to look cool."

"Cool?"

"With-it. Hip. Happening."

"I know what's going to happen. You're going to act like a fool."

"Did you say cool?"

I shook my head. "I know another thing that's going to happen. I'm going to take a shower."

I did. Then I got dressed. Gray slacks, white shirt, and a navy jacket. I settled on the living room sofa and began reading an article in this week's edition of *JAMA* while I waited on Evan. When he finally appeared, he had decided on gray slacks, a white shirt, and a navy jacket.

"You should change," he said.

"I got here first."

"But I'm the one who needs to look cool and this is my coolest outfit."

"Mine, too."

"But Jill doesn't care what you wear."

"I'll tell her that and see if she agrees."

"But . . ."

I waved him away and stood. "I'll change jackets."

I chose a black one.

Chapter 6

Sam greeted Evan and me at the door. He wore not only his typical gray suit, blue vest, and red bow tie but also a big smile. Bigger than I had ever seen. Sam was always formal and professional, and when he smiled, it was warm but quick, as if he was simply being polite. Playing his role as the friendly gatekeeper of Ellie's domain. Tonight he was beaming. Maybe he'd expected someone else, but the smile didn't evaporate when he opened the door and saw us, so that theory didn't fit. Beyond his smiling face, I heard music and the chatter of conversation, punctuated with laughter.

"Dr. Lawson. Mr. Lawson. Welcome."

"Thanks, Sam," I said. "Hope we're not too late."

"Not at all, sir."

"You look happy, Sam."

"I am, sir. This place always livens up when Miss Nicole visits. Ellie glows whenever she's around."

That explained the oversized smile.

"So the excitement hasn't caused her any problems?" I asked.

"Quite the contrary. She's the life of the party." He stepped back and waved a hand. "Please, enjoy yourselves."

The party, small by Ellie's standards, only sixty or so

people, was in full swing. The crowd was mostly Nicole's friends, young, attractive, and attired in designer rags. Rags with four-figure price tags. It was obvious that several of the women, though only in their twenties, were not strangers to the plastic surgeon's knife. The gathering filled the great room and spilled out through the open doors onto the rear patio. Tux-clad waiters and waitresses circulated with trays of champagne and food.

Evan immediately grabbed a glass and a plate, which he topped with two fat shrimp and a half dozen lobster bites. He popped some lobster in his mouth and spoke around it. "This is great, isn't it?"

I took a flute of champagne. "The food or the party?"

"Both." Evan took a gulp of champagne. "Let's mingle."

"Are you going to embarrass yourself tonight?"

"Moi?" He flattened one palm over his chest. "Wouldn't dream of it."

"Wouldn't dream of what?" I turned toward the voice. It was Divya. "I was wondering if you were going to make it," she said as she glanced at her watch.

"Wardrobe issues," I said. "Evan couldn't decide what to wear."

She looked at him. "You look very nice, Evan R. Lawson."

Evan bowed. "As do you, Divya Katdare." He extended his plate toward her. "Shrimp?"

"No, thanks." Then she raised her glass. "I could do with a little more champagne, though."

As if he had heard her request, a waiter appeared. Divya exchanged her empty flute for a full one.

"Have you met the bride-to-be yet?" Divya asked.

"No. Just got here."

"Come along and I'll introduce you."

We found Nicole on the back patio. Her face reflected the setting sun, and the warm ocean breeze lightly jostled her perfectly layered blond hair. She was even more beautiful than her pictures. A rich caramel tan, a flawless smile, and the bluest of blue eyes I'd ever seen.

"I'm so glad you could come," she said as I shook her hand. "Ellie raves about you."

"I pay her to say that."

"Oh, I thought she paid you." Her eyes literally twinkled when she smiled.

"Very good."

"Evan R. Lawson," Evan said. "CFO of HankMed."

He extended his hand and Nicole took it.

"I know about you, too," Nicole said. "Ellie said I should watch out for you."

"Me? Why would she say that?"

I wonder.

"Something about a reformed wolf in sheep's clothing." Nicole laughed.

Yes, her laugh was musical. She was a living, breathing cliché of feminine beauty. I swear.

She extracted her hand from Evan's. "I'm just teasing you. I understand you have a girlfriend. Is she here?"

"No. She's in California right now."

"What part?"

"Orange County. She's with her parents. Visiting family."

"I want all of you to meet my parents." Nicole looked around, finally settling her gaze on a woman who could be only her mother. An older version of Nicole, a younger version of Ellie. She wore a red silk dress that clung to her lean curves. Nicole waved her over. She headed our way, her walk that of a runway model. She was followed by a man in a dark blue suit with a yellow tie and a pale blue shirt. One of those with the white collar and cuffs. He also walked like a runway model.

Nicole introduced Evan, Divya, and me to her mother, Jacqueline, who said we should call her Jackie, and her father, Mark. Jackie's handshake was firm, Mark's less so. One of those limp dismissive shakes as if he couldn't really be bothered. I did notice that he wore gold and opal cuff links, the fiery opals catching the remnants of the sunlight.

"Congratulations on the wedding," I said.

Jackie threw an arm around Nicole and pulled her close. "We're so proud of her."

"Where's the lucky groom?" Divya asked.

"Mark has him working late," Jackie said.

"Ellie told me that he works for you," I said to Mark.

"That's right. I have a Wall Street investment firm. You've probably heard of it. Crompton and Associates?"

I hadn't. "Sure. Evan probably has, too. He worked in the Manhattan financial world at one time."

Evan, whose attention had been on the crowd, suddenly dropped back into our conversation. Sort of.

"Heard of what?" he asked.

"Crompton and Associates," Mark repeated.

Evan shook his head. "Nope. Never heard of it."

Mark seemed annoyed but went on. "We do business with all the big firms in New York and internationally. Last count, twenty-two different countries."

"And he makes Robert work too hard," Jackie said.

"If he's going to learn the business, he has to be there."

Jackie gave him a soft punch on the arm. "But this is your daughter's party. He should be here."

"He just called," Nicole said. "He's on the expressway and making good time. Should be here in an hour or so."

"That's wonderful," Jackie said. "He'll at least make it for part of the reception."

"I hope he got those documents he was working on squared away," Mark said. "I better call him." He pulled a cell phone from his pocket and walked away, out toward the garden.

No good-bye. No "Excuse me a sec." No "Nice to meet you." I got the impression that in his head business trumped people.

A young woman walked up. Rich black hair that hung to her midback, white slacks, and a dark green silk blouse that deepened her intensely green eyes. She was so striking even Evan seemed slightly dazed, not a condition I often see.

"This is Ashley," Nicole said. "My best friend and maid of honor. This is Hank, Grandma's doctor. And his brother, Evan."

Evan found his voice. "Evan R. Lawson, CFO of Hank-Med."

"And this beautiful lady is Divya, Hank's PA," Nicole continued.

"Nice to meet all of you," Ashley said. "Ellie's told us all about you and what you guys do for her."

"We try," I said. "I understand you and Nicole are staying here until the wedding."

She hooked her arm with Nicole's. "It's going to be like two weeks of partying."

A waiter flowed by, stopping to offer mini crab cakes. This time I took one. Evan took three.

Nicole declined, saying, "I've got to lose some weight before the wedding."

She didn't.

"Go see my guy," Ashley said. "Remember him?"

"That nutritionist?" Nicole asked.

"Every time I need to drop a few. You know how well it works."

"Cool. Can you get me in?"

"No problem."

"Who is this guy?" I asked.

"Dr. Julian Morelli. He's like so beautiful."

I laughed. "Beautiful?"

Ashley laughed. "Okay. Hot."

"How does he help you lose weight?" I asked.

"Mostly by encouraging exercise and a better diet. And he mixes up these special herbs and vitamins."

A commonsense hint: Beware of anyone who sells health products that they make themselves. The FDA, for all its warts, does a good job of keeping some very bad stuff off the US market. And nutritional products, now called "nutraceuticals," a new buzzword that makes them sound medicinal, aren't scrutinized by anyone. The herbs and spices these folks cook up could contain arsenic or almost any other toxin. They could've been mixed up in a rusty bucket or a dirty cat box in someone's garage. You just never know.

"What kinds of herbs?" I asked.

"I don't know," Ashley said. "He does blood tests to see what's out of balance and then like puts together a custom mixture to fix it."

"I see."

"All I know is that they work. They give you energy and kill your appetite, and like the pounds literally melt away."

"That's what I need," Nicole said.

I started to say that she didn't need to lose weight. That magazine models and Hollywood stars shouldn't be the arbiters of beauty. That she should be careful of homemade concoctions. Instead I decided that talking shop at Nicole's party or offering medical advice to someone who wasn't one of my patients might not be the best idea.

Besides, I was distracted.

Through the open doors I saw Jill and Ellie come down the stairs and go into the great room. I excused myself and headed their way.

Chapter 7

I hugged Ellie and then Jill, giving her a peck on the cheek.

"When did you get here?" I asked Jill.

"A few minutes ago. Ellie was showing me her latest redecorating projects. The drawing room and a couple of the upstairs suites."

"Small stuff," Ellie said. "Not moving any walls this time." She laughed.

Ellie always had some construction project going. Like the partially complete dance floor out by the gardens. She could never leave things static; instead she was constantly looking for change. I could think of only a couple of times that I had been here when there weren't workers hammering away at something.

"The party is great," I said.

"Isn't it?" Ellie scanned the room. "All these wonderful young people. So much energy and laughter. Makes me feel young again." She looked back at me. "Did you meet Nicole?"

"Yes. She's almost as pretty as you."

"Liar."

"Isn't that what you pay me for?"

She nudged Jill. "Watch out for him. He's a charmer."

"I know."

"How are you doing?" I asked Ellie.

"Never better. But it helps knowing you're here in case I get my flutters." She flashed a mischievous smile. "*That's* what I pay you for." Another laugh and then she excused herself to "go mingle with the young folks."

"How'd your meeting go?" I asked Jill.

"Boring. A rep from one of our surgical-equipment suppliers wanted to jack up his prices, so I told him we'd take our business elsewhere. He backed down."

"Why am I not surprised?"

"Are you trying to tell me something?"

"Yeah. You're good at your job."

"Not that I'm stubborn?"

"No comment."

"Chicken?"

"Absolutely."

We exchanged our champagne glasses for fresh ones and walked outside. The ocean was flat and the onshore breeze felt clean and cool.

I was going to introduce Jill to Nicole but didn't see her. Instead we took the steps that led from the patio down to the massive gardens that seemed to extend to the horizon. We decided to walk out to the end of Ellie's property. No small hike. Took a good fifteen minutes. We stood in the soft sand and watched the pale blue evening sky fade to a rich cobalt blue, unmasking hundreds of stars. I had one arm around Jill, her head resting against my shoulder. Not a single word passed between us. Every day should end like this.

Once the sky darkened, we made our way back toward the house, this time weaving through Ellie's massive garden. Clusters and rows of trees, sculpted hedges, and stone walls partitioned the garden into square, rectangular, even circular areas. Several sections exploded with roses and other flowering plants, their aromas dense in the night air. A few held marble fountains and sitting areas. One large rectangular section was filled with sculptures, a couple as tall as fifteen feet. Reminded me of the Louvre.

We got lost a couple of times and laughed about being like Alice in the maze of the Queen of Hearts. Fortunately, we didn't run across a Mad Hatter, a White Rabbit, a Dormouse, or anyone wanting our heads, but just before we reached the patio, we did see Nicole. She stood near an evergreen shrub at the garden's edge, staring skyward. I glanced up, thinking she must be looking at the moon or maybe a shooting star. No moon, only a scattering of stars, none of them moving.

"Nicole, I want to introduce you to Jill Casey."

Her gaze remained locked skyward as if she hadn't heard me.

"Nicole?"

No response.

I touched her arm and again called her name.

She looked at me. Blankly.

"Are you okay?" I asked.

"Who are you?" she asked.

"Hank. Dr. Lawson. We met earlier."

She stared at me for a beat, but said nothing.

"I'm your grandmother's doctor. Remember?"

No response. She glanced at Jill and then turned her eyes back to me. "Why are you here?"

Now I was getting concerned. "Your party."

"Party?" Her gaze again rose to the night sky.

I grabbed her arm and gave it a shake. "Nicole?"

She looked at me, her face expressionless, her pupils slightly dilated but no more so than would be expected in the dim light that filtered down from the patio.

"Are you okay?" I asked.

Nicole's brow furrowed and her eyes narrowed. "Who are you?"

"I told you. I'm . . ."

"Dr. Lawson?"

I turned to see Sam, standing on the patio's edge, one hand waving me toward him. "There's been an accident."

Chapter 8

As soon as I entered the house, I heard voices, some high-pitched and stressed, others more like moans, even a sob or two. The guests had gathered near the bottom of the spiral staircase that led to the second and third floors. I pushed through the crowd.

An elderly man sprawled on the marble floor, moaning, his face frosted with sweat. His breaths came in labored gasps. An elderly woman sat on the bottom step, near his head, and dabbed his face with a wadded napkin. His left leg was laterally rotated in an awkward position and I knew instantly it was either a hip fracture or dislocation. I knelt next to him.

"I'm Dr. Lawson."

The man's head rotated back and forth, grunts and groans escaping his open mouth.

"This is my husband, Jim," the woman said. "Jim Mallory. I'm Louise." Her voice broke. "Help him. He's in so much pain."

"What happened?"

Jim found his voice and between grunts said, "Stupidity. That's what happened." He grimaced. "I was coming down the stairs . . . talking . . . not paying attention. Missed a step."

He swallowed hard. His wife wiped his face. "Must have tumbled down a dozen of them. My hip hurts like a bitch."

"Let me take a look."

"You're Ellie's doc. Right?" Jim asked.

"That's right."

Someone behind me said, "We called the paramedics."

Divya appeared. "I'll go get my bag from the car."

I checked the pulse in his left ankle but found none. "I need some scissors or a knife."

I heard a click behind me and one of the young men extended an open black-handled switchblade toward me. Normally I'd ask why he carried a switchblade, but right now I didn't care. Mr. Mallory took priority.

I began at the cuff and worked upward, the knife easily slicing through the fabric. After I divided the pant leg up to the groin, I checked for pulses higher up but again found none. His thigh was neither swollen nor discolored. A good sign. Meant he wasn't bleeding into his thigh. At least not massively. Of course, that could change at any time.

I unbuckled and removed his belt. Using the knife, I cut his pants completely away and then slit up the side of his blue boxers. Now I could see his hip. A large ugly bump protruded laterally, indicating a hip dislocation. I heard several gasps behind me.

I spun on my heel and looked at the crowd. "Everybody move back and give us some space here."

Almost reluctantly the curious onlookers began to shuffle backward. Not too far. No one wanted to miss something as exciting as this. I saw Ellie and Sam to my left, near the back of the group. Both of their faces were creased with concern.

I nodded toward Sam and then jerked my head toward the crowd.

He moved to the front of the group, turned, spread his arms, and began herding everyone back toward the great room. "Let's move back, everyone," he said. "Give Dr. Lawson room to work."

Divya appeared with her bag and the portable EKG machine. Evan followed.

"That looks bad," Evan said.

Divya grabbed his arm. "You're not helping."

"But look at—"

I tossed a frown at him, halting him in midsentence before turning back to Jim. "It probably looks worse than it is." Maybe, maybe not. I wasn't sure yet. But Jim needed good news about now. "We'll take care of it."

"Can you do something about the pain?"

"I'm working on it."

Divya began setting up an IV system. I inserted a needle into Jim's arm, secured it with a strip of tape, and connected the IV line. Divya attached the other end to the plastic fluid bag. I didn't have anything to hang the bag on, so I looked back toward the crowd, found Mr. Switchblade, and motioned to him. He hesitated a beat as if he wasn't sure what to do, so I motioned again. "Come here." Sam stepped aside and let him pass. "Hold this." I handed him the bag.

Divya filled a syringe and inserted the needle into the IV line's side port. "Dilaudid, two milligrams," she said. She pushed the plunger. "That should help."

Jim clutched his chest and began gasping for breath. His sweating increased.

"What is it?" I asked.

"My chest," he gasped.

"Jim has heart problems," Louise said. She was rummaging through her purse. "He gets angina whenever he's stressed."

This would definitely qualify as stress.

His pain was likely a simple bout of angina, easily relieved with nitroglycerin, but other possibilities lined up in my brain.

Louise retrieved a small bottle of nitroglycerin and fumbled with it, the obvious arthritis in her hands making it difficult. Before she could open it, Divya handed me the nitro spray she keeps in her bag.

"Open wide," I said to Jim. He did and I pumped two quick sprays into his mouth. "Close your mouth."

Divya began hooking up our EKG machine.

"Feeling better?" I asked.

He took a couple of deep breaths. "My chest does. Can't say the same for my leg."

While Divya ran the EKG, I took a closer look at his hip. Still no swelling, still no pulses, and now the leg appeared paler and felt much cooler. I couldn't be sure without X-rays, but it looked more like a dislocation than a fracture, which meant the out-of-position bone was pressing on the femoral artery, blocking blood flow. It needed to be reseated and it probably wasn't wise to wait for the medics. With little or no blood flow to his leg, time was critical.

Divya handed me the EKG. Sinus tach about 120 but otherwise normal. No evidence of an acute MI.

I explained the situation to Jim and his wife.

"How can it hurt and feel cold and numb at the same time?" Jim asked.

"The dislocation hurts. The coldness and numbness are because the dislocated bone is compressing the artery and the nerves."

"So what does that mean?"

"It means I need to pop it back in place."

"Sounds painful," Jim said.

"Only for a minute and then it'll feel much better."

"Then do it."

I looked at his wife, confusion and fear on her face. "It'll be okay," I said.

If this worked, that is. Reducing a dislocated hip is sometimes impossible without general anesthesia. The muscles around the hip are very powerful and they react to injury by contracting and resisting movement. It's a self-protective mechanism. The muscles seem to know they should immobilize the injured hip. To reduce it, I had to overcome this contraction. Not an easy proposition. The fact that Mr. Mallory was old and had the muscle atrophy that comes with age would help. Hopefully enough.

Divya gave him another two milligrams of Dilaudid.

Jim lay slightly rotated toward his right side, so I eased him flat on the floor and then looked at Evan.

"Get over here and hold him so he won't slide across the floor while I do this."

"Me?"

"Yes, you."

A young man stepped up. "I'll help."

"Good. You and Evan each grab him under his arms and hold on."

Mrs. Mallory moved out of the way so that Evan and the young man could kneel near Jim's head. Each grabbed an arm, high, near his armpit.

"Ready?" I asked.

Jim nodded.

I raised and flexed Jim's left knee. He grimaced.

"I'll have this done in a minute," I said. The words *hopefully* and *with luck* came to mind, but I kept them to myself.

I wedged my left forearm behind his bent knee and then grabbed his ankle.

"You guys ready?"

"Got him," Evan said.

"Jim, take a deep breath."

With my forearm, I pulled his knee toward me while I also tugged and slightly rotated his lower leg. I felt the ball of his hip slide downward. He moaned. I twisted his leg inward sharply and released the traction. I felt the ball snap back into the socket.

Jim let out his breath. "Oh, that's much better."

"Told you," I said. "Now we need to get you to the hospital for some X-rays."

I checked for pulses, finding that his popliteal and pedal pulses were now strong. "Everything looks good."

"Is it broken?" Mrs. Mallory asked as she hovered behind me.

I looked up at her. "I don't think so, but the X-rays will tell us if I'm right. Looks more like a dislocation."

Her eyes glistened with tears. "That's better, isn't it? Better than a fracture?"

"Yes, it is."

She sobbed.

I stood and gave her a hug. "He'll be just fine."

She laughed and cried at the same time. "Thank you."

I turned back toward Evan and the young man who had helped. "Good job."

"Don't tell Evan that," Divya said. "He'll be insufferable."

Evan looked at her. "This PA thing isn't all that hard. Maybe we should swap jobs."

Divya gave me a look that said, "Told you so," and then began packing things back into her medical kit.

I shook hands with the young man. He was tall, handsome, with thick dark hair. He wore a tan suit, a white shirt, and a red tie, loosened at the collar. "Thanks."

"No problem. Glad I could help."

"Who are you?"

"Robert Woolrich."

"The groom?"

"That's right."

Nicole appeared and hugged him. "There you are."

He kissed her cheek. "I just got here. Walked in and saw this."

"And he saved the day," I said.

"No, you did," Robert said. "I just helped."

"But you're my hero," Nicole said with a laugh as she hugged him.

She seemed completely normal now. Had I misread things outside on the patio? Had she simply been distracted? Being the center of attention at a party and a wedding closing in can do that, but deep down, I didn't buy it. Something was going on with Nicole. I just hadn't figured out what yet.

I heard sirens approaching and looked down at Jim. "Sounds like your chariot has arrived."

Chapter 9

The next morning Divya and I got an early start. We saw a new patient and three follow-ups before stopping for coffee. The plan was to head back to Shadow Pond and update some of our medical records, but on the way we stopped by Ellie Wentworth's. I couldn't shake the image of the confused and disoriented Nicole I had seen in the garden last night. I wanted to believe that it was nothing, but that little voice that says all is not well kept whispering in my head. I learned years ago to never ignore such murmurings.

We found Ellie outside, supervising the workers who were preparing the dance floor for the wedding. She was more casual than I had ever seen her. Blue jeans, a blue work shirt, untucked, and a floppy hat to protect her from the sun.

"Hank. Divya. What are you doing here?"

"Checking on you," I said.

She said something to one of the workers and then waved a hand toward the garden as she climbed the steps up to the patio. "I'm doing just fine, but I'm glad you stopped by anyway." She rubbed her hands together as if knocking off dirt, but I noticed that her hands were clean. "How about some lemonade?"

By the time we returned to the parlor and sat down,

three glasses of lemonade appeared, carried by one of the kitchen staff. It was cold and perfect.

"So you're doing okay?" I asked.

She looked at me over the rim of her glass and gave a sly smile. "Yes, but that's not why you're here. Is it?"

One thing you can say about Ellie is that very few things get by her. She seems innately able to read faces and body language, and sometimes I believe she has a cosmic antenna dialed in to thought waves.

"I want to talk with Nicole."

"About what?"

"I should talk with her before I say anything."

"Hank, are you trying to scare me?"

"No. It's probably nothing."

"That's not waylaying my concern."

"Sorry. Is she here?"

Ellie sighed and shook her head. She picked up the phone and buzzed Nicole's room. When she hung up, she said Nicole would be right down.

Nicole appeared in less than a minute. She wore jeans, hems frayed, no shoes, and a pink T-shirt, its hem tied in a knot, exposing her tanned abdomen.

"What's up?"

"Hank wants to talk with you," Ellie said.

"About what?"

Ellie nodded to me.

"Let's step outside."

Nicole followed me to the patio. I led her down to one end, away from the men who were working in the garden.

"Do you remember seeing me last night? With Jill? Right down there?" I pointed toward the area where we had run into her at the party.

Her brow furrowed, but she didn't say anything.

"You seemed confused."

"Probably too much champagne."

"I don't think so." I smiled, trying to relax her. It didn't seem to be working. She wound one finger in the knotted

T-shirt and stared toward her bare feet. "Did you take anything else last night?"

"Of course not. Why would you think that?"

"You looked disoriented. You didn't remember me and yet we had met just thirty minutes earlier."

"I'm not good at remembering people."

"And you didn't seem to know where you were or what was going on."

"I'm fine."

"You didn't take anything?"

She rolled one foot up on its side. "I told you I didn't."

"Have you ever had periods where you were confused or disoriented or maybe dizzy before?"

"I don't want to talk about this. I'm fine. I just have a lot on my mind."

That was possible, of course. I just didn't believe that was the whole story.

"You sure?" I asked.

"Of course. Now I have to get cleaned up. Ashley and I are going shopping."

"What if I arranged a time to examine you and draw a few blood tests?"

"I don't need any of that."

"Probably not, but it would make me feel better."

"I don't have time to deal with all this. I'm getting married and I have a whole list of things to get done."

"Like shopping?"

"Of course. There are a half dozen parties to go to. Before the wedding."

"Will you at least think about it?"

"No. I told you I don't have time to deal with this."

She turned and walked inside. I followed. Nicole headed for the stairs without saying a word to Ellie and Divya on the way by.

"What was that all about?" Ellie asked me.

I hesitated. Should I tell Ellie anything? Worry her needlessly? Would Nicole consider our talk confidential?

Of course she didn't really say anything, so I had nothing to reveal anyway. She wasn't my patient, so expressing my concerns to Ellie wouldn't be a breach of any kind. But was it fair to Nicole? Or was it fair to Nicole if I ignored my concerns? If something was wrong with her and I ignored my gut, how could I ever justify that? I decided that saying too much was better than saying too little.

"I'm worried about Nicole," I said.

"Why?"

I told her about Jill and me running into Nicole in the garden the night before and how her behavior had been odd.

"She seemed disoriented," I said. "Confused. She didn't know who I was and yet she had met me just a half hour earlier."

"With all the excitement and people here last night it probably slipped her mind. Not that you aren't memorable, but you know how young people are."

That sounded reasonable. I would have bought it had lines of concern not appeared in her forehead. I could read people fairly well, too.

"You don't really believe that, do you?" I asked. "There's something else, isn't there?"

Ellie sighed and placed her lemonade on the coffee table. She stared at the glass but didn't speak for a minute, as if trying to sort out what to say and how to say it. Finally, she nodded slowly. "Yes, there is something else." She looked at me. "A couple of years ago Nicole got into drugs and alcohol and some other bad behaviors. Mark and Jackie got her help at one of those clinics up in the Finger Lakes region. When she left, I thought it was all behind her. But when she was here a couple months ago, I saw hints of the old behavior. I confronted her about it." She picked up the lemonade and took a sip. "She didn't take it well and we had a big fight. Of course we made up later and she promised that she wasn't using anything, but I could tell something wasn't right."

"Something like what?" Divya asked.

"I don't know. Nothing I could put my finger on. She just didn't seem her usual self."

"What about now?" I asked. "Have you seen anything since she arrived that would raise suspicion?"

"Honestly I haven't had much time with her. There's been so much going on and so many people here that we haven't had a chance to sit and chat. But to answer your question, I haven't noticed anything out of the ordinary."

"What types of drugs was she using?" Divya asked. "Back then?"

"I'm certain about alcohol and marijuana. She told me herself. She said all the kids did it." She took a deep breath and let it out slowly. "Like that made it okay. I suspected more. Maybe even cocaine. I know her father, Mark, used that some. A few years ago. But my Nicole? I prayed she wasn't using that." Her shoulders sagged and she sat back more deeply into the sofa.

I sat down next to Ellie and took her hand. "I could be wrong. Maybe she was just stressed from all the people and the party and her upcoming wedding. That's a lot of stress for a young woman."

"You don't believe that," Ellie said, more a statement than a question.

No, I didn't. "I've been wrong before." I smiled.

"Hank, you can't con a con artist. Remember, I'm from Texas and we're professionals at that stuff."

I laughed. "Okay. I won't try. Still, I could be wrong. Keep your eyes open and let me know if Nicole does anything odd."

"How would you describe odd for a twenty-five-year-old?"

She had a point. "Just let me know if she has any episodes of confusion or she appears disoriented. Seems out of it. Things like that."

"You're making me nervous."

"I'm sorry. I probably shouldn't have said anything."

"No, I'm glad you did. If there's something wrong with Nicole I want to know about it. Whatever it is." She laid an open hand across her chest.

"Are you okay?"

"Oh, I'm fine. And yes, I've been taking my medicines regularly." The twinkle was back in her eyes.

"Make sure you do." I stood. "You call me if anything changes. With either you or Nicole."

By the time Divya and I said our good-byes and reached her SUV, my cell phone was buzzing. I pulled it from my pocket and looked at the screen. Jill.

"I have the lab results on that waitress friend of yours," she said.

"She's not a friend. She's a patient."

She laughed. "I'm just yanking your chain."

"Funny."

"Actually her labs are not exactly normal."

I listened while she went over the test results, and then thanked her, telling her I would swing by her office later.

I closed the phone, slipped it into my pocket, and looked at Divya. "Got time to go by and see Miranda Randall with me?"

"Of course."

Chapter 10

I called Miranda. She was at work. When I told her that we needed to go over her lab results, she asked if it could wait until she got home. I told her it would only take a few minutes. She said she had a break due in twenty.

It took us only ten minutes to get there, so Divya and I sat at Panama Joe's polished oak bar and sipped iced tea. Behind the bar, extending its entire length and reaching the ceiling, a shelved glass wall held hundreds of bottles of liquor of seemingly every variety. Two waitresses loitered near the far end, chatting, waiting for the two bartenders to complete their drink orders. Sunlight slanted through the open double doors that led to the deck, where we had had lunch the day of the great jellyfish massacre. A warm breeze followed.

"Has Evan said more about the van?" Divya asked.

"No. But he will. You know how he is when he gets an idea in his head."

"I'm amazed when he has anything in his head."

"You know my brother too well."

I felt a tap on my shoulder and turned to see Miranda.

"I only have ten minutes," she said.

"Is there somewhere private we can talk?"

She looked around. The lunch crowd had descended and

the tables were mostly filled, the noise level rising by the minute. "We can go outside. Would that work?"

I paid for our iced teas and we followed Miranda into the front parking lot. Moving away from the entrance, we settled beneath a shade tree near the edge of the asphalt.

"All of your lab tests were normal except, as I expected, your thyroid. It's overactive. Producing too much hormone. That's what's causing your symptoms."

"Why is it doing that? Did I do something to cause it?"

"No. It's not your fault. You have what we call Hashimoto's thyroiditis."

Her eyes widened. "That sounds scary."

"It does, doesn't it? But it's not. It's actually common and easily treatable."

"What is it? Some awful Japanese disease? I've never been to Japan."

I laughed. "It's not awful and it's not Japanese. Hashimoto is the doctor who discovered it over a hundred years ago, so it's not exactly new and exotic."

"Then what the hell is it?"

"An inflammation of the thyroid gland. It's in the family of autoimmune diseases. Things like lupus and scleroderma. In these, the body builds antibodies against itself. In Hashimoto's, these antibodies attack the thyroid gland. It becomes inflamed and produces too much hormone."

"Am I contagious or anything like that?"

"No," Divya said. "You can't catch it and you can't pass it to anyone. It just happens."

"Oh, lucky me."

"We have medications for it," Divya said. "You will feel much better in just a day or two."

"I already feel a little better from the ones you gave me yesterday."

"Those helped with the symptoms," I said. "The new ones will correct the problem."

"Are they expensive?"

"No," Divya said. "Besides, we might be able to get them through the Hamptons Heritage free clinic."

"Free? I didn't know they had such a thing."

"Jill Casey, the administrator, set it up," I said. "She's also the one that did your lab testing for free. She's arranged for an endocrinologist to see you about this."

Miranda looked at me. "You know I don't have insurance, right?"

"It's a free clinic," Divya said. "It's designed for people in your circumstance."

"So what do I need to do now?" Miranda asked.

"Divya will write you a prescription for two medications," I said. "One will prevent the thyroid from making so much hormone, and one will block its release into the bloodstream. Your thyroid levels will come down and all your symptoms should improve. Then we'll have you see the endocrinologist and he'll pick up the ball from there."

Miranda blew a wayward strand of hair from her face. It didn't stay, so she settled it behind one ear. "I don't really have time to deal with this. I can barely cover my rent and it seems like I have to work all the time to do that." She looked up at the sky, took a deep breath, and let it out slowly. "Why does this have to happen now?"

"Like you said, lucky you." I smiled. "There's nothing to be afraid of. This won't turn your world upside down. You simply have to take some medications and then life will go on as before."

She dabbed one eye with a knuckle. "Are you sure?"

"Of course I am. I'm a doctor." I smiled again. "Take the medications and this'll be behind you in no time."

She glanced at her watch again. "I have to get back to work."

Divya handed her the prescription. "Take this over to the free clinic and they will give you the medications. We've already talked to them, so they'll have everything waiting."

Miranda folded the prescription and stuffed it into the pocket of her jeans. "I don't know how I'll ever repay you."

"You don't have to," I said. "Just get better."

Again she knuckled a tear from one eye. "Maybe a free appetizer next time you're in."

I laughed. "We never turn down free food."

Chapter 11

After leaving Miranda and Panama Joe's, I headed back to Shadow Pond. Divya had a luncheon engagement with her parents, something she was not looking forward to, since she was sure they would continue pressuring her to leave HankMed and get back to the life she was born to. She loved her parents but hated these discussions, which she saw as interference in her life. Not to mention the healthy dose of guilt they always dropped on her for not following cultural and family traditions. I told her not to worry, that she was tough and had weathered their lectures before. She gave me a hug, saying that's exactly what she needed to hear.

I expected to find Evan at home, but when I got there, everything was quiet. No Evan. I wasn't sure whether that was a good thing or not. Evan out of sight usually meant he was up to something. My money was on his van scheme, but the possibilities were endless.

I had planned to drag him out for lunch, so I called his cell. No answer. I left a message, asking him to call back. I then called Jill to see if she was free. She wasn't. Two meetings and a handful of catastrophes. I asked her what catastrophes, but she said she didn't have time to explain and hung up. I stared at the phone for a minute, considered calling her back, but thought better of it. Best not to rile her when she was already riled.

I rummaged through the refrigerator and cabinets. Didn't take long to realize that a trip to the store wouldn't be a bad idea. I finally settled for peanut butter on crackers and the latest issue of *JAMA*. I stretched out on a patio lounge chair and began reading. The peace and quiet was wonderful. So wonderful that soon the magazine dropped to my chest and I fell asleep.

Evan parked next to a fully tricked-out bright blue van at Fleming's Custom Shop. As he stepped out of his car, Rachel Fleming walked out the showroom door. Tall and thin, she wore tan slacks and a navy blue silk shirt, cuffs rolled to her elbows. The soft curls of her light brown hair framed her face. Her brown eyes sparkled in the sunlight when she smiled.

"Well, if it isn't the CFO of HankMed," she said.

"At your service." Evan offered a half bow.

"Ready to buy that new van?"

"Actually I stopped by to see you."

"Liar."

"Okay, so I am here to talk about the new HankMed van, but seeing you is a big bonus."

"How sweet of you to say that." She pulled the door open and held it for him.

Once inside she led him to one of the vans on the showroom floor. She opened up the driver's door and let him crawl into the front seat. He settled in and placed his hands on the steering wheel.

"This one is cool."

"Full leather throughout. State-of-the-art navigation system. Bluetooth and iPod connections. Everything voice activated. It even has a hard drive where you can dictate notes while driving."

"You're kidding."

"We just finished this one. It's for a local attorney. He

D. P. Lyle

wanted to be able to dictate letters and whatever while behind the wheel." She indicated a button on the steering wheel. "Simply press the button and start dictating. Press it again when you're done. You can then wirelessly upload it to a laptop or to a thumb drive through this USB connection." She pointed to a slot just left of the navigation screen. "This would be perfect for dictating medical notes, too."

Evan pressed the button several times, but nothing happened.

"The ignition has to be on for it to work." She stepped aside. "Let me show you what's in back."

Rachel swung open the side door while Evan climbed between the front seats and settled into one of the rear captain's chairs.

"Look up," Rachel said. "That's a forty-two-inch plasma screen that swings down. Grab the handle and give it a tug."

Evan did. The screen folded down in front of him. "This is so cool."

"You can attach a laptop or DVD or whatever."

"You guys are amazing." He spun the chair around, now facing the rear compartment. The third row of seats had been replaced with a folding worktable on one side and filing drawers on the other. "This is like a rolling office."

"That's exactly what the client wanted. For HankMed this rear area would be configured for medical equipment and storage. We can customize it to fit your exact needs."

"You've sold me. Now if I can just get it past my brother." Evan climbed out and walked a lap around the van, ending back where he started. "Impressive."

"Want something to drink? Coffee?"

"Sure."

Evan shoved the side door closed. Rachel screamed. Evan froze. Two of her fingers were trapped in the door.

My lounge-chair nap didn't last long, but somewhere along the way it must have descended into a deep sleep, complete with a vivid dream. Evan and I were kids. We were at some oceanfront resort with our father. We played on the beach while he sat at an umbrella-shaded table talking with two men I'd never seen before. Dad wore swim trunks and an open shirt, the two men suits and ties. For some reason the table was near the water's edge and gentle waves lapped at Dad's feet.

Somehow I knew Dad was running a scam on the men. Not a big leap. Dad was always running a scam or two. Not sure what this one was, but the men were angry, shouting and pointing fingers, faces red and distorted. Dad stood and tried to leave, but the men handcuffed him and told him he was under arrest.

Evan began crying.

I ran to Dad, but before I could reach him, the dream evaporated.

I woke to the trilling of my cell phone. In my confused state it took several rings before I recognized the sound and answered.

It was Evan. He talked rapidly, mostly to me, but also to someone else. Took a minute before I realized that he was at the van dealership and the other person was Rachel Fleming. Finally I was able to calm him down enough to understand what was going on. When I did, I told him I'd be right there.

Traffic was light, so it took only thirty minutes to reach Fleming's Custom Shop in Westhampton. A salesman led me to a back office where I found Evan and Rachel.

Rachel's pictures didn't do her justice. She was much prettier in person. Of course right now she wasn't at her best. Her hand lay on her desktop, beneath a plastic bag filled with ice.

"This is my brother," Evan said. "He's the doctor. He'll fix it."

Rachel lifted the ice bag from her hand and I could see that her middle and ring fingers were swollen and purple.

"Ouch," I said. "Fingers and car doors don't mix."

"It was an accident," Evan said. "She was showing me

this cool van and I closed the door. Her finger got in the way."

"Got in the way?" She shook her head and looked up at me. "I was going to go over to one of those urgent cares or maybe the hospital, but Evan said you could take care of it. Can you?"

I pulled a chair around, scooted up next to the desk, and sat. "Let me take a look."

"It hurts like the devil," she said. "Throbs like it's going to explode or something."

The middle finger was slightly swollen with a small blood pocket beneath the nail. We call this a subungual hematoma. The ring finger hadn't fared as well. It had a much larger hematoma and appeared to be slightly out of line near the distal knuckle.

"It's not going to explode, but the blood that's collected beneath the nails makes it feel that way. First thing to do is release the pressure."

"That doesn't sound like fun."

"It will only take a minute. Do you have a paper clip and a cigarette lighter?"

"I've got plenty of paper clips, but I don't smoke. I bet one of the guys in the back has one."

I looked at Evan. "Go see if you can find a cigarette lighter and a pair of pliers."

"Pliers?" Rachel asked. "What are you going to do? Pull my fingernails off?"

"Yes, and then the wings off a couple of butterflies."

She laughed.

"Maybe I'll pull out Evan's nails, but not yours."

"I like you," Rachel said. "I wish my doctor was funny."

While Evan was gone, I examined Rachel's fingers more thoroughly. The nerves and blood vessels were intact, but the middle phalanx of her ring finger wasn't so lucky.

"Looks like you have a fracture. Should be simple to reduce, but I'll have to give it a tug to do it. You okay with that?"

"Does it hurt?"

"Only for a very brief second."

"Jesus." She sighed and extended her hand toward me. "Go ahead."

I carefully pinched her finger between my thumb and forefinger and said, "Here goes." I gave the finger one quick pull. She flinched and gave out a soft whimper. I felt the bones settle back into position, the slight off angle now reduced. "There, all done."

"It still hurts."

"That's the hematomas . . . the blood pockets. Fractures don't hurt much. Those do."

Evan returned with a pair of well-worn pliers and a yellow plastic cigarette lighter. I unfolded one end of a paper clip so that it extended out at a ninety-degree angle. I grasped the clip with the pliers and began heating the extended tip with the lighter's flame.

"What kind of medieval device is that?" Rachel asked.

"One that works," I said. "In the ER we have fancy drills for this, but they require applying pressure, which can be painful. This will burn through the nail. No pressure needed."

The clip was now heated, so I angled the tip directly down on top of one fingernail. It immediately began to smoke as the hot tip bored through, and when it reached the hematoma, there was a slight hiss and a squirt of dark blood. Startled, she jerked her hand back.

"Doesn't that feel better?" I asked.

"It does." She examined her finger and the small charred hole in the nail. "This sure messes up the expensive manicure I got yesterday."

"Let's get the other one done."

Releasing the second hematoma was as easy as the first. I then pulled a roll of tape out of my bag.

"I'm going to tape these two fingers together. Sort of a poor man's splint."

I tore off three strips of tape and then applied them one

at a time, wrapping each securely around her two fingers. After I finished, she examined her hand.

"Not very fashionable," she said.

"But effective. I'll write you a prescription for a pain med."

"And that's it?" she asked. "I just wait for it to heal?"

"I'll need an X-ray of your fingers. You can either run by Hamptons Heritage or I can have Divya, my PA, swing by and do it here."

"If we had a HankMed van," Evan said, "you'd have an X-ray machine here with you. Right out in the parking lot."

Rachel laughed. "Who's the salesperson here?"

I shook my head. "Are you two going to gang up on me?"

"Would it help?" Rachel asked.

"Probably not."

She glanced at her watch. "I have a couple of errands to run over near the hospital, so I'll go by there."

"After I'm sure everything is lined up properly, I'll devise a splint for you. It'll take four to six weeks to heal."

"Six weeks?" She looked at Evan. "You owe me big-time."

"How about lunch?"

"It'll take a lot more than that. At least a very expensive dinner." She laughed. "When your girlfriend gets back, that is."

"I think I can handle that," Evan said. "You and Paige will hit it off. Like you, she's smart and pretty."

"Is he always this charming?"

"In his own mind," I said.

"At dinner we can talk more about the employee health plan I told you about," Evan said.

"What plan?" I asked.

"Evan proposed a program for our employees." He shrugged. "It actually looks good. My father is working the numbers, so we'll see."

"We'd be happy to help if we can," I said.

"Of course that means you'll definitely have to buy that van."

"What van?" I asked.

"We've been working on a really cool one," Evan said. "It'll have computers with big screens and big comfortable chairs in back. It'll have room for a portable X-ray machine, a sonogram, oxygen tanks, and even a folding treadmill for doing stress tests."

See what I mean? Evan's van scheme wasn't going to simply fade away. When he gets focused, he never lets go.

"The treadmill will slide beneath the floorboard and can be pulled out and set up in just a matter of minutes," Rachel said. "There's also a place for a fairly large medicine cabinet so you can carry most of your drugs with you."

"Sounds like you've got it covered," I said. "But we don't need a van."

Rachel shrugged. "You might change your mind once you see it."

"Can't afford one either," I said.

"I bet we can make you a deal you can't refuse."

"You sound like the Godfather."

She laughed. "Would it help if I were?"

"It wouldn't hurt."

"But I don't have a horse's head to make my point."

Beautiful and funny. I liked Rachel.

"Just take a look at what Rachel put together," Evan said. "I mean, she even sacrificed her hand to make the sale."

"I think you sacrificed her hand."

Rachel laughed and then said, "Maybe the CEO should bail out the CFO by taking a look at what I can offer."

I knew I didn't have a chance. She was charming and I felt at least somewhat responsible for what Evan had done. I'm not sure why, but it had been that way most of our lives. Evan always meant well but seemed to attract trouble like a black sweater attracts lint. Regardless, I caved.

Rachel gave me a tour of their facility, including the

three conversions they had under way. She showed me sketches of what she suggested for the HankMed van. Not something she had simply scribbled on a piece of paper, but rather professional drawings, showing both exterior and interior layouts. She had obviously put a great deal of thought and effort into it.

"I'll make you a copy of the sketches so you can take them home. Just look at them and give it some thought. Hopefully you'll change your mind."

"Will do. No promises, though."

"I understand. If you decide not to, that's okay. At least I'll get a fancy dinner out of it." She jerked her head toward Evan.

"And a broken finger," I said.

She held up her hand. "No way I could forget that."

Chapter 12

When Evan and I returned to Shadow Pond, we found Divya, sitting at the table on the patio with a wineglass and bottle, each half-empty. From where she sat, she had a view down the slope and over Shadow Pond's elaborate gardens. She seemed deep in thought and didn't hear us until we stepped onto the patio. She turned and looked at us.

"Where have you guys been?" Divya asked.

I told her what had happened to Rachel.

She looked up at Evan. "You're such a charmer."

"It was an accident. Those things just happen."

Divya let out a brief laugh. "To you, but not the rest of us."

"Where did the wine come from?" I asked.

"Boris."

"Boris?"

"He saw me sitting here and took pity on me. He asked if I needed anything. I told him no, but he had Dieter bring over the wine anyway. Want some?"

"Sure."

Evan retrieved two wineglasses from the kitchen, and filled each, handing one to me. We sat at the table with Divya. I took a sip. Outstanding. I picked up the bottle and examined the label. A 2005 Château Lafleur Pomerol. I know little about wines, but this one looked and tasted expensive.

"It is," Divya said, obviously guessing what I was thinking. "Maybe two hundred a bottle."

Loose change for Boris, but still. "He took pity on you for what?" I asked.

"My parents can be so infuriating sometimes."

"Are they still upset with you about Raj?"

Raj was Divya's former fiancé. Her arranged fiancé. She and Raj had agreed that marriage wasn't in their future. Friendship seemed a better fit. Divya's parents felt otherwise.

"Oh, yes, they're still unhappy about that, but this is something else." She opened her purse and pulled out an envelope. "Take a look at this."

I slid the letter from the envelope and unfolded it. It was on her father's stationery and was addressed to the International Federation of Red Cross and Red Crescent Societies.

"What is this?"

"My parents' latest scheme. It's a letter of introduction to the president of the International Red Cross. They want me to work with them and with the World Health Organization." She crossed her arms. "Help with some of their outreach programs."

"And leave HankMed?" Evan asked.

"I would have to move to Geneva."

"Are you considering doing this?" I asked.

"Of course not. I'm perfectly happy right here. But they seem to think I need to be doing something bigger. More international." She took a deep breath.

"Maybe they see you capable of bigger and better things," I said. "Which of course is true."

"What could be bigger than HankMed?" Evan said.

Divya looked at him for a beat and then said, "I can't believe I actually agree with you. For once." She took a sip of her wine. "This is what I want to do. I don't want to travel all over the world and deal with people I don't know. Here, we have a practice that is very personal. I like that. I don't want to give it up."

"What did you tell them?" I asked.

"That there was no way I would consider it. That I was perfectly content where I am and with what I'm doing."

"I take it they didn't agree."

She shook her head. "That's why I'm here and they are finishing their lunch without me."

"The Red Cross's loss is our gain," Evan said.

"What do you want?" Divya asked. "Must be something big, since I know how difficult it is for you to be nice."

"Can't I just be nice without any strings attached?"

"There is a first time for everything."

"Since Evan is being so nice, you can hang with us tonight," I said. "Not that we're going to do anything exciting, but you're welcome to share our boredom."

She poured each of us a little more wine. "I'm going to a party this evening."

"Party?" Evan said.

"Nicole and her friends are getting together at a restaurant and she's invited me to join them. Jill, too."

"Then Hank and I should be there. It'll be fun."

"It will be fun because you will not be there."

"We just might be," Evan said.

"It's a party for Nicole and her *female* friends," Divya said. "Do you understand what that means?"

"Of course I do. It means a room full of potential Hank-Med clients."

"Really? You want to go solicit clients?"

"It worked at Ellie's party the other night."

"How so?" I asked.

"I lined you up three new clients. The uncle of one of the guys there and the parents of one of the women."

"Really?"

"Yeah. Donald something and Mr. and Mrs. Palumbo."

I was impressed and said so.

Divya looked at Evan. "The problem is that trouble always follows in your wake."

"That's not true."

"Rachel the van girl might feel differently."

"The van girl? You make her sound like a homeless person."

"Or a superhero," I said. "I can see the movie marquee now . . . *The Adventures of Van Girl.*"

"That would be awesome," Evan said. "She could have a cool outfit."

Divya rolled her eyes. "You honestly want to know why I don't want you at this party?"

"Why?"

Divya looked at me as if asking for help. I preferred not to engage, so I merely shrugged.

My cell phone rang. It was one of the radiologists over at Hamptons Heritage Hospital. He had a report on Rachel Fleming's X-ray. He talked, I listened, and then I thanked him and hung up.

"That was the X-ray report. Looks like Rachel's finger is fractured. Middle phalanx of her ring finger. It's in good alignment. I'll run over there and make a better splint for her."

"I'll take care of it," Divya said. "Then I have to go home and get ready for tonight." She stood.

"You're really not going to tell me where the party is?" Evan asked.

"Not a chance." She picked up her purse. "I'll talk with you tomorrow. We have a couple of new patients to see in the morning." She left.

"Since the party is out, what do you want to do?" I asked.

Evan shook his head. "I'm going to the party. Want to come?"

"We're not invited. It would be rude to crash a wedding party."

"It is never rude to take advantage of an opportunity."

"I thought it was a party, not an opportunity."

"Same thing."

Sometimes my brother amazes me. Right or wrong, true or false, his confidence level is off the chart. The fact that his attempts at rounding up business are often odd and awkward and he mostly strikes out doesn't seem to bother him. In psychiatric terms it's called intermittent reinforcement. It's part of the old classical conditioning scenario and is the most powerful motivator known. Regardless of what you're attempting, if you're successful every time, it becomes boring, and if you are never successful, it becomes frustrating. But if you win every now and then, if you hit it out of the park just one out of ten times, you can't quit playing the game. That's the way Evan is with business. About one out of ten potential clients fall for his shtick and that's all he needs.

"So exactly how are you going to find out where this party is?"

"Lawson. Evan R. Lawson."

"So now you're James Bond?"

"I would make a great superspy. Even better than James Bond."

"This delusion is based on what?"

"I'm smart. I'm stealthy. I'm crafty."

"Don't forget humble."

He stood. "I'm going to shower and get ready. Sure you don't want to come?"

"I'm sure."

"Your loss."

"I still don't see how you're going to find out where the party is."

"Simple. I'm going to go stake out Divya's place and follow her."

"I don't know about a superspy, but you would definitely make a good stalker."

Chapter 13

Evan was in full James Bond mode. He parked his car half a block from Divya's place, shadowed by a tree, and sandwiched between a bright red Chevy pickup and a silver Mercedes. He wore a New York Yankees baseball cap pulled down low and wraparound sunglasses.

Lawson. Evan R. Lawson.

While he waited, he surfed the radio stations and munched from the bag of Cheetos he had picked up at a small mom-and-pop grocery store. As he settled on Fleetwood Mac doing "Gold Dust Woman," he realized he was thirsty. Should have remembered water.

Did James Bond ever forget stuff like that? If so, did he simply dial up Q on his wristwatch phone or some other high-tech gadget and have it delivered by airdrop?

That would be so way cool.

Evan glanced at his own watch. He needed one with cooler features.

Where was Divya? Time to go. The party was waiting.

His thirst grew. He studied the house he had parked near. Maybe they'd give him some water if he asked. Or . . . he eyed the garden hose that nestled in the shrubbery near the front door. As he debated the wisdom of sneaking across the yard for a quick drink, Divya's garage door jerked to life. Her Mercedes SUV backed out. He slid down in the seat and peered over the dash, watching as she drove by without so much as a glance.

Lawson. Evan R. Lawson.

He nearly lost her in traffic a couple of times, mainly because Divya shattered the speed limit and changed lanes at will, but after flashing through a couple of yellow lights, he caught up, just as she turned into the lot at Castellano's, a trendy East Hampton restaurant. Like James Bond would do, Lawson, Evan R. Lawson, rolled on past and did a lap around the block before pulling up to Castellano's valet stand.

Inside, a cacophony of voices and laughter as well as the rich aroma of marinara sauce filled the air. He walked into the crowded bar. The bar along the left side was two deep, mostly women occupying the stools, men standing at their shoulders, no doubt vying for a hookup. The dozen tables were filled. No Divya or Ashley or Nicole in sight. He moved into the only slightly more sedate dining room. Red leather booths lined the walls and four-top tables filled the room. Flowers rose from the necks of the straw-wrapped Chianti bottles that topped each red-checkered tablecloth. Still no one he recognized. He returned to the hostess stand.

A slim young brunette with a model's smile asked, "Can I help you?"

"Evan R. Lawson."

"I'm Brianna."

"I'm looking for my friends, but I didn't see them in the bar."

"Is it the wedding party? Or should I say prewedding party?"

"That's it."

"They're in our private room. Near the back."

Evan looked that way.

"I'll show you," Brianna said.

Evan fell in behind her as she wove through the dining

room. Few of the diners looked up as they passed, some
talking, others devouring forkfuls of pasta, one woman
wiping marinara sauce from the face of her high-chair-
strapped daughter.

"Here you go." Brianna pushed open a door.

"Thanks."

The spacious private room was a mirror image of the dining room. Same tablecloths and Chianti bottles on each of
the eight tables. Along one wall and beneath a row of multi-
paned red-curtained windows a long table held bowls of
pasta, trays of fried calamari, a platter of antipasto, sliced
loaves of Italian bread, small bottles of olive oil and balsamic
vinegar, and an array of wine bottles and goblets. About
thirty young women talked, laughed, and sipped wine.

"Evan?"

He jumped and then turned to see Ashley.

"What are you doing here?" she asked.

"I stopped by for a bite to eat. I was in the bar and I saw
Divya come in and head this way. Then I remembered there
was some party or something for Nicole, so I thought I'd
say hello. I hope I'm not interrupting."

"Not at all. Come on in and have some wine with us."
She balanced a glass of wine in one hand and hooked her
other arm with his. "But since you're the only guy here, I
might have to protect you from some of the girls."

Divya stood near the bar that had been set up for the private party, talking to Jill.

"How is the clinic going?" Divya asked.

"Good and bad. We're up and running, but it seems like
it's almost day-to-day. We have all the doctors we need
lined up and a great staff. The money?" She extended her
hand, flat, palm down, and waggled it. "That's the problem.
We can't seem to find a stable funding source and so I'm
scrambling all the time."

"I don't envy you your job. Dealing with money is never
pleasant."

"True." Jill started to take a sip of wine but hesitated, looking past Divya. "Is that Evan?"

Divya turned. "That rascal. He's harassed me all day about this party. Wanted me to tell him where it was."

"Did you?"

"Of course not. I'll have a word with him."

Divya marched toward Evan, Jill following. He looked up and smiled.

"What are you doing here?" Divya asked.

"Evan was here having dinner," Ashley said. "He saw you come in and like figured out this must be where Nicole's party is."

"I'm sure that's exactly what happened," Divya said. "He's been hounding me all day about this party."

"Is that true?" Ashley asked.

"Of course not," Evan said. "She likes to make trouble."

"With you that never proves difficult."

Ashley laughed. "Either way, I'm glad you're here."

Evan gave Divya a smug look. She frowned back.

Evan felt a tap on his shoulder and turned. It was Esther Palumbo. He had met her at Ellie's party and had set up her parents as HankMed patients.

"Hi, Evan," she said. "I wanted to say hello and thank you for getting my parents in to see your brother."

"Glad I could help."

"My dad needs the help. Too many bad habits."

"Hank can fix those for him."

"We'll see. He's pretty stubborn."

"So is my brother."

Esther laughed. "I want to introduce you to one of my friends. She's looking for a new doctor for her mother."

Lawson. Evan R. Lawson. CFO on the case.

With Jill and Divya at Nicole's party and Evan somewhere playing James Bond, I had a quiet evening at home. I read a little, and then watched an old movie while eating microwave popcorn. Hitchcock's *Rear Window*. One of my favorites. Jimmy Stewart and Grace Kelly. Doesn't get much better than that. I'd seen it a dozen times and would probably watch it a dozen more.

Around eleven o'clock I grew bored, so I had a dish of strawberry ice cream. The perfect cure for boredom. After that, I crawled into bed with the latest James Lee Burke novel. I got through the first four chapters before the phone rang.

It was Evan. He had obviously found the party. I could barely hear him over the background din of voices and music.

"Hank? Hank? Can you hear me?"

"Barely. And no, I am not coming to the party."

"No, that's not it. It's Nicole. She's missing."

I closed the book, set it aside, and swung around to sit on the edge of the bed. "What do you mean?"

"She was here and then she was gone. No one knows where she is."

"Was she behaving oddly beforehand?"

"I don't know. I've been chatting with Ashley and some of the other girls, so I wasn't really paying attention to her." I heard him turn and say something to someone, but I couldn't make it out with all the background chatter. Then he was back. "Jill said that she saw her maybe forty-five minutes ago and that she appeared okay then."

"Where are you?"

"Castellano's. In East Hampton."

"Maybe she went home. Or took off somewhere else."

"She doesn't have a car. She came with Ashley."

"Did you check the other bars in the area?"

"Not yet. That's why I'm calling you. Where do you think we should look?"

I wasn't sure why he thought I would know the answer to that, but I realized sitting here talking on the phone wouldn't resolve the issue. I stood. "I'll be right there."

"Castellano's is on—"

"I know where it is. I'll be there in a few minutes."

It only took about twenty minutes to change clothes and drive over to the restaurant.

"Welcome to Castellano's," the attractive young brunette who stood behind a reception podium said. "Would you like a table?"

"No, thanks. I'm looking for the wedding party."

"It's in one of our private rooms. Just go straight through the dining area and turn left at the fireplace. You'll see it."

I found the room and immediately saw Evan talking with Ashley, Jill, and Divya near the far wall. I walked over.

"Any news?" I asked.

"No," Ashley said. "I've called her cell phone like a million times and all I get is her voice mail. She always answers her phone."

"Maybe she turned it off or is in a place too noisy to hear the ring?"

Ashley shook her head. "No, something's wrong. This is the way it is when she has one of her spells."

I glanced at Jill and then asked Ashley, "What kind of spells?"

"I don't know."

"Tell me what happens. What she does."

"I don't know how to describe them. She just seems like out of it and goes off by herself. When she comes back, she like doesn't remember where she was or what she'd been doing."

"She do that often?"

"Like every couple of months or so." She shrugged. "At least as far as I know."

"How long do these episodes last?" Divya asked.

"An hour or two. Sometimes longer."

"Has she taken any drugs tonight?" I asked.

"No. I did see a couple of the guys over there doing some coke. At least that's what it looked like to me."

"Did you see Nicole using?"

"She hasn't done that for like a couple of years. I know that for sure."

How many times had I heard that? One thing you learn as a physician is that people either lie about or play down their drug and alcohol use. Particularly to their friends and their doctor. If they say they have a couple of glasses of wine with dinner each night, it's more like four or five. If they say they rarely smoke pot, it's three times a week. People don't like their weaknesses and vices exposed, so they fudge the numbers. Human nature.

"Some people are able to hide it," I said. "Even from their closest friends."

"Not Nicole. She and I tell each other like everything. Everything."

I looked across the room at the two guys that Nicole had indicated. They were laughing and chatting with a couple of girls. I excused myself and walked over.

"How are you guys doing?" I asked.

Four faces turned toward me, all smiling, one of the girls wiping laughter tears from her eyes.

The crying girl said, "We're having too much fun." Another wave of laughter rolled through them.

"Have you seen Nicole Crompton?" I asked.

"Who wants to know?" one of the guys asked. He was tall and thin, with slicked-back black hair. The collar of his blue shirt was turned up in back. He was ultracool. Don't believe it? Just ask him. Odds are he'd tell you.

"I'm Dr. Hank Lawson. I'm looking for Nicole."

His smile evaporated and his brow creased. "Is something wrong?"

"I don't know. Have you seen her?"

His head swiveled as he looked around the room. The other guy and the two girls also scanned the room. Finally the guy said, "I saw her an hour ago. Maybe a little longer. I'm not sure."

The others nodded in agreement.

"Did you share any of your goodies with her?" I asked.

"I don't know what you're talking about."

"Sure, you do. Peruvian marching powder? You share any of that with her?"

He cupped a hand behind one ear, turning his head slightly. "Sorry, but I can't hear you."

"Look, I'm not trying to cause trouble and I don't really care what you do or don't do. I'm trying to find Nicole. All I'm asking is, as far as you know, did she do any drugs tonight?"

He looked nervous. His gaze bounced around the room but finally came back to me. "Not that I saw."

Again, the others nodded in agreement. Easy to see the social hierarchy here.

"Did she mention that she might be going somewhere? Maybe another bar?"

He shook his head.

"You didn't see her leave? Or see her talking with someone you didn't know?"

"Nope. Nothing like that."

I thanked them and then rejoined Evan, Ashley, and Jill.

"Where's Divya?"

"She went to talk with the bartender," Jill said. "Any luck?" She nodded toward the couples.

"They don't know anything."

Divya walked up. "I talked with the manager and a couple of the bartenders," she said. "None of them saw Nicole leave or saw her talking with anyone unusual. They suggested she might have gone to one of the other bars or restaurants in the area. There are several in easy walking distance."

"Let's go check them out," I said.

"Should we call the police?" Jill asked.

"No," Ashley said. "Her parents would like absolutely freak if we did that."

"What would they do if something was wrong and we didn't call them?"

"There's nothing wrong. She's done this before. Like all the time. She'll come home. She always does."

"You sure?" I asked, still not feeling comfortable with this.

"Yes, I'm sure. Let's just look for her."

That's what we did. We went to a dozen restaurants and bars. Both Ashley and for some reason Evan had photos of Nicole on their cell phones. We chatted with the receptionists and the bartenders and even a couple of managers, but none had seen Nicole that night. One of the bartenders knew her but said he hadn't seen her in a few months.

Everything was a dead end and by two o'clock in the morning we had run out of options. The bars were closing. Ashley tried Nicole's cell phone but again got her voice mail. Jill suggested, for the third time, calling the police.

"No way," Ashley said. "Really. Her parents would like go ballistic."

"But she could be in trouble," Jill said.

"She will be if we call Mark or Jackie." Ashley dropped her cell phone into her purse. "She's done this in the city. Don't you think here in the Hamptons is safer than there?"

She had a point. Not one I was comfortable with, but what were we going to do? Call the police and tell them that Nicole had walked away from a party? That no one had seen her abducted or anything sinister like that? She was an adult, which meant she had a right to come and go as she pleased, and I could just hear the police telling us as much.

"She could be home already. In bed," Ashley said.

"Let's call and see," Evan said.

"She's not answering her phone, and if we call the house, we'll wake everybody up. That's the last thing Nicole needs." Ashley sighed. "Believe me, she'll turn up. She always does."

I still didn't like this, but we weren't accomplishing anything and the streets were now deserted. No one out, no traffic. Running around here in the middle of the night didn't seem to make much sense either. "You promise you'll call me the minute you hear from her?"

Ashley nodded. "I will."

"And if she doesn't turn up by sunrise, we will tell her parents."

Ashley hesitated.

"That wasn't a question. I'm saying that if you don't tell them, I will."

Ashley nodded. "I promise."

Chapter 14

The call came just after seven a.m. I was asleep. Something I enjoy at that hour. I fumbled the phone, twice, before I brought it to my ear. Apparently my voice betrayed my sleep deprivation because Ashley said, "Sorry I woke you up, but I told you I'd call as soon as I heard from Nicole."

Now I was awake. I sat up on the side of the bed as a sense of dread swelled in my chest. One thing you learn practicing medicine is that phone calls at odd hours are almost never good news. Someone was ill or injured. Or worried, maybe even panicked, by some new or odd symptom. Even worse, a patient you thought was stable had taken an unexpected downward turn.

This one wasn't so bad.

"She came in around four," Ashley said. "We talked until she finally fell asleep."

"Where was she?"

"She doesn't remember."

"Doesn't remember or just has a fuzzy recollection?"

"She said like the last thing she remembered, she was in the women's room at the restaurant, brushing her hair. The next thing she knew, she was like standing in front of a bank. Middle of the night. No one around. Everything totally dark and deserted."

"How did she get home?"

"She called a cab."

"I'll be right there."

"She's like asleep and when she goes out after one of these adventures, she's like impossible to wake up."

"I want to talk to you anyway," I said.

I showered, shaved, put on fresh jeans and a white shirt, sleeves rolled to my elbows, and in forty-five minutes stood at the door of Westwood Manor.

"Dr. Lawson," Sam said as he opened the door. "What brings you by?" He gave a quick glance over his shoulder. "Did she call you?"

"No, Sam. I'm here to see Ashley."

He hesitated a beat.

"About Nicole."

Sam nodded as he stepped back to let me enter. He led me to the kitchen, where Ashley sat at the breakfast table drinking coffee. She offered me a cup. I accepted and settled in the chair across from her.

Ashley looked tired, face drawn, eyes puffy and red, hair tousled. Even at her young age, two hours of sleep wasn't enough. Add to that the stress of looking for Nicole until two and then doing a couple of hours of friend-to-friend psychotherapy when Nicole finally showed up. Yet, even with all that and no makeup, hair combing, or any of the other things women do before stepping out of their rooms, she was beautiful.

"I want some straight information," I said. "Okay?"

"About what?"

"You know about what. I'm concerned about Nicole. Her behavior. I've already talked with Ellie and I know about her past drug use. I asked you last night, but here in the light of day I'll ask again. . . . Is she still using?"

Ashley stared into her cup, running one finger around its lip. She then pushed her hair back from her face and gazed out the window. Delaying tactics.

"Listen, Ashley, you're her best friend. You're the only

one who can help her. The only one who can tell me the truth."

She looked down and seemed to work on a cuticle with a fingernail. She sighed and then looked up at me. "Like what do you want to know?"

"Is Nicole using drugs again?"

"No. Not really."

"That sounds like a qualified no. Tell me about it."

"She like smokes a little pot every now and then. She probably drinks a little too much on weekends and at parties, but like who doesn't? But like nothing heavier than that."

If she said *like* one more time, my head might explode. Where did that come from? Who first started talking with every third word *like*? Probably started out in like California, dude.

"Don't hold out on me," I said.

"That's it. I swear."

"Other than these episodes, have you noticed anything odd about her behavior recently?"

"Like what?"

First appropriate use of the *like* word so far.

"Anything out of the ordinary. More irritable or short-tempered? A change in her sleeping patterns? A change in her eating habits or her weight?"

"Not really. Maybe she's like gained a couple of pounds from all the parties we've been doing around the city as a run-up to this wedding. But not enough that anyone would like notice."

"Yet she thinks she needs to lose weight?"

She shrugged. "Name a girl our age that doesn't. It's a battle we fight like all the time."

I refrained from telling her it was a battle they didn't need to fight, that they all looked perfectly healthy, that movies and commercials were created to make them feel that way. Instead I asked, "Has she seen that nutritionist of yours yet?"

"Yesterday. He put her on a program and guaranteed she would lose like ten or twelve pounds before the wedding."

Ten or twelve pounds she didn't need to lose. "Does the program include taking vitamins and other supplements?"

"Of course. Julian always prescribes those types of things. I mean like they boost metabolism and lower appetite. That's why his program works better than anybody else's."

She looked at me as if she couldn't fathom that a doctor wouldn't know that. I wrote it off as a reflection of a young and unseasoned mind. Maybe *gullible* was a better word.

"So she might've started these supplements yesterday?"

"I know she did. She like took some at lunch and more last night at dinner."

That still wouldn't explain her behavior at the reception the other night.

"But none before yesterday?"

She looked at me quizzically. "She just saw him yesterday. That's when she got the pills."

"She didn't take any of yours?"

"I'm not on the program right now, so like I don't have any."

"How does the program work?"

"Julian does all these blood tests . . . for things like vitamins and minerals and things he calls neurotransmitters. Not sure what they are." She twisted a strand of her thick black hair around a finger. "Then he gives you supplements for like four weeks and then retests everything. Usually everything is back to normal."

"And that's it? Four weeks?"

She nodded. "Every three months he does more lab tests, and if things are like messed up again, he will give you another four weeks of treatment."

"You know these blood tests aren't real, don't you?"

"What do you mean?"

"There are no blood tests for neurotransmitters."

"Sure, there are. I do them all the time."

This was going nowhere. Time to get back to Nicole.

"Tell me about Nicole's spells. Where she gets lost or confused."

Now Ashley used both of her hands to push her hair back. She gathered it into a ponytail, which she tossed over one shoulder, the dark waves covering half her chest. "It's like she's there and then she's not. She seems to get this odd expression and then goes off somewhere. I've like tried talking to her during a couple of these episodes, but it's like she doesn't hear me. I remember one . . . maybe three or four weeks ago. . . . We were at a bar and she was like talking to this guy. I came over to make sure everything was okay. . . . You know us girls have codes."

"Codes?" I asked.

"You know. Private signals."

"What was your code?"

"Tugging on one ear. If either of us does that, it's a signal that we like want to dump the guy we're talking with and the other will come over and do the extraction."

"Extraction?"

"Like a hostage rescue."

I smiled. "Did she give you the signal that night?"

"No. I just thought she looked uncomfortable. It turned out she actually liked the guy. Not that she would've like done anything, being engaged, but a little innocent flirting never hurts."

"Okay, so she was chatting with Mr. Wonderful. What happened then?"

"She disappeared. I went to talk with some other people and looked back a few minutes later, and she was like gone. The dude was still sitting there on the barstool. I asked him where she was, and he said she like went to the restroom but hadn't come back yet. I went to check on her, but she wasn't there."

"Did he say anything about her behavior? Maybe something odd happened before she left?"

"I didn't ask, and I didn't see her again until early the next morning."

"What did she say when she came home?"

"That she couldn't remember anything that happened or where she had gone or whether she'd been with anyone or not."

"Exactly like last night?" I asked.

She nodded.

"Did that seem to bother her? Was she scared that she might've done something wrong?"

"When these things started a couple years ago, she like freaked out. Now it's like she's used to them and doesn't worry about it. I worry more than she does."

"Do you think they're getting worse? More frequent or lasting longer?"

"Definitely. I think in the first year it happened like twice. In the last six months it's happened at least a dozen times. Not always like last night. Sometimes they only last a few minutes. But there's been at least three or four episodes where she disappeared for hours." She rested her elbows on the edge of the table. Her eyes glistened with tears. "What's wrong with her?"

"I don't know. There are several possibilities. It could be drugs." Ashley started to say something, but I held up a hand. "I know she would probably tell you if she were, but *probably* is the operative word here. Many people, particularly those that have gone through any type of rehab before and were embarrassed by it, will hide any future use. Even from their closest friends. They don't want their friends to see them as a failure."

"No way. I would know. Nicole would like for sure tell me. There is no doubt about that."

"There could be other causes. Some physical, some psychiatric. Some minor, some much more serious."

"Like what?"

"I don't think we should go into that right now. I need to talk with her, examine her, and get a few tests done."

"Never going to happen. Her mother would hit the roof. She like refuses to even consider that something could be wrong with Nicole. Ever. Even when she went through the rehab thing, her mother refused to accept that it was drugs. She told everybody that Nicole was like exhausted from working so hard in school. Talk about denial."

"Then I'll need your help."

"Me? For what?"

"Convince Nicole to get checked out."

"I can't do that. She'd get like mad or something."

"You're her best friend. Wouldn't you do anything to help her?"

Again she twirled a strand of hair around one finger. "I suppose so."

"Then talk to her. That's all I'm asking."

Chapter 15

Ashley refilled our coffee cups and then said she would go check on Nicole but doubted that she would be awake yet. Before she headed upstairs, Ellie came in. She stopped short, looked at me, at Ashley, and then back to me.

"What's going on?"

"I'm just getting some coffee to go back upstairs." Ashley eased past Ellie and headed out of the room, tossing me a nervous glance on the way out.

I was on my own.

"I came by to talk with Ashley about Nicole."

Ellie poured herself some coffee and sat down across from me. She wore a light blue silk robe over a navy blue gown, her makeup perfect. She looked more like she was ready for a party than just crawling out of bed. "You're still worried about her behavior at the party?" She added cream and sugar and took a sip.

How much should I tell her? Would telling Ellie about last night betray Nicole? Technically, Nicole wasn't my patient, so there were no real ethical restrictions, but was that fair? And what about Ashley? Did she expect me to keep everything she had said confidential? Probably. Would she consider sharing this with Ellie a breach of that confidence or was she tired of taking care of Nicole's secret? Did she want Ellie to know? Lift some of the burden from her?

They don't teach you how to handle these situations in medical school. You have to unravel them on your own out here in the real world. The wrestling match in my head didn't last long, since I knew deep down that the truth would be best and that Ellie needed to know everything. If Nicole got angry or felt that I was unnecessarily digging into her life, I'd deal with that later. Same for Ashley. Right now Nicole's health was my major concern.

"Not just at the party," I said. "Last night she had another episode."

Ellie's gaze fixed on me. "What do you mean by 'episode'?"

"This is between the two of us, okay?"

"Hank, you're talking about my granddaughter. My only granddaughter. The only part of this family that I truly have left."

I let the fact that her daughter, Jackie, was still part of the family slide, and told Ellie everything that Ashley had said to me about Nicole's spells and how they seemed to be getting worse. I told her about Nicole's disappearance last night and her apparently not remembering any of what happened.

I could see the anguish in her face as she stared at me and said, "What does all this mean? What could possibly be wrong?"

"There are several possibilities. She should have a complete examination and have some tests run."

"There is nothing wrong with my daughter."

The voice was harsh and angry. I turned to see Jackie standing in the kitchen doorway. She wore knee-length black formfitting pants and a white T-shirt beneath an unzipped two-toned purple hoodie, each sporting the Nike swoosh. An iPod was strapped to one arm and earbuds hung around her neck. Looked like she was going for a walk or maybe to the gym. Disturbingly, her face appeared tight, jaw set, and her hands were squeezed into fists at her sides.

"Jackie," Ellie said, "don't get all wound up. Just hear what he has to say."

"I don't care what he has to say. He's got you fooled but not me." She looked at me, her eyes dark and angry. "I know about you. How you neglected and killed that man. How you fled out here to the Hamptons to prey on old women."

Ellie stood. Now her hands were balled into fists at her sides. "Don't you dare. Don't you say one more word about Hank. If it wasn't for him, I'd probably be long dead." She leaned forward, flattening her hands on the tabletop, and looked Jackie directly in the eye. "Or maybe that's what you want? Can't wait to get your hands on all the money."

Jackie's anger vibrated through her entire body. "Mother, how could you say that? Just because I'm worried that some quack has you fooled?" She looked back at me. "But he doesn't have me fooled. And he absolutely will not touch my daughter. Not now. Not ever."

This was getting uncomfortable. I wasn't sure what to do. Something else they don't teach you in med school. Maybe get up and run out the door. But leaving Ellie to fight my battle didn't seem right.

One thing I did know was that illness, even the prospect of illness, can bring out the good, the bad, and the very, very ugly in some people. Most are quietly brave, but some, like Jackie, become volcanic. Usually the best way to defuse these people is to agree with them.

"Mrs. Crompton," I said, "you're right. I did lose my job. Not for the reasons you imagine, but I lost it nonetheless. I didn't want to be here doing this, but here I am. I do know what I'm doing, and just as important, I care about the people I see. Including your mother. But right now, I'm more concerned about your daughter."

"Nicole is none of your concern and she never will be."

"Then have her see someone else. I can suggest an excellent internist."

"She does not have a problem. She's just stressed from the wedding and all the plans."

"That's entirely possible," I said. "But there are other possibilities."

Jackie crossed her arms over her chest and jutted her chin toward me defiantly. "Okay, Doctor, what did your infinite wisdom tell you the problem is?"

"I'll tell you what any physician would tell you. When a young woman Nicole's age begins to exhibit abnormal behavior, drugs are commonly the cause." Jackie started to say something, but I went on, cutting her off. "To be honest, I don't believe that's the problem. Neither does her friend Ashley, and she knows Nicole better than just about anyone."

"I know darn well it's not drugs and I will not have my daughter treated like a junkie."

Okay, agreeing with her didn't seem to help, so I decided to go in another direction. Fear. The greatest motivator and most sobering emotion humans possess. "There are a few other important considerations."

Jackie walked toward the counter, spun, and rested against it, her arms still crossed over her chest, her face even tighter. "Let's hear them."

"She could have a brain aneurysm or a tumor. She could have an encephalitis . . . a brain infection. Maybe some hormonal problem with her pituitary or thyroid. Maybe she has diabetes and her blood sugar is all over the place. Each of these can cause erratic behavior."

"What erratic behavior?"

"Aren't you aware she's been having episodes of confusion and disorientation? Loss of memory?"

"Oh, please."

I nodded. This wasn't going anywhere.

"Nicole doesn't have a brain tumor or that encephalo-whatever," Jackie said. "She's just stressed."

"Maybe. But these things must be ruled out. Mild schizophrenia or some other psychiatric disorder, too."

Jackie came off the counter, her face contorted in anger. "My daughter is not crazy. My daughter does not have a psychiatric problem. No one in our family has ever had a psychiatric problem and she is definitely not the first."

"Mrs. Crompton, you're missing the point here. There are many things that could cause Nicole's odd behavior, and whatever it is, it needs to be evaluated and corrected. Not necessarily by me, but by someone. Doesn't that make sense?"

"What makes sense is for you to leave my daughter alone."

"You don't have to like me," I said. "You don't have to think I'm a good doctor. What you do have to do is pay attention to your daughter. Get this looked into because whatever it is, it's probably not going to get better on its own."

My cell phone buzzed. I looked at the screen. It was Divya.

"I need to take this." I stood, walked past Jackie, out of the kitchen, and into the foyer. I flipped open the phone. Divya told me that Mrs. Maria Mendez called about her husband, Oscar. Said he was more confused than usual and that she was headed over to see him. I needed to get away from Jackie, give her time to think about what I had said—if she would, that is—so I told Divya I'd meet her there.

Chapter 16

The shaded walkway that led from the street to the home of Oscar and Maria Mendez was uneven and cracked from the tree roots that twisted beneath it. That was the only bit of disrepair visible; the remainder of the property was meticulously groomed. By Maria. That was her nature. The house was a light green stucco with white shutters, and the odor of fresh paint greeted me as I knocked. Maria answered. Inside it was as orderly as outside.

I found Oscar sitting on the sofa, with Divya next to him. She appeared to be completing her neurological examination as she tapped his patellar tendon with a rubber reflex hammer.

"His neurological examination is unchanged from my last exam," Divya said. "I found no evidence that he's had another stroke."

Oscar Mendez was well-known in the Hamptons. He'd run a bicycle-repair shop for many years, catering to everybody from weekend pedalers to hard-core racers. He reputedly could make any bike smoother and faster. Until his first stroke three years earlier. It didn't do much physical damage in that he could still use all his extremities, but mentally he didn't fare so well. His confusion and memory impairment forced him to sell his shop and retire.

A year later, he had a second stroke and his dementia worsened.

Maria was as steadfast a spouse as anyone would ever want. She doted on him and took his episodic confusion, crying jags, and temper outbursts in stride. She had seen them before in her father, and she knew that none of this was personal but rather the broken wiring of a stroke-damaged brain.

"He's been so confused the past couple of days," Maria said. "His ups and downs seem worse. He constantly sleeps or gets agitated and cries. He can't remember how to make coffee." She wound a handkerchief into a knot around one of her fingers. "What's wrong?"

I knelt on the floor in front of Oscar and looked him in the eye. "Oscar, how are you doing today?"

He stared at me blankly for a minute and then smiled. "Dr. Lawson, what are you doing here?" He then looked at Divya. "Divya, you, too? I get to see both of you today?"

Then I saw the spark of realization in his face as he suddenly remembered that Divya had been there for a while. He closed his eyes and swallowed hard.

"It's okay, Oscar," I said. "Sometimes I forget Divya's around, too." I gave her a quick wink. She smiled, knowing what I was doing.

If you can't fix it, make it seem less serious.

This is the tragic part of dementia. Contact with reality comes and goes, in an almost cruel manner. Sometimes I believed it would be better for the person to remain confused all the time. That way he would never know he was confused. But these moments of lucidity, where everything suddenly, if briefly, makes sense, must be maddening. That's what I saw in Oscar's face. The frustration of knowing that something had happened and yet he was completely unaware of it. I knew his days were likely filled with such episodes.

I reached out and touched his hand to bring his attention back to me. "I'm going to ask you some silly questions, but I want you to answer them as best you can."

I began a mental-status exam, asking his name, the date, where he was, and the name of the president. He answered all the questions perfectly, proving he was oriented to time, place, and person. I evaluated his memory by asking what the name of his old bicycle shop had been and then saying five words and asking him to repeat them in the proper order. He aced it. I asked him to repeatedly subtract seven from one hundred. He stumbled on a couple of the numbers. To test his cognitive abilities and abstract thinking, I asked him to explain what is meant by "A penny saved is a penny earned" and "Don't cry over spilled milk." He didn't do so well. Not uncommon in multiple-stroke dementia.

Oscar took two meds for high blood pressure and an SSRI for his episodic anxiety. A year earlier, he had accidentally doubled up on his blood pressure meds and ended up on the floor. When I saw him, his blood pressure was down to seventy, but a few hours in bed and avoiding those medications for twenty-four hours resolved that issue. After that, Maria took over dispensing his meds.

I asked Maria, "He's been taking his medications regularly, hasn't he?"

"Oh, yes. I have one of those weeklong pill containers and every Sunday I set up his medicines for the week. I keep the bottles locked up like you told me."

"His vital signs are normal today," Divya said.

I stood and motioned for Maria to follow me. I led her into the kitchen, where I sat down at the table. She sat across from me.

Concern etched her face as she asked, "What is it? What's wrong with Oscar?"

It's always best to have these types of discussions out of earshot of the patient. Even those that are the most demented and confused often hear and understand bits and pieces of what is said. In their scrambled and often paranoid reasoning, such shards of information can be misinterpreted and this can induce fear and panic, and even aggression, meant to be self-protective.

This conversation was for Maria only.

"I think it's simply his dementia worsening," I said.

She wound the handkerchief into an even tighter knot. Tears collected in the corners of her eyes. "He's been doing so well. It's just the past couple of days that he's been out of it."

"That can happen. Remember when I told you things would wax and wane, but they would soon begin doing more waning than waxing? I'm afraid that's what's going on here."

"There's nothing you can do to help him?"

"Unfortunately there isn't. We just don't understand this disease very well. Not yet anyway."

She dabbed a tear from one eye with the wadded handkerchief. "I don't know what I'm going to do."

"We discussed the options."

"Go to one of those places? Oscar would never do that."

"You could have someone come and help you at home."

"We can't afford that. Besides, I can take care of him myself."

"For how long?" I reached across the table and took her hand. "You're not twenty anymore. This will take a toll on you."

She sniffed, turned her gaze toward the lemon tree that grew just outside the kitchen window. "It already has."

"It might be time to consider some assisted-living arrangement."

She swallowed hard and then shook her head. "No. I'll keep doing this as long as I can." She looked back at me. The tears that welled in her eyes seemed to magnify them to large brown orbs. "He's a good man. We promised each other fifty-two years ago that we were together forever. That included sickness and health."

I hate these situations. The ones where there is no solution. The ones where I don't have any tricks in my bag or clever words of comfort. I had nothing to offer.

"I understand," I said. "Just think about it."

She didn't respond but rather dropped her gaze to her lap, where her hands continually wound and unwound the handkerchief.

Divya and I said good-bye, telling Maria that one of us would come back by in a couple of days and check on Oscar. Outside, I opened the door to Divya's SUV for her.

"It's so sad," she said. "They've lived together all those years and now this. I don't know which one I feel for the most."

"It's an uncomfortable situation and unfortunately there isn't a thing we can do about it."

"You want me to see the two new patients? They're both over in East Hampton, so it's easy for me to go from one to the other."

"That would be great. I'll go see the three follow-ups and meet you back at the house."

"Works for me."

Chapter 17

The three follow-ups were scattered, two in Southampton, the other in Westhampton. If traffic cooperated, a couple of hours should do it. I was making good time on one of the back roads when I came on an odd scene. A wad of cars, blocking the road, doors flung open, apparently abandoned by the drivers. Beyond, they seemed to have gathered, along with a group of road-crew hard hats, near a bridge abutment. I pulled onto the shoulder, got out, and hurried toward the bridge. I passed a man, cell phone to his ear, screaming for the person on the other end to hurry up and get the medics rolling.

As I approached the crowd, I saw a mangled bicycle on the roadside and then something really odd: a young man pinned to the bridge abutment. Literally. As if he were a butterfly on a collection board.

I pushed through the crowd until I reached the impaled cyclist. A large, thick-armed man stood nearby, hands clinched at his sides, frozen as if he wasn't sure what to do.

"I'm Dr. Hank Lawson," I said. "What happened here?"

The big man turned, a grim look on his face. "You're a doctor?"

"Yes."

"Man, am I glad you're here." He wore an orange reflective vest over a black T-shirt. "I'm not sure what happened. I think he lost control of his bike and took a header into the bridge. Hung himself up on that rebar."

The injured man, who looked to be twentysomething, wore a bicycle outfit: black pants and a bright blue shirt with SHIMANO in white lettering across the front. The shirt was torn and bloody. A piece of rebar protruded from his right lower chest. His face was pale and contorted in pain, his breathing labored and raspy.

Someone behind me said that the medics had been called, but they were at least twenty minutes away.

"I'm Dr. Lawson," I said to the cyclist. "Let's see what we can do here."

I gently ripped away his shirt. He groaned.

"Sorry, but I need to get a better look."

"Go ahead," he said, his voice weak, almost a whisper.

The rebar had entered his chest from behind, just beneath his right scapula, and had come out in the area of his seventh or eighth rib. Blood soaked his chest and right pant leg, and pooled on the ground beneath him. Each breath produced a gurgling sound and bloody bubbles erupted from his chest.

I used his shirt to wipe away the blood and could now see the wound more clearly. It was large, half as big as my fist. The real problem? It was a sucking chest wound. Not that all chest wounds don't suck, but a real one constitutes a true medical emergency.

With this type of injury, not only does the lung on the side of the injury collapse and therefore become useless, but the entire chest becomes less effective. When we take in a breath, the diaphragm moves downward and the muscles between the ribs expand the chest. This creates negative pressure that pulls air through the mouth and nose and into the lungs. When the chest has another opening, such as a large wound, air is more readily pulled in through that wound than it is into the good lung. Means one lung is useless and the other can't get a good breath. Not a healthy situation.

Sucking chest wounds are seen in war injuries from large-caliber rounds, shrapnel, and things like that, but are uncommon in the real world and particularly from a bicycle accident.

"What's your name?" I asked the young man.

"Owen. Owen Cooper." He spoke between gasps.

"Okay, Owen. We're going to help you." I turned toward the men who had now formed a semicircle around us. "We need to get him down."

"Are you sure?" the big man said. "We were afraid to touch him."

"If we don't take care of his chest wound, he won't live to see the paramedics." I looked him in the eye. "What's your name?"

"Paul Doocy. I'm the foreman here."

"Get a couple of your guys and let's gently lift him off his rebar and get him on the ground."

He hesitated as if unsure what to do.

"Look, I'm a doctor. A former ER doctor. I know how to handle this, but I need your help. I take full responsibility."

Now Paul didn't hesitate. He snapped a finger at a couple of his guys. "You heard the doc. Let's get him down."

I looked back at Owen. "This is going to hurt, but there's no other way."

"Just do it. I can't stand this anymore."

I nodded toward Paul. "Let's go."

Two men grabbed Owen's upper arms. Paul wrapped his massive arms around the young man's legs. He lifted while the other two men slid Owen from the metal spike. I stabilized his chest as best I could as the rebar disappeared back into his chest.

"Oh, Jesus," Owen moaned.

"Quickly," I said. "Get him off there."

The men pulled, Owen groaned, and then he was free.

"Lay him down. Here on the grass."

Air and bloody foam squished in and out of the ragged

opening with each breath. Visible bone spicules meant that
at least one rib had been trashed. I grabbed the shirt I had
ripped off him, wadded it into a ball, and pressed it against
the wound. He moaned and recoiled, but I held it steady.

"You have what we call a sucking chest wound and we
have to close it."

Sweat dotted Owen's face and his pulse was weak and
rapid, maybe 120. He was descending into full-blown shock
and I had nothing to work with. I wished Divya were here.
Her SUV had IV fluids and all the bandages I needed. I
had none of that.

The wadded shirt didn't make a good seal. I needed
something airtight, something that wouldn't let air move in
or out. That would make the other lung, the good one, more
efficient, more able to move air and to supply oxygen to the
blood and the brain. Plastic wrap, petroleum jelly on cloth,
even a trash bag, would work, but I didn't have any of those
either.

I nodded toward the mangled bicycle. "Look in the seat
pouch. See if there's a spare inner tube."

One of the guys stood the bicycle upright while another
unzipped the bag that hung beneath the seat. He began
pulling things out. A couple of Allen wrenches, a bottle of
sunscreen, a granola bar—make that two—and a pair of
tightly wrapped inner tubes.

"Toss me those tubes," I said. "Anybody have a knife?"

Three pocketknives appeared. Nice to know that road
crews were so well armed. I took the largest of the knives
and snapped it open. I cut a twelve-inch section out of one
of the inner tubes and then slid the blade down its length.
Now I had a black rubber rectangle. I slapped it over the
wound.

"Hold this," I said to Paul.

He knelt beside me and placed his large hand over the
rubber patch.

Owen moaned.

"Hang in there," I said. "We're almost finished here."

I cut the other tube crosswise and stretched it out on the ground. It looked like a long snake. I slit it lengthwise, and opened it out flat. I then divided it into two long strips. I wrapped them around Owen's chest, positioning one across the top of the patch and the other near its lower end. I stretched and tied each securely. I listened but couldn't hear any air leak.

"You feeling any better?" I asked Owen.

"A little."

His voice sounded stronger and that awful sucking sound had faded. I heard sirens in the distance.

Chapter 18

Although Divya wasn't really in the mood to deal with Evan on the two new patient consults, she hadn't really objected when he climbed into her SUV as she was backing out of her parking space. She just wasn't up for an argument, so she simply said, "Buckle up."

But a moment later she slipped the SUV into PARK as she looked at him and asked, "Why are you so eager to come with me today?"

"Who says I'm eager?"

"You jumped in the car while it was moving."

"Slowly."

"It was still moving."

"This isn't the first time I've gone with you to see new clients."

"Unfortunately that's true," Divya said.

"You like my company."

"I do?"

"My new marketing campaign is to get to know all our clients."

"You already do."

"No. I know most of them but not all."

"So this is going to be a regular event? You tagging along with me all the time."

"Sure."

Divya sighed. "I suppose I have nothing to say about that?"

"Why would you? It's a great idea."

"It's an idea all right."

"Since I set up our clients' accounts, I think they'd like to meet me. Know who they're dealing with."

"I'm not sure anyone is prepared to deal with you."

"I'm the CFO. I take their money. Wouldn't you want to know who you're giving money to?"

"That would be Hank and I. The actual earners."

"I'm an important cog in the machine."

"You're a cog all right."

"You know what I mean," Evan said. "An essential part. Component."

"I know what a cog is. Even a component. I'm trying to understand exactly what this machine is. The one you are cogged into."

"The HankMed machine."

"Silly me. I thought it was a medical practice."

"And a business. One that should run like a well-oiled machine."

"You make it sound like a Chicago political outfit."

Evan twisted toward her in his seat. "Anybody ever tell you you're funny?"

"Constantly."

"They're lying."

Divya rolled her eyes. "Why did you choose today to launch your new and improved CFO patient-relations scheme?"

"Never thought of it before."

"I thought maybe it was to aggravate me."

"You have to admit this will make any money issues go more smoothly."

"Somehow you and smooth don't belong in the same sentence."

"Still not funny."

She refrained from saying that she was amazed he could have formulated such a plan on his own. Or, and most important, that she thought his idea actually made sense. That would have stroked his ego and puffed out his chest more than she could handle today, maybe any day.

Instead she said nothing. Evan no doubt had an agenda and he wasn't going to be swayed from it.

She slipped the SUV in gear and pointed it down the long treelined drive that led away from Shadow Pond. Evan rode shotgun, as he called it. To her, that was an odd American expression. She remembered reading somewhere that the term had originated in a 1920s pulp-fiction story but had first reached a wide audience in the movie *Stagecoach*.

"Have you ever seen the movie *Stagecoach*?" she asked.

"John Wayne? You bet. Probably a dozen times. Why?"

"No reason. Just wondering."

"I love old John Wayne westerns."

"I thought you loved James Bond?"

"Him, too."

The first patient visit went well, taking only forty-five minutes. Evan stayed in the client's living room, saying he needed to call a couple of clients and then Paige to see how things were going in California. At least he was out of the way and occupied. A good combination.

Divya interviewed and examined the middle-aged man in the den. All was okay except for some indigestion and mild right-upper-abdominal discomfort, symptoms that suggested he might have gallbladder disease. She drew some blood, scheduled an abdominal ultrasound over at Hamptons Heritage, and told him she'd call when all the test results came back.

Back in her SUV she asked Evan, "How's Paige doing?"

"Great. Just getting up. She said her dad had some meeting in Beverly Hills, so she and her mom were going to the Beverly Hills Hotel for breakfast."

"Sounds nice. Better than the bagel I had."

As they neared the next patient's home, a huge mansion in East Hampton, Evan's real agenda became clear.

"You have no idea who this guy is?" Evan asked.

"Nathan Zimmer. Works on Wall Street."

"Not just works on Wall Street. He *is* Wall Street. He's one of the hottest investment bankers around. He won't talk to anyone unless they have over a hundred million dollars in business to conduct."

"Actually he's fifty years old and has high blood pressure."

"I'll let you worry about that. I'm more interested in how he makes his money."

"You do know this is a medical visit and not a high school economics class?"

"Maybe it's a multitasking opportunity."

Divya pressed on the accelerator and swung the Mercedes SUV hard through a sweeping left curve, pressing Evan against the door. He righted himself as they came out of the curve, and looked at her.

"Are you trying to toss me out?"

"I wouldn't dream of it. But if you want to open your door, I can try that maneuver again."

Evan ignored her and went on about Nathan Zimmer. About how he'd made his first billion by the time he was twenty-five and was considered a moneymaking wizard. How his clientele list read like the Forbes 400. How he appeared almost weekly on the pages of the *Wall Street Journal* and was a fixture on many of the financial television shows. He had been married and divorced twice, had no children, loved to hunt big game in Africa, and fished for marlin all over the globe. Six years earlier, he had almost reached the summit of Mount Everest, nasty weather forcing a harrowing descent. *Vanity Fair* had done a huge story, Nathan gracing its cover.

"How do you know so much about Mr. Zimmer?" Divya asked.

"When I worked in New York, this was the guy everybody listened to. Sort of the guru of finance."

"From what I've seen of the medical history he sent, if he doesn't start taking care of himself, he won't be a guru much longer."

"That's your job. Keep this guy around so I can learn from him."

She laughed. "It is all about you after all."

"I'm just saying that HankMed can always benefit from sound financial advice."

"If we have Evan R. Lawson, CFO, why do we need Nathan Zimmer?"

Divya turned into a long Italian-cypress-lined drive that passed between a pair of massive gates and led to Nathan Zimmer's home. The drive ended at a cobblestone circle that surrounded a three-tiered fountain. She settled the SUV between a midnight blue Bentley convertible, top up, and a bright red Ferrari, top down.

Divya began climbing the marble steps that led to the entry but stopped when she realized Evan was no longer with her. She turned to see him snooping around the cars.

"Are you going to stay out here or are you coming in?"

"You have to admit he has great taste in automobiles. I'd love to own either one of these."

"Maybe Mr. Zimmer will teach you how to do that."

Evan began to climb the stairs. "Let's hope."

"I don't want your little lovefest with Mr. Zimmer interfering with why we're here."

"Wouldn't dream of it."

A handsome young man in a gray suit and an open-collared black silk shirt answered the front door. His blond hair swept casually across his forehead and he smiled warmly.

"I'm Todd Hammersmith," he said. "Mr. Zimmer's assistant. Welcome." He stepped aside, letting them enter.

Divya shook hands with him. "I'm Divya Katdare, Dr. Lawson's PA."

Evan pumped his hand. "Evan R. Lawson, CFO of HankMed."

"Oh yes, we spoke on the phone." He led them through a massive entry foyer. "Nathan is on the patio."

The house was modern, glass and steel, straight lines and sharp angles everywhere. The south-facing wall was all glass and looked out over a broad patio that was embraced by a series of marble statues and more Italian cypresses. Beyond, a pair of tennis courts and an Olympic-sized pool, complete with two diving boards and a ten-meter platform, nestled in the parklike grounds.

Nathan Zimmer sat at a round teak table, shaded by a huge lemon yellow umbrella. He wore red jogging shorts, a white Shinnecock Hills golf shirt, black rubber flip-flops, and wraparound sunglasses. His tightly curled black hair had retreated significantly and was lightly salted at the temples. An open seventeen-inch MacBook Pro and stacks of papers littered the table before him. A pulsing Bluetooth device hung from his left ear. He didn't look up as they approached but rather kept shuffling through papers and talking.

"You've got to get those reports out today. I promised the client we would have this wrapped up before the weekend, but if the bank in Zurich doesn't get the paperwork today, they'll never be able to transfer the funds in time." While he listened, he motioned for them to sit down, and then went back to his conversation. "Tell him if he misses the deadline on this, he'll be working somewhere else tomorrow." He reached up and touched the Bluetooth device and then smiled at them. "Welcome."

After the introductions were made, Divya asked, "Is this a bad time?"

"No worse than any other. Seems like there aren't enough hours most days."

He picked up a pack of cigarettes, Marlboros, shook one up, and clenched it between his teeth. He lit it and took a deep drag, exhaling the smoke up and to his left. "I guess I shouldn't be doing this in front of you."

"You shouldn't be doing it all," Divya said.

"Yeah, I know. But it keeps me calm, and from chewing heads off. Even when they deserve it."

"I saw the article on you in *Forbes*," Evan said. "I really liked the part about how you made your first billion."

Divya frowned Evan's way, but he seemed to ignore it.

"That was a long time ago now," Nathan said. "I was young and stupid then."

"A billion dollars by age twenty-five seems smart to me."

"Or lucky," Nathan said.

"I've looked over your medical history and all of your recent tests," Divya said. "I just have a few questions for you."

Nathan raised the index finger of one hand toward her and then with the other pressed the Bluetooth device.

"No, I did not say you were fired," Nathan said. "But if you don't get this goddamn report to the folks in Zürich in the next couple of hours, I might reconsider." He listened for a minute and then said, "I don't want excuses, I just want it done. Now."

"See?" Evan whispered to Divya. "That's how you run a business. Take charge. No prisoners."

Divya looked at him but didn't respond.

Nathan continued his conversation. "Put Bridget on." He stubbed his cigarette out in an ashtray that held the remnants of a dozen others. "What kind of questions?"

Divya stared at him for a beat before she realized he was talking to her. "About your current medical status."

"Didn't Todd send you all of that?" He gave a quick glance toward Todd, who had taken a position to his left.

Todd started to say something, but Divya jumped in. "Yes. The records were very thorough and gave me what I needed about your past, but I have a few questions about what is going on now."

"And why is that?"

His response surprised her and it must have shown on her face, as Nathan raised a finger and waggled it. She realized he was back to his phone conversation.

"I don't care if she's talking to the goddamned president, you tell her to get her ass on the phone right now." He pulled another cigarette from the pack and lit it. "Ask away." When Divya didn't respond, he said, "That was for you."

Divya retrieved her pen from her purse and flipped open her notebook. "Have you had any chest pain or shortness of breath?" Divya asked.

"No chest pain. Yes, shortness of breath."

"When? With exercise or does it happen at rest?"

"When I'm riding my bike or jogging or sometimes even just climbing the stairs in the house."

"How long have you had this symptom?"

"Twenty-four hours?"

Divya began noting that in the chart, but as he continued, she realized he was back to business.

This was getting confusing.

"You're telling me that you need another day to finish something you've been working on for a month? Is that what you're telling me, Bridget?" He listened for maybe two minutes and then said, "How about this? If you don't get that report out within two hours, you'll be out walking Wall Street. You understand?" He took a long drag from his cigarette and exhaled smoke as he spoke. "Maybe six months."

Divya sat there waiting. Nathan opened one hand toward her.

"The shortness of breath," he said. "It's been going on about six months."

Divya made a note and then asked, "Any coughing?"

He shook his head. "That's what I'm telling you. I don't care what it takes—get the report done and get it done now."

It went that way for the next twenty minutes. Nathan spoke with Bridget and someone named Phil and back to Bridget and maybe a couple of other people. She couldn't keep up with all the players and could never tell when Nathan was talking to her or to someone who she presumed was over at his Wall Street office. Ultimately, she did get the information she needed.

Nathan finally agreed to turn his phone over to Todd long enough for Divya to give him a quick physical exam, run an EKG, and draw some blood.

"I'm going to change your blood pressure medications," Divya said. "And we've got to develop a plan for you to stop smoking."

Nathan nodded as he seated the Bluetooth device into his ear.

"I want you to try either the patches or the gum first," Divya said. "Many people find either of those to be quite successful. If not, there are other medications we can consider."

"What is going on there today?" Nathan said.

He was back to his call. She wasn't sure he had heard what she had said and was waiting for another break in his call to repeat it, but Nathan lit another cigarette, stood, and walked toward the edge of the patio, facing out toward the ocean. "Bridget, you're responsible for all this. That's why you're in charge there. Remember when I hired you? Didn't I tell you that you had my backing?" He listened for a few seconds. "If he's not doing his job, fire him." He walked along the edge of the patio and was soon far enough away that Divya could no longer hear what he was saying.

The visit was obviously over.

"As you can tell, he works a little too hard," Todd said as he led them back into the house. "I'll have his prescription filled and will pick up some of the patches and gum and let him decide which he wants to use."

"Make sure he does," Divya said. "His blood pressure is too high and they don't call cigarettes coffin nails by accident."

Todd laughed. "You're quite charming. It has been a pleasure meeting both of you."

They had reached the front door and Todd pulled it open.

"I'll call as soon as I get the lab results," Divya said. "And to make a follow-up appointment to see how his blood pressure responds to the new medication."

Once they were back in the SUV, Evan said, "Easy to see how he made all his money. Talking about large and in charge. Bet he made a few million while we were here."

"He might even get to enjoy it," Divya said. "If his blood pressure and bad habits don't kill him first."

Chapter 19

The ambulance made a wide turn and backed into the receiving ramp, its red lights flashing, its siren now dead, its backup beeper sounding a rhythmic electronic warning. I had followed it from the scene. As I pulled into an empty space, I saw Jill and two nurses waiting near the pneumatic sliding doors that led into the emergency department. The ambulance's rear doors flew open and one of the medics jumped out. The nurses helped him ease the stretcher to the pavement and then through the entry doors.

I trailed them into the major-trauma room, where Dr. Andrew Weinberg, the ER doc on duty, waited. A nurse was setting up a surgical tray.

"Hank," Weinberg said. "What's the story here?"

I quickly ran through what had happened and what I had done in the field, while Weinberg inspected my makeshift dressing. He poked at it and then shook his head.

"I've never seen anything quite like this."

"Neither have I," I said. "Best I could do under the circumstances."

"Clever." He ran a gloved finger around the edge of the rubber patch, checking its seal. "Looks like it's working." He turned to one of the nurses. "Let's get blood for a type and cross-match, CBC, electrolytes, and then get X-ray down here for a stat chest film."

"BP is eighty-eight over fifty, pulse one thirty, and respirations thirty-two," one of the nurses said. "O_2 sat is eighty-six."

"Put him on a one hundred percent rebreather," Weinberg said. He then asked me, "Any other injuries?"

"Not that I saw. His abdominal and neurological exams were normal."

An X-ray tech rolled a portable machine into the room and began setting up to do the chest X-ray. I walked out to the nurses' station, leaving Weinberg with his new patient. Jill was leaning against the counter, talking on her cell phone.

"All right, Mrs. Cooper," she said. "The doctors are with him now." She listened for a minute and then said, "Don't rush and get yourself in an accident. I'll see you when you get here." She hung up the phone.

"His wife?" I asked.

She nodded. "How's he doing?"

"Hurting but otherwise okay."

She took a couple steps to the left so she could see into the trauma room. "How exactly did this happen?"

"He said he wasn't paying attention and was going pretty fast. When he looked up and saw the road crew working on the bridge, he jerked his bike to the left and lost control. Probably hit the front brake too hard. The bike flipped and he was thrown against the abutment. Landed on a four-foot-long piece of rebar."

"Bizarre."

"That hardly does it justice."

The X-ray tech completed taking the films, backed his machine out of the room, and parked it against the wall. He grabbed the film cassettes, settled them under one arm, and scurried toward radiology.

Trauma surgeon Dr. Stephen Holmes nodded to Jill as he walked by and into the trauma room.

"Looks like they've got everything in control here," Jill said. "Can I buy you a cup of coffee?"

"Cafeteria coffee?"

"Unless you've installed a cappuccino machine in your Saab."

"Not yet, but I'll look into it."

We walked downstairs to the cafeteria and grabbed some coffee; then Jill walked me out to my car.

"What does the rest of your day look like?" she asked.

"I was supposed to be doing follow-up visits when this happened. Divya, being the trouper that she is, stepped in for me. I was thinking I would head home and go for a run."

"How about dinner tonight?"

"You buying?"

She laughed. "Better than that. I'm cooking."

"How could I say no to that? I'll bring the wine."

"Make it around seven."

When I got home, I tugged on red jogging shorts, a white T-shirt, and my well-worn running shoes. Evan wasn't there, so I walked over to the tennis courts and found him volleying with the automatic ball machine.

"Want to go for a run?"

"I'd rather hit tennis balls. It's too hot to run."

"I'll be having dinner at Jill's tonight. What are you up to?"

"As soon as Divya gets back, I'll get those new accounts up to date and then I'm going to see Rachel Fleming. She has some updated sketches for me."

"Van girl? Try not to injure her again."

"It was an accident."

"My point exactly."

"Funny."

"And we still don't need a van."

"We'll see."

Evan was like a bulldog with a new chew toy. He had this van idea in his teeth and wasn't going to let go. I admired his focus even if it was misplaced. Relentless came to mind. As did committed and persistent. And let's not forget annoying.

I left Evan to his ball machine and headed toward the beach road, where I turned east and ran along the shoulder. It felt good and I soon found my stride. There's nothing quite like a peaceful run at the end of a stressful day. Just as I was turning around and heading back home, I realized that I had not slept much the night before. Maybe a shorter run would've made more sense. Too late now.

I came up behind two ladies power walking, each with hand weights and exaggerated strides. As I pulled up next to them, I recognized them. Rose Maher and Amanda Brody, two of my patients. Rose owned several local boutiques and Amanda ran a thriving shipping business with her husband. I knew that they were both fitness freaks. Vegetarians and gym rats. Heavily into yoga and yogurt.

I slowed to match their pace.

"Dr. Lawson," Rose said. "Good to see you out running."

"I didn't think you ever had the time to do that," Amanda said.

"How is everything?" I asked.

"Never better," Rose said. "Amanda and I are on a new diet program and we've each lost over ten pounds."

"In just the last couple weeks," Amanda added.

"That's a lot for two people who didn't need to lose weight in the first place."

"You know us," Rose said. "The vanity twins?"

Both of them laughed.

"How did you do it?" I asked. "More exercise and less carbs?"

"We're seeing a wonderful nutritionist," Rose said. "Julian Morelli. Do you know him?"

"No, but I've heard of him."

"Apparently, he's been around for years, but we just discovered him," Amanda said. "He practiced in the city be-

fore he moved to the Hamptons. A couple of years ago."
She looked at Rose. "Isn't that about right?"

"Exactly," Rose said. "He's got this new program that
makes weight loss simple."

"Simple doesn't always work," I said.

"It does this time," Amanda said. "He's got us on more
fiber and more exercise as well as his own special vitamins
and herbs."

"What vitamins and herbs?"

"I'm not sure, but they definitely work. I've never felt
better and the pounds are just falling away." She lifted her
shirt and pinched the very small amount of flesh around
her midsection, proving that she didn't really need to lose
weight, see Julian Morelli, or swallow a bunch of mystery
meds.

"So you're not really sure what he's giving you?" I
asked.

Rose laughed. "I don't really care as long as it works."

Chapter 20

By the time I finished my postrun shower, Divya had arrived. She and Evan sat at the table, working quietly alongside each other, neither sniping at the other. Amazing.

"Sorry about piling all that work on you today," I said.

"Not a problem," Divya said. "How is the cyclist doing?"

"Last I heard, very well." I grabbed a bottle of water from the fridge. "The two new-patient visits go well?"

Before she could answer, Evan jumped in. "I'll say. I got to meet Nathan Zimmer."

I looked at Divya. "Evan went with you?"

"Unfortunately. He has some new scheme where the CFO meets all our patients."

I took a swig of water. "I don't see much good coming out of that."

"You're about as funny as Divya."

I shrugged. "So why is meeting Nathan Zimmer such a big deal?"

He gave an exasperated sigh. "He's only the hottest dude on Wall Street. The guy is worth billions. Many billions. More billions than Boris."

"Exactly how many billions does Boris have?"

"I don't know, but Nathan Zimmer has more."

"I believe Hank is more interested in his health than his portfolio," Divya said.

"And?" I asked. "How is his health?"

"Blood pressure too high and he chain-smokes. I upgraded his blood pressure meds and told him to try either the nicotine patches or gum."

"Sounds good."

Evan picked up a piece of paper and waved it toward us. "The contract he signed is even better. He's paying us twice our normal fee."

"Why is that?"

"He demanded it."

"He demanded to pay more? That doesn't sound like a financial genius."

"He said you get what you pay for and he wanted to make sure he paid top dollar." Evan slid the contract into his briefcase. "Someday all our patients will pay top dollar."

"I doubt it."

"If you leave everything to me," Evan said, "money will be the least of your problems."

"I didn't realize that spending an hour with Mr. Wall Street would rub off on you," Divya said. "Simply being around the man has given you the Midas touch? Is that how it works?"

"It's not what you know—it's who you know."

Divya raised an eyebrow. "I must have missed something. Exactly when did you and Mr. Zimmer become such good buddies?"

"We will be. After I turn on the old Evan charm."

Divya leaned back and crossed her arms over her chest. "Modesty is such an overrated virtue."

Things were now back to normal.

"As much as I enjoy listening to this argument, I have plans." I picked up a bottle of wine from the kitchen counter and headed toward the door. "Don't wait up for me."

*   *   *

Jill's front door stood open to capture the evening breeze. I rapped my knuckles on the frame. She yelled for me to come in. I found her standing at the stove, glass of wine in one hand, a wooden spoon in the other.

"Smells wonderful. What is it?"

"Creamed corn. One of the things my mom used to make." She raised her wineglass. "I just poured the last of the bottle, so you might want to open that." She aimed the spoon at the wine bottle I held.

"Anything I can do to help?"

"Got it under control. I made that marinated chicken you like, green beans with almonds, and the corn. Too much of everything, of course, so I hope you brought an appetite."

"Starving."

I opened the wine, poured a glass, and sat at the table. Jill turned off the burner, saying that it needed to sit for a few minutes. She sat across from me.

"I called the hospital a few minutes ago," she said. "Mr. Cooper is already beginning to wake up. His nurse said they would have the ET tube out shortly."

"He seemed to be in good shape. He'll heal quickly."

"You have more than a couple of fans there. All the nurses and even Dr. Weinberg were very impressed with your patchwork."

"Just used what was available."

"It worked."

"Any news on the clinic?" I asked.

"Still scrounging for money, but at least we have enough banked to keep the doors open. Barely."

"It'll all work out. I'm sure of that."

"Glad you're so confident. I have my doubts. The board is very good at stonewalling and delaying."

"They'll ultimately pony up the money, because the free clinic is needed."

"Maybe I should have you talk to the board."

"Probably not a good idea."

"Why do you say that?"

"I'm not on staff there. Have nothing to do with Hamptons Heritage. And I'm new to the Hamptons."

"So?"

"They wouldn't listen to me."

She shrugged. "They don't listen to me either."

"There you go."

Jill served the food and we dug in. It was great. Even better than it smelled. I told her so.

"You're just saying that to be nice. You're used to Evan's cooking and he's pretty good."

"Yes, he is. But this is still delicious. One of the best things I've had in a long time."

"Do you think complimenting my cooking will get you anywhere?" She raised an eyebrow and smiled.

"I thought it was the other way around. I thought you were feeding me food and wine to take advantage of me."

"Probably."

"No complaints on this end."

We finished the meal and then Jill served dessert. Strawberry shortcake. Homemade biscuits, bright red strawberries, and fresh whipped cream. It doesn't get much better.

I licked whipped cream from the back of my fork and then asked her, "Do you know Julian Morelli?"

"Yeah."

"What's his specialty?"

"He's not a medical doctor. He's a PhD. Nutrition science. Why?"

"His name has come up a couple times. Seems that Nicole is seeing him to lose weight, though I have no idea why."

"Because women always feel they're overweight." She forked a strawberry into her mouth.

"Apparently Ashley has seen him off and on for years. She arranged Nicole's appointment. Then while I was jogging, I ran into a couple of my patients who also see him. Seems that everyone thinks he's the weight-loss guru."

"That's the rumor. I know a couple of the nurses at the hospital go to him and they love him. They say his clinic is unbelievable."

"Where is it?"

"In Southampton. Overlooking the ocean. Prime real estate from what I hear, so he must be doing well."

"Weight loss is big business. Just look at the *New York Times* nonfiction best-seller list every week." I took another bite of strawberry shortcake. "Maybe I should write a book about it."

"Just don't get any whipped cream on it."

"Beautiful and funny. No wonder I'm smitten with you."

"Smitten? All this time I thought it was purely physical. But smitten?"

"You're getting less funny."

"No, I'm not. Besides, you'll laugh at my jokes anyway."

"Why is that?"

"Because you think it'll get you into my bed."

"Won't it?"

Now she licked whipped cream from her fork. "We'll see."

Chapter 21

The next morning, I followed Jill into town. We stopped by her favorite coffee shop, where I picked up a large dark roast, she a double cappuccino. Much better than hospital cafeteria coffee. Even I thought so. Jill is a bit of a coffee snob—me, not so much. Medical students, interns, and residents spend so much of their lives in hospitals and are so chronically sleep deprived and fatigued that coffee becomes essential for survival. Any coffee. If it's hot, dark, and caffeine loaded, it'll do.

Caffeine in hand, we headed to the hospital. I walked her to her office, where a stack of phone messages had already accumulated on her desk, so I left her to deal with them and went up to the ICU to check on Owen Cooper.

He was sitting up in bed, two IV lines running to bags of fluids above his head, and a chest tube extending from the right side of his chest to the suction bottle on the floor. He was reading the newspaper, which he folded when I came in.

"How are you doing?" I asked.

"Still hurts but overall not too bad."

"It'll get better day by day."

"I've already been out of bed. Even to the bathroom. With their help, of course."

"I'll let you get back to your paper. I just wanted to see how things were going."

"When I get out of here, I want to hire you to be my doc. My wife's, too."

"I'm flattered."

"Flattery's got nothing to do with it. Everybody here says that if you hadn't been there, I might not be alive. To me, trust is everything. I trust you."

"I appreciate your vote of confidence. Of course I'll see you and your wife. We'll talk when you're up and around."

After I left the hospital, I drove to Ellie's. She was in the parlor, sitting on one of the Louis-the-whatever sofas reading *Architectural Digest*. I asked how she was doing.

"Hank, I know you're not here to see me."

"That's not exactly true."

"I'm fine." She looked out the windows toward the back patio. "She's out there. Reading." She looked at me with that mischievous twinkle she so often has. "Just in case you want to wander in that direction."

I did.

Nicole lay on a lounge chair, a book propped on her abdomen, oversized sunglasses on her face. She wore a yellow bikini that looked as though it had been made from a couple of handkerchiefs. Her hair was pulled back into a golden ponytail and a nearly empty coffee cup rested on the table beside her. Below the patio and out toward the garden, several men worked on the new circular dance floor for the wedding reception. Two of the men balanced on ladders as they strung lights from the dozen fifteen-foot poles that surrounded the area.

Nicole looked up as I approached. She slipped a finger into the book she was reading to hold her place and closed it.

"Great day, isn't it?" I asked.

"A lazy one so far." She looked out toward the ocean. "I was going to go to the gym this morning but decided to have a cup of coffee and read instead. Maybe I'll go later, after Ashley gets up."

"She's sleeping in today?"

Nicole laughed. "She sleeps in every day she can. Except when I wake her up."

"How're you doing?" I asked.

"I'm fine. Really, I am. I wish you would quit worrying about me. And quit making Ellie worry."

"I think she worries on her own. And so do I."

"I've never felt better. I've already lost four pounds in only two days."

"On Julian Morelli's program?"

She nodded. "He's a genius. You should see his clinic. Fab-u-lous. Packed. I've never seen so many people."

"That's what I hear."

She blew a strand of hair from her face. "I just want to look good for my wedding. I know it's silly, but wedding pictures are forever. You only get one chance to make them and then you have to look at them for the rest of your life. I want them to be perfect. I want to be perfect."

"There is a saying in medicine that the enemy of good is better. Anytime you try to make something that is good better, trouble always seems to rear its head."

"I don't understand."

"All I'm saying is that you are a beautiful young woman who doesn't need to change in any way. You do not need to lose an ounce to be perfect. That's a myth."

"I just want the wedding and the pictures and everything else to be perfect. Is that asking too much?"

"Everyone wants their wedding to be memorable. I just don't want you to wreck your health in the process."

"Julian Morelli has a great reputation and he apparently had a huge following in the city before he came out here. Many of his old clients drive or take the train out here just to see him. He's that good." She slid a bookmark into the book and placed it on the table beside the lounge chair. "I met one woman there who had lost fifty pounds this year."

She rolled toward me, propping herself up on one elbow. "She looked marvelous. Lean and fit. And she's sixty years old."

I nodded but said nothing.

Nicole continued. "I've never seen anything like it. It sure works for me."

"Have you had any more of those spells? Where you get confused?"

She swung her legs off the lounge, sat up, adjusted the bathing suit top, and then said, "I told you. Those are nothing. I've had them for years. They only happen when I'm stressed or fatigued."

"Like now? With the wedding?"

"Exactly."

I heard someone behind me and turned to see Jackie walk out. She wore white slacks and a white shirt, and had a white cable-knit sweater draped around her shoulders. It was her gold sandals that caught my eye.

"What's going on here?" Jackie asked.

"Just enjoying the day," I said.

"Dr. Lawson, did I not make it clear that I do not want you bothering my daughter?"

"He's not bothering me, Mother. We were just talking about books." She glanced at me with a conspiratorial smile.

"Are you sure?" She walked over and picked up the book. It was the latest Lisa Gardner thriller.

"We were just talking about her books. Seems that Hank is a big fan, too."

Jackie dropped the book back on the table and stared at me.

"I've read just about everything she's written," I said.

Jackie ignored me and looked back at Nicole. "I'm going into town to do some shopping. Want to go? Maybe pick out a dress for the party this weekend?"

Nicole stood. "Let me go wake Ashley. I'm sure she'll want to go. Then I'll jump in the shower. Say half an hour?"

"That's fine."

Nicole picked up her book and towel, said good-bye to me, and headed into the house.

"Look, Dr. Hank, I meant what I said. Stay away from my daughter."

I wanted to say that Nicole was an adult and could make her own decisions, but instead I said, "We were talking about books."

"That better be all."

Chapter 22

After Jackie delivered her ultimatum, she blew past me and back into the house. I stood on the patio, looking out toward the flat ocean.

Was I out of line?

Nicole wasn't my patient, so what right did I have to stick my nose into her life? Why was I making a curbside diagnosis when the evidence was flimsy at best? So she acted a little strange at a party. And did a disappearing act after drinking in a bar. She wouldn't be the first twenty-something to pull a stunt like that. Maybe Ashley read things incorrectly. Maybe I did, too.

No doubt Nicole was under pressure. Wedding pressure. Psychiatrists have long said that life's great stresses revolve around birth and death, a change of residence, a new job start, an old job loss, a major change in health status, and divorce and marriage. Nicole might simply be reacting to such pressure.

Still, it could be something else and it was that feeling I couldn't shake. By far, drugs would be the most common answer. There is an adage in medicine that says that common things occur commonly. That was likely the case here but . . . maybe not.

I turned back toward the house. Through the window I

saw Jackie and Ellie talking. Ellie sat on the sofa, Jackie standing over her, looking down, hands waving animatedly. I assumed the conversation was about me. I could almost hear it. Jackie telling Ellie, in not so bashful terms, that I was not to have any contact with Nicole.

Time to leave.

As I pulled open the door, I heard a crashing sound behind me and turned. One of the workers lay on the newly constructed dance floor beneath an aluminum ladder. He was holding one side of his chest and grimacing. Two of the other workers yanked the ladder off him as I ran down the stairs.

I knelt next to the man. Rhythmic grunts accompanied his shallow breathing. Beads of sweat dotted his face. I assumed he had fallen from the ladder, since he was one of the men who had been stringing lights earlier, but I asked anyway.

"He was reaching out, trying to wrap the light strand around that pole, and the whole ladder came down," one of the men said.

"I'm Dr. Lawson. What's your name?" I asked the injured man.

He managed to grunt out, "Jesus."

"Okay, Jesus, let me take a look."

I tugged his hand away from the ribs he was holding and lifted his work shirt. A three-inch-wide red welt slashed diagonally across the left side of his chest. He had not just fallen off the ladder but fallen on one of its side rails.

I reached out and touched his chest. He winced.

"I know this hurts, but just bear with me a second," I said.

He nodded.

I continued my examination, palpating along his ribs, and located the truly painful area along his seventh and eighth ribs. At least bruised, possibly fractured.

I stood. "I need to run to my car. Don't move him until I get back."

As I headed back up the stairs toward the patio, I saw that Ellie and Jackie had stepped outside.

"What happened?" Jackie asked.

"Jesus fell off the ladder. He might've broken a rib or two."

Ellie's hand came up to her throat. "That's awful."

"Don't let him move," I said. "I'll be right back."

It took me only a couple minutes to grab my medical bag. I also called Divya. She said she was on the way. When I walked back onto the patio, I saw that Ellie had settled into a chair, Jackie hovering next to her. Ellie's eyes glistened with tears.

"What's the matter?" I asked her.

Ellie sniffed back tears. "What's going to happen next? First poor Jim Mallory falls down the stairs and now this. I'm starting to believe this wedding is cursed."

I squatted next to her so I could look her in the eye. "No, it's not. Things like this just happen. Don't get yourself all worked up." I checked her pulse. Regular and not too fast, considering.

"Don't bother with me. Take care of Jesus."

I walked back down the steps to where Jesus was now stretched out on his back, one hand pressing over his injured ribs. His breathing was easier but obviously still painful.

Falls such as this are similar to automobile accidents. The most obvious injury is not always the end of the story. There can be other, less apparent but often more serious injuries bubbling beneath the surface. A broken leg, or in this case a rib, might be the focal point of the victim's symptoms while occult injuries to the head, neck, or abdomen go unnoticed. One thing you learn in emergency medicine is to never assume anything. Always look for the devil that hides in the details.

I checked his blood pressure, normal at 120 over 80, and his pulse, slightly elevated at around 110. I then did a quick head-to-foot examination. His neck was supple and nontender and his neurological exam was normal. His lungs were clear, but as I laid my hand over his chest, I could feel a slight pop with each breath. No doubt he had broken at least one rib. I moved on to his abdominal examination and detected some left-upper-quadrant tenderness, not an unexpected finding with left-sided rib fractures. But he was in so much pain that he tightened his abdominal muscles every time I touched him. It's a situation we call guarding and it makes a reliable examination very difficult. The concern was that something was going on in his abdomen, but his reaction to the pain was preventing my uncovering it.

As I pressed my fingers into his belly, I said, "Take a deep breath and let it out slowly." As he did, he grimaced. "Sorry. Let's try it one more time." Again he took a breath and again he grimaced, tightening his muscles each time.

"Something for the pain," Jesus said.

"It's coming. As soon as my assistant gets here."

Divya arrived a few minutes later. "What happened?"

I told her the sequence of events and then said, "Looks like a couple rib fractures on the left side. Might be something going on in his belly, too."

"Should I call nine-one-one?" Jackie asked. She stood at the edge of the patio, looking down at us.

"No," Jesus said. "No hospital. No insurance."

"You hush up, Jesus," Ellie said. "I'm paying for this."

"That might not be necessary," I said. "If it's just a couple of broken ribs, we can treat it here. We can get a portable X-ray out here to make sure."

"No hospital," Jesus grunted.

"Draw me up some lidocaine," I asked Divya. "A nerve block will knock out the rib pain and then maybe I can do a better examination."

Divya filled a syringe with lidocaine and handed it to me. We removed Jesus's shirt and rolled him up on his right side. The movement caused him to moan.

"Can you Lie in this position for a couple minutes?" I asked.

"Anything. *Por favor.* Make the pain go."

"I'm going to inject an anesthetic drug that should block the pain."

He nodded but said nothing.

"It'll sting a little."

"Is okay."

Divya opened a pack of Betadine-soaked gauze, and I cleaned the area just to the left of the spinal column where the seventh and eighth ribs originated.

"Hold still."

I eased the needle into the area just beneath the seventh rib where the bundle of intercostal sensory nerves lies. These transmit pain signals from the ribs to the spinal cord and on to the brain. Blocking them would relieve Jesus's discomfort. I repeated the process along the eighth rib.

"That's it," I said. "You should feel better in a minute."

Jesus seemed to breathe freely for the first time. "Is better already."

Divya and I rolled him onto his back again. He winced and grabbed his belly with both hands. Sweat trickled into one eye, causing him to blink. He swiped it away with the back of one hand. His breathing became more labored.

I listened to his lungs again, still clear, still inflated and working well. One concern in any rib fracture is a pneumothorax caused by the broken rib puncturing and collapsing the lung. That wasn't the situation here.

I moved to his abdomen, which I could now examine more easily. As I pressed my fingers into the left-upper quadrant, he moaned. I could now feel a mass in the area.

"I think he's ruptured his spleen."

Divya checked his blood pressure. "I'm getting eighty over fifty. Pulse is one thirty."

I looked up toward Ellie and Jackie. Sam had joined them. "Sam, call nine-one-one."

Sam turned and hurried inside.

"No hospital," Jesus said.

"Jesus, we don't have any choice. I think you've ruptured your spleen and you're bleeding into your abdomen. If we don't get you to the hospital and get it fixed, you'll bleed to death."

His level of consciousness was dropping. His head rolled from side to side and he murmured, "No hospital."

Divya started an IV. "I've got a liter of lactated Ringer's."

"Run it wide open," I said.

My cell phone buzzed. I answered. It was Nathan Zimmer. He sounded distressed. He spoke rapidly, telling me he was having chest pain and was short of breath.

"Calm down, Mr. Zimmer. I want you to call nine-one-one."

When it rains, it definitely does pour.

Divya looked at me with a raised eyebrow.

"I'm not going to call the paramedics," Nathan said. "I want you to come over here and tell me what's wrong."

"I'll be glad to do that, but I think you should call now. And I want you to chew an aspirin."

"I'll take the aspirin, but I'm not calling the medics."

I heard sirens in the distance. I looked down at Jesus. He was awake again and his breathing was less labored.

"Hold on just a second, Mr. Zimmer." I muffled the phone against my chest. "Check his blood pressure again."

Divya did. "Better. It's ninety-five over sixty."

I heard commotion up on the patio and turned. The medics had arrived and were carrying a stretcher toward us.

I pressed the phone to my ear again. "Okay, Mr. Zimmer. I'm on the way."

"Hurry up." He disconnected the call.

"What was that?" Divya asked.

"Nathan Zimmer. Having chest pain. He's refusing to call the medics, so I'll have to go see him."

"I'm not surprised. He probably thinks he can't be away from his phone and computer long enough to go get medical help. And he's probably smoking right now."

I told the medics that Jesus had a couple broken ribs and probably a ruptured spleen. They placed an oxygen mask over his face, hooked him up to a cardiac monitor, and loaded him on the stretcher.

"No hospital," Jesus said. "They'll send me back to Mexico."

"Jesus, right now no one cares whether you're here legally or illegally. Understand? You don't have a choice." He started to say something, but I stopped him. "If we don't get you to the hospital and get this taken care of right now, you're going to die. Understand?"

He nodded.

"Let's roll," I said.

Chapter 23

While accelerating, braking, and sliding through turns as if she were in the Monaco Grand Prix, Divya brought me up to date on Nathan Zimmer's history. During a lull in the story, I made the mistake of suggesting she might want to slow down. Actually what I said was, "Are you trying to kill us?"

"No. I'm merely responding to an emergency call." She jumped on the accelerator a little more forcibly.

"Try to avoid trees."

She frowned at me. "You sound like Evan."

Ouch. I shut up and held on.

By the time we reached Nathan's house, smoke drifted from the brakes and heat waves danced above the hood. I stepped out on wobbly legs.

"Next time I'll drive, Dale."

She lifted her bag from the backseat. "Dale? Who's Dale?"

"Earnhardt. Famous NASCAR driver. Died when he plowed into a wall."

"In case you didn't notice, I hit no walls." She slung her bag over her shoulder. "Or trees."

"Sometimes luck is on your side."

"Maybe I'm a better driver than Dale."

I had no comeback for that.

Todd, Nathan's assistant, led us through the house and out to the patio. On the way he told us that Nathan seemed worse than he had been just a few minutes earlier. More pain and very short of breath. He had tried to convince Nathan to let him call 911, but he had refused, saying it was just indigestion from the chilaquiles he had had for breakfast. Todd argued, but Nathan, "the most stubborn man I've ever known," said he'd wait until I arrived.

Todd's diagnosis?

"I think he's having a heart attack. My father had three of them before he died, so I've seen them before."

Todd pushed through a large glass door that opened to the patio. We followed. Nathan reclined on a lounge chair, cigarette hanging from his mouth. Sweat slicked his face, his shirt damp from perspiration. An open laptop and a cell phone sat on the patio next to him.

"What did I tell you?" Divya said, indicating the cigarette.

"It's about time," Nathan said. "I could've died waiting for you."

I yanked the cigarette from his mouth, dropped it on the patio, and crushed it with my shoe. "I'm Dr. Lawson. Do you think smoking right now is a smart move?"

"I was nervous. Smoking calms me down." He laid a clenched fist on his chest. "Didn't help this darn pain much, though."

"Gee, I wonder why not."

Divya inserted an IV and hooked up a bag of half-normal saline. I dragged a chair over and she hung the bag from its back. She then began attaching EKG leads, beginning with his ankles and wrists.

"Did you take the aspirin like I said?" I asked.

"That didn't help either." He looked at Divya. "And those bloody patches and that gum don't help at all. I've tried both and they just make me want a cigarette more."

Divya had finished hooking up the limb leads and now

unbuttoned his shirt so she could position the EKG's precordial leads. Three nicotine patches decorated his chest.

"What are these?" I asked.

"Ask her. She told me to use them."

I now noticed that he had gum in his mouth. "Wait a minute. You put on the patches AND you're chewing gum?"

He nodded.

"And smoking," Divya said.

Nathan looked at her. "I told you the patches weren't working."

I peeled off the nicotine patches and had him spit out the gum.

Divya now had his shirt completely undone, revealing two more patches on his abdomen. She removed those.

"I figured the more the better," he said. "Isn't that how it usually works?"

"That's not how this works. Nicotine is dangerous. Particularly in someone who could have coronary disease."

"I never had that before."

"Not that you knew of, anyway," I said.

Nicotine does several nasty things, like constricting, or narrowing, arteries, including the coronary arteries, which supply blood to the heart. If someone already has atherosclerotic narrowing of these vessels, any further constriction can reduce the blood supply to the heart muscle and result in tissue damage and death. This is what happens in a heart attack. In medical terms a myocardial infarction, or MI. By any name it can be deadly.

Divya finished the EKG tracing and handed the strip to me. It showed that Nathan was indeed in the midst of an acute MI, one that appeared to involve the front, or anterior, wall. Not the best place. MIs in this area tend to do the most damage and are the most life threatening.

"How is the pain now?"

"Worse than when I called you but better than it was ten minutes ago."

"You're having a heart attack. We've got to get you to

the hospital." I looked at Todd. "Call the paramedics right now."

He glanced at Nathan as if awaiting permission.

"Now," I said.

Todd flipped open his cell phone.

Divya retrieved a spray bottle of nitroglycerin from her bag. "Open wide." Nathan did and she pumped two quick sprays into his mouth. "Close your mouth and let it absorb."

"When did this start?" I asked. "The pain?"

"Maybe an hour ago. It started in my jaw. I thought I had a toothache or something like that. But then it moved down to my neck and chest, like it is now." He opened and closed his left fist a couple of times. "Even my arm feels heavy and numb."

"What did you think this was?" I asked. I always ask this question. Particularly of men who are great deniers. I've heard some outlandish diagnoses. Everything from insect stings to allergies to sleeping on the wrong side to cold air from a nearby window air conditioner to bad chili. Nathan fit the last category.

"I had chilaquiles for breakfast. I thought that was it."

"Really? That's your story?"

He sighed. "Okay. You win. I thought it might be my heart."

"You sure this has been going on for less than an hour?"

"About that. It sort of comes and goes. Not really gone, more like it would get better and then worse. Back and forth."

"That's because there's a clot sitting in your artery that's getting bigger and smaller. As the clot grows larger, it blocks the artery more completely and the pain increases. Then the body starts destroying it, and as it gets smaller, the pain lessens."

"Heparin. Ten thousand units," Divya said. She injected the drug into the IV line's side port.

"What's that?" Nathan asked.

"A blood thinner. Helps reverse the clotting."

"Why did it clot in the first place?"

"A plaque, a cholesterol plaque, in your artery cracked. The body doesn't know the difference between a cracked plaque and a gunshot wound. All it sees is a breach in the system. And just like there's no screen doors on a submarine, the body knows to patch up any breach. So it forms a clot to seal the crack. Unfortunately, the clot can grow large enough to block the artery and cause a heart attack."

"That doesn't make sense."

I smiled. "The body also makes certain enzymes that destroy the clots and that's why the clot gets bigger and smaller."

"Sounds like a screwy system to me. Like the body can't decide what to do."

"It's actually very elegant. And necessary. If you cut your finger, the blood in that area clots, which is a good thing. Keeps you from bleeding to death from a minor injury. But what's to keep this process from spreading through the entire system and clotting all the blood?"

"Those enzyme things?"

"Exactly."

He thought about that for a minute and then said, "It is clever."

"I can't take credit for it. I didn't invent it."

"No wonder medical school takes so long."

"Yes, it does."

"I'm glad you didn't cut classes the day they talked about heart attacks."

I laughed. "I was definitely there on heart attack day."

Todd had walked away to call the paramedics and now came back toward us. He snapped his phone closed. "They're about twenty minutes away."

"Any reason he can't get tPA?" I asked Divya.

"No history of severe hypertension or of a previous stroke. His blood pressure right now is one thirty over seventy."

"You've never had ulcers or nosebleeds or problems with bleeding during surgery?" I asked Nathan.

"Don't know about surgery, since I've never had any, but no to everything else."

"How much do you weigh?"

"Why?"

"So we can give you the right dose of this medication."

"What medication?"

"Remember that clot we talked about? This drug breaks it up."

"I had a business associate once who got that and bled like crazy."

"That can happen. It can also abort this heart attack you're having." I sat down on the edge of the lounge chair next to him. "Listen to me. This heart attack. It's a big one. We have to get you to the hospital so a cardiologist can open the artery up. But every minute that goes by, more damage is being done. That's damage that can't be reversed. This drug will save heart muscle and that's the name of the game. How well you do down the road depends on what we do right now."

"You aren't much for sugarcoating, are you?"

"Not in a situation like this. I know you're scared, but just let us do what we need to do and everything should work out fine."

"I'm not scared. I just don't have time for all this."

"There's never a good time for a heart attack," Divya said.

Divya drew up the tPA, tissue plasminogen activator, a clot-busting drug, and handed me the syringe. I inserted the needle into the IV line.

"Here goes." I pressed the plunger.

"Will I feel anything?"

"Hopefully, this'll make the pain better."

That's exactly what happened. By the time the medics arrived, Nathan's pain and the massively elevated ST segments on his EKG had begun resolving.

The medics carted him through the house and loaded him into the ambulance. I climbed in back with him. We roared up the drive, Divya on our tail.

I hoped she didn't think this was a race.

Chapter 24

The emergency department was slammed. That was obvious from the moment we pulled up to the receiving ramp. Two other ambulances sat nearby, one with red lights still pulsing, the other silent, except for the two medics who worked in its open rear doorway, stuffing soiled towels and empty medication boxes into a plastic hazardous-materials bag.

Inside chaos ruled: nurses and doctors scurrying from one room to another, an X-ray tech maneuvering a portable machine into one of the cubicles, a lab tech drawing blood from a young woman in another, Dr. Andrew Weinberg putting a chest tube in a middle-aged man in the major-trauma room, shouted orders flying from every direction, and the cries of several babies echoing from the packed waiting room.

It reminded me of my days in the ER. Days when one catastrophe piled on top of another, when time for contemplation was a lost commodity and you had to move on instinct, when the decisions you made and actions you took made a difference right then and there.

Real medicine. At its purest.

I missed it.

Near the nurses' station, Jill stood like a calm oasis in the middle of the storm and directed traffic.

"Where do you want Mr. Zimmer?" I asked her.

"Over here, cubicle six. I saved the last monitored bed we have for him."

We rolled Nathan into the cubicle and slid him from the stretcher onto the treatment table. A nurse, whose name tag read Susan Foster, RN, began swapping the medics' portable cardiac monitor for the hospital one.

"I'm putting him on our portable, since he'll be going directly to the cath lab." Once she got the electrical cables attached, she adjusted the IV flow rate and then began wrapping a blood pressure cuff around Nathan's arm. "How are you feeling?" she asked him.

"Better. The chest pain is almost gone."

"We gave him tPA at the scene," I said. "Looks like he reperfused. His pain resolved and the ST elevations have decreased."

"That's what cigarettes will do for you," Susan said.

He gave her a quizzical look.

"I can smell them on you. We ER nurses have pretty good noses." She smiled. "Especially for things like cigarettes. I bet you get religion after this and put those things down."

"Maybe."

"That's usually how it works," Susan said. " 'Maxwell's silver hammer' hits you in the head and you begin to see things a little differently. Sort of a wake-up call. Seen it a million times."

Dr. Walter Edelman walked in. He was young, maybe midthirties, and had been on staff for only a couple years but was arguably the best cardiologist. I had met him a few months earlier when I brought in another patient almost identical to Nathan Zimmer. An acute MI, tPA, the whole deal.

"Hank," Edelman said. "How's it going?"

I wasn't sure if he was asking about me or about Nathan. I went with the latter. "Much better. Looks like the tPA worked."

Edelman introduced himself to Nathan and then said,

"The cath lab is waiting. First thing we'll do is an angiogram to see what we're dealing with and then maybe put in a stent or two. I'll explain it on the way, but let's get you out of this chaos and down to the lab, where it's much quieter."

While the nurse began preparing for the transfer, I told Nathan, "You're in good hands here. Just do what Dr. Edelman says and everything will work out."

"You saying I'm a difficult patient?" he said with a smile.

"Let's go with stubborn."

"I guess I can't argue with that."

"I'll check on you later."

"Thanks, Doc. I owe you."

As I exited the cubicle, I saw Divya come through the double doors and work her way through the chaos.

"Looks like you guys are having fun today," Divya said.

"Big accident over on the highway," Jill said. "I hear there were six cars involved and two fatalities. We have four of the injured here already and two more on the way."

Divya's cell phone buzzed. She pulled it from her purse and walked away to answer the call.

"Thanks for dinner last night," I said.

Jill gave me a knowing smile. "Thank you for dessert."

"But you made the strawberry shortcake," I said.

She punched my arm. "You know what I mean."

"My favorite part, too."

She propped a fist on her hip and cocked her head to one side. "Are you saying my cooking is second-rate?"

"Compared to the rest of the night? No contest."

"I'll remember that. Next time I'll just order in pizza."

"That works for me."

Divya returned. "That was Maria Mendez. Apparently Oscar is worse. She said he was confused and talking nonsense."

"Let's run over and see him," I said. "Then you can drop me back at Ellie's so I can get my car."

Jill walked out to the parking lot with us. Divya climbed in her Mercedes SUV and cranked it up.

"Pizza tonight?" I said.

Jill laughed. "All of a sudden you're a pizza fan?"

"You make it sound so appealing."

"Can't do it tonight. I have a meeting that'll last until ten or so."

"The exciting life of a hospital administrator. Maybe tomorrow, then?"

"That'll probably work. Now you go get some work done." She pulled open the car door for me.

The sound of a racing engine and then the screech of tires caused both of us to flinch and then turn. A dark blue four-door sedan slid to a stop behind one of the ambulances. A man jumped out, waving his arms and screaming.

"Help me. Help me. It's my daughter."

I sprinted in that direction. He ripped open the back door. Inside, a young girl, looked to be mid- to late teens, lay on the backseat. Her breathing was labored and erratic and she was unconscious. I immediately climbed in and reached for her neck to check her pulse. Slow and weak and then nothing. Her face and her entire body went limp.

"She's in cardiac arrest," I shouted. I immediately began doing chest compressions. "Get a stretcher out here."

Jill ran into the ER just as Divya appeared with her medical bag. She pulled out an Ambu bag and a face mask. She seated the mask over the girl's mouth and began pumping air into her lungs.

As I continued the CPR, the man climbed into the front seat, now on his knees, arms resting on the seat back, eyes wide.

"What happened?" I asked.

"I don't know. She had been out for a run and then came home and then . . ." A sob racked him.

"Relax. Take a deep breath. Tell me what happened."

I glanced through the car's rear window and saw Jill and one of the nurses rolling a stretcher toward us.

"She had some water. She said she felt dizzy." He

squeezed his eyes shut as if preventing more tears. "Then she gasped once and fell to the floor."

While the two nurses stabilized the stretcher, Divya and I lifted the girl out of the car and onto the stretcher. I climbed on top of her, straddling her hips, and continued CPR. Divya led the way, never missing a beat with the Ambu bag.

Jill and the nurse rolled the stretcher into the cubicle vacated by Nathan Zimmer. I climbed off and stood beside the bed, continuing the chest compressions. One nurse started an IV while another hooked her up to the cardiac monitor. As soon as the final patch was in place and the last cable connected, a rhythm appeared on the monitor screen.

V-tach.

"Charge the defibrillator," I said.

One of the nurses placed the portable defibrillator on the bed, while the other used a pair of scissors to cut away the girl's shirt and bra. I smeared electrode paste just to the right of her sternum and to the left of and below her left breast. The defibrillator whined as it charged.

"Ready," the nurse said. "Four hundred watt-seconds."

I pressed the two paddles against the girl's chest and rested my thumbs on the red buttons at the top of each. "Clear," I said, and then depressed both buttons.

There was a soft pop and the girl quivered slightly as she took in a quick breath. She then began to move around, waving first one arm and then the other. I looked up at the cardiac monitor and saw that she was now back into a normal sinus rhythm.

"Let's give her a one-hundred-milligram lidocaine bolus and then start a drip at two milligrams a minute. O_2 at one hundred percent. Get an EKG, blood gases, and draw labs for electrolytes, a CBC, and a chem panel."

The girl was now becoming combative, swinging her arms and kicking her legs. This often happens after a cardiac arrest. The brain, which has been deprived of oxygen, suddenly receives blood flow and oxygen again. The result is a period of confusion and disorientation. Not unlike waking up from anesthesia. These victims don't know where they are, or what's going on, and often feel threatened by the confused images that come at them from the fog. Some can become completely out of control and can harm themselves and others.

"Get some soft restraints," I said. "Call radiology and tell them we need a stat chest X-ray."

Dr. Weinberg came into the cubicle. "You sure are keeping us busy today, Hank. What have you got here?"

"Not sure. Young girl was brought in by her father because she collapsed at home and then she arrested in the parking lot. We started CPR immediately. Why she arrested, I don't have a clue."

I moved out of the way to let Weinberg begin his examination. The girl was now his patient. I stepped out of the cubicle.

"Good job," Jill said. "Both of you."

"Thanks," Divya said. "I'm glad we were there."

I saw the girl's father, standing at the receptionist's desk, probably giving them the insurance information. The clerk handed him something, which he stuffed into his pocket. He nodded and stepped away, turning toward us. His face said it all: confused, anxious, terrified. Divya and I walked over to him.

"I'm Dr. Hank Lawson," I said. "This is Divya Katdare, my physician assistant."

"Tony Gilroy. That's my daughter, Valerie. How is she?"

"Better. She suffered a cardiac arrest due to a very dangerous arrhythmia. That's corrected now and she's beginning to wake up."

He nodded, fighting back tears.

"Tell me exactly what happened."

"Just as I said. She'd been out jogging, came in and had a glass of water, grabbed her chest, and collapsed."

"Did she have a seizure or anything like that?"

He shook his head. "She just fell. Very slowly. I was

standing right there. Everything seemed to be in slow mo-
tion. I froze. I couldn't move. I just stood there. I couldn't
help her." A sob racked him.

"What happened then?"

"Her breathing was all raspy and irregular. I shook her.
Tried to wake her up. But she wouldn't respond. I was going to call nine-one-one but decided I could get her here
faster."

Not always the best call but in this case the right one.
Had he waited on the medics and had she arrested at home
before they arrived, this could have gone badly.

"Does she have any medical problems?" Divya asked.

"No. She's very healthy. Exercises all the time. Really
pays attention to her diet. Runs cross-country. She's just a
freshman, but she made the varsity track team."

"Does she use any kind of drugs?" I asked.

"No. I'm sure of that."

I refrained from mentioning that most parents thought
that.

He swiped a hand, fingers trembling, over his mouth. "Is
she going to be okay?"

"I think so. Dr. Weinberg will take care of her here in the
emergency room, but she'll be admitted to the hospital
while all this is sorted out."

"You're a doctor. Aren't you going to treat her?"

"I don't practice here. Dr. Weinberg runs the emergency
department. He's very good."

He nodded. "Thanks for saving her." He looked down
toward the cubicle where his daughter lay and swallowed
hard. "She's all I've got. We lost her mother a couple years
ago. It's been tough on Valerie, but she's a trouper. Tough
as they come."

Chapter 25

Maria Mendez was right. Oscar was confused. Very confused.

He didn't know his name. He didn't recognize Maria. He didn't know where he was or what day it was, and had no idea who Divya and I were or why we were standing in his living room, looking down at him sitting on the sofa.

Oscar did not sit quietly. He jabbered on and on, mostly nonsense, occasionally putting together something that sounded like a sentence only to fall apart before he finished. He stared wide-eyed at nothing and waved his arms around as if protecting himself from a squadron of invisible insects. He burst into hysterical laughter and then fell into equally hysterical sobbing.

"He's been like this all morning." Maria sat on the other end of the sofa, out of reach of Oscar's flailing. Crying had puffed and reddened her eyes, and her face appeared pale and drawn.

I pulled a chair over near Oscar and sat. "Oscar, how are you doing today, partner?"

Oscar's head snapped in my direction, but he didn't look at me but rather past me toward the front window. "The tangerines have been bouncing all day. Did you see them? I think they belong in the airplane."

Maria sniffed, tears welling in her eyes. "See what I mean?"

"Who am I?" I asked.

"Don't you know?" he asked, his eyes widening in surprise, now looking at me. Then his gaze was gone, this time up toward the ceiling. "I think ice cream would be nice. And cherries. Do you like cherries? I do."

"Oscar, look at me." He did. "What did you have for breakfast today?"

"Tangerines. I saw tangerines everywhere."

I turned to Maria. "Anything unusual happen? Like maybe a fall?"

"No. Everything's been normal. He actually had a very nice breakfast this morning. Ate more than he usually does."

"Tangerines?" I asked.

A quick nervous laugh escaped her lips. "I don't know where he came up with that. We haven't had tangerines in years. In fact, Oscar doesn't like fruit of any kind."

"He's still taking his medicines regularly?"

"Oh yes. Like I told you the other day, I take care of that. Make sure he never misses any of them."

"Can I take a look at his medicines?" Divya asked.

Maria stood and left the room, returning a few minutes later with a paper bag filled with prescription bottles and a pale blue plastic pillbox, one of those with three small compartments for each day of the week.

"Every Sunday morning I organize all of his pills and put them in this." She handed the box to Divya and sat back down on the sofa. "He takes some of his medicines three times a day, so I have everything set for breakfast, lunch, and dinner."

While Divya moved to the kitchen table and began going through Oscar's meds, I conducted a neurological exam. It wasn't easy. I couldn't hold his attention long enough to get through all the necessary tests, but we muddled through.

"I don't see any change in his physical status," I said. "There's no evidence he's had a stroke or anything like that."

"Then what is it?" Maria asked.

"Most likely a worsening of his dementia. Remember? I told you this is how it usually goes?"

Her knuckles whitened as she gripped the front edge of the sofa. "This quickly? I mean he's been up and down for months. But this? I've never seen him like this."

"It's unpredictable, Maria. It can happen just this way."

"You might want to look at this," Divya said.

Maria and I walked to where Divya had Oscar's pillbox and bottles arrayed on the kitchen table. Oscar began muttering more about tangerines and now began talking about someone or someplace named Rosarita. When I asked, Maria said she had no idea what he was talking about.

Divya held up a brown plastic medicine bottle. There were only a half dozen pills inside.

"These pink oval pills?" Divya said. "These are his anti-anxiety meds. Citalopram. Based on the last refill date, he should still have over twenty-five of these left." She then pointed to the pillbox, where she had opened each of the twenty-one compartments. "See these same pills here, and here, and here?"

I saw the problem immediately.

"Maria, this is a once-a-day medication, but it looks like he's been getting it three times a day," I said. "Probably for a week or more."

Maria collapsed into the chair across from Divya. Her face tightened as if holding back tears. "I'm always so careful."

"It's easy to do," I said.

She looked at Oscar, who was staring at the TV, which was off, and muttering to himself. "I've poisoned him."

"No, you haven't. Even if taken correctly, these medications can cause some very strange behavior, particularly in someone who has dementia like Oscar. Taking too many makes that more likely. Now all of his odd behavior makes perfect sense."

"What do we do?" Maria asked. "Will he ever be his old self again?"

I nodded. "He should be fine. We'll just hold this medicine for a few days and then restart it at the proper dose."

I could see the fear and anxiety on her face when she looked up at me. "This is my fault."

"It's an honest mistake, Maria. It happens all the time."

"You mean to old folks. Like me and Oscar."

"That might be true, but I mess up things like this, too," Divya said.

"You're just being nice." She sighed heavily, her shoulders slumping. "I know you're both wondering if I'll do this again. If maybe next time something bad will happen to Oscar."

"You'll have to be more careful," I said. I laid a comforting hand on her shoulder. "Maybe you should reconsider what we talked about before. Some assisted-living arrangement."

Maria tugged a napkin from the green plastic holder that sat in the middle of the table and dabbed her eyes. "I don't . . . we don't want to do that." She looked up at me. "Unless we have to."

"You don't have to make that decision right now, but I do wish you would consider it."

Again, she looked toward Oscar, her gaze resting on him for a full minute before she spoke. "I owe him so much." She sniffed back tears. "Like swallowing my pride and doing what's best for him."

I sat in the chair next to her and took her hand. "Let me talk to Jill Casey. She's the administrator over at Hamptons Heritage. She'll have one of the hospital social workers come talk with you. Show you the options. Even take you around to look at some of the places. Then you can make a decision."

Maria nodded, and took in a deep breath, letting it out slowly. "I guess I should do that."

Chapter 26

Divya dropped me at Ellie's estate to pick up my car. She headed back to my place to work on her notes and to have some sort of quasi marketing meeting with Evan. His idea. Not something she looked forward to.

Better her than me.

I drove to Hamptons Heritage.

I walked into the emergency room and immediately ran into Jill.

"Looks a lot quieter around here now," I said.

It did. Where there had been disorder earlier, everything was now calm. No one was in the trauma room or either of the two major treatment rooms, and only a handful of people sat in the waiting area.

"Probably the calm before the next storm," she said. "What're you doing here?"

"I came to see you."

"Liar." She laughed. "I know you too well, Hank Lawson. You're here to see how all the patients you brought us today are doing."

"That, too."

"Come on. I'll go upstairs with you."

"Is that because I don't have privileges and shouldn't be

wandering around the hospital or because you just want to hang out with me?"

"Let's go with the former."

"Maybe both?"

"Maybe not." She smiled.

"Now look who's lying."

We first stopped by to see Jesus Morales, who was light one spleen but otherwise doing well. ICE hadn't been called, at least not yet, so he was happy and anxious to go home.

"It'll be a few days yet," I said.

"I'm fine. A little pain, but I can handle it."

I was sure he could. "See that bag of yellow fluid?" I pointed to the IV bag that hung above his head. "That's fluids and vitamins and antibiotics so you'll heal properly. Can't shortcut that stuff or bad things might happen."

He held out one of his hands, palm down. A large scar ran diagonally across its back. "See that? Piece of sheet metal. Know what I did?"

"What?"

"Nothing. No doctor. No hospital. I washed it with whiskey every day." He made a fist. "I'm a fast healer."

"This is a little different, Jesus. Be patient."

We then visited Nathan Zimmer in the cardiac ICU. He was sitting up in bed, stacks of paper on his tray table, half-glasses resting on his nose. Todd sat in an adjacent chair, his MacBook Pro on his lap, fingers struggling to keep up with Nathan's rapid-fire dictating.

"Does Dr. Edelman know you've turned his cardiac unit into an office?" I asked.

Nathan didn't look up, his eyes racing across the page he held. "They took my phone. Some BS about it interfering with the electronics in here. I think it's a power play."

"Actually, it's true. Cell phones can interfere with the monitors."

"Pardon my skepticism."

"You should be resting, not working."

"I told you I didn't have time for this," Nathan said. Now he looked at me and then to Jill. "Who is this lovely creature?"

I started to answer, but Jill beat me to it.

"This creature is the hospital administrator," she said.

Nathan perked up. "I'm glad they sent the big boss to see me."

Jill laughed. "I'm simply trying to keep Han—Dr. Lawson—out of trouble."

Nathan looked from Jill to me, back to her. "How long you two been sleeping together?"

"Mr. Zimmer . . . ," Jill began.

He raised a hand. "Don't protest. It's obvious." He gave me a thumbs-up. "Good job."

Jill shook her head. "You are definitely as advertised."

"And then some," Nathan laughed.

"You should listen to Dr. Lawson and put the work aside. Relax a little."

"Trust me," Todd said. "This is relaxing for him. If he couldn't do business, he'd climb the walls and drive the nurses crazy."

"I feel like nothing happened," Nathan said.

"Well, something did happen," I said. "Something very dangerous. You dodged a very big bullet. You got two stents and hopefully everything is going to be okay, but you could've easily died long before you got here."

"But I didn't. Thanks to you. And Dr. Edelman."

Most people, after suffering a life-threatening event, get religion. They want to know what they did wrong and how they can make things better and will this ever happen again and all the normal things that cross someone's mind after a brush with mortality. Many of them want to start turning their diet and exercise regimen upside down immediately. These people you often have to hold back until everything is settled and then get them into a rehab program where they learn how to do things properly.

Nathan wasn't that way. I'd seen people like him, too.

They forget the fear and anxiety. Forget how close to death they were. Forget everything except what came before and jump right back into the same arena.

The truth is that type A people can't be made type B. The stress of change is much worse than the stress of driving forward. Nathan was type A plus, so I didn't argue with him.

"It's good to see you doing well," I said.

"Are you still going to' be my doc? After I get out of here?"

"Wouldn't miss it." I smiled and waved as we left his room.

After we left the cardiac ICU, Jill said, "He's a piece of work."

"Oh yeah."

"Come on, I want to show you something," Jill said.

"What?"

"Valerie Gilroy's labs."

"What about them?"

"You'll see."

We walked down the hall to the medical ICU. One of the nurses found Valerie's chart and slid it across the counter toward us. Jill flipped it open to the lab section and turned it toward me.

"What do you make of these?"

I took a few minutes to thumb through the pages, reading each of her lab reports in turn. The results were not what I expected. Her potassium and magnesium levels were frighteningly low, her thyroid studies were off-the-chart high, and she had a digitalis level of 4.5, which was over twice the upper limits of the therapeutic range. Then there was the drug screen. Amphetamines. What the heck?

"What is all this? Her lytes and her thyroid are screwed up and she has digitalis and amphetamines in her system?"

Jill shrugged.

"Does her doctor know about these?"

"Yeah. Said he'd talk with her after he finished office and made evening rounds."

"Athletes sometimes use amphetamines to improve performance. Thyroid hormone, too. The low electrolytes could be from diuretics. To keep her weight down. Foolish, but I've seen this combination before." I thumbed through the remainder of her chart. "Why was she taking digitalis?"

"She wasn't. At least not that she knew."

This made no sense and I said as much.

"Both she and her father swear she takes nothing except for some vitamins and a couple of different types of protein powder. She says it helps with her running."

"Where does she get the vitamins and the powder?"

"I don't know."

"I want to talk to her."

Jill led me down to cubicle three, where we found Valerie, bed cranked up to a sitting position, chatting with her father. He sat in a chair next to her bed. She looked remarkably well. Much better than when I saw her sprawled in the backseat of her father's car. She had an IV in each arm, and the cardiac monitor above her head beat a steady rhythm.

Tony stood. "Dr. Lawson. Ms. Casey." He nodded to Jill.

I walked to the other side of the bed and looked down at Valerie. "You look great. How're you feeling?"

She gave me a quizzical look. "Who are you?"

Tony answered. "This is Dr. Lawson. He saved your life today."

"Along with some other people," I said.

"Sorry. I don't remember."

"I wouldn't expect that you would," I said with a smile. "Are you feeling okay?"

"Fine. Except for these burn spots on my chest." She fingered a circular red area just to the right of her sternum.

"I'm afraid that's my fault," I said. "Those electrical paddles will do that sometimes."

"I hope they don't leave scars."

"They'll fade in a couple of days."

"Good. No bathing suit until they do."

"I understand you're on the track team," I said. "Cross-country, too?"

"Yeah. I'm pretty good. Aren't I, Dad?"

"That's because you work hard at it."

"How much do you run each week?" I asked.

"It varies. Anywhere from twenty to forty miles."

"At least," Tony said.

She laughed. "I love it." She glanced at her father. "I'm maybe a little compulsive about it."

Tony laughed. "That's an understatement."

"I guess you have to watch your diet," I said. "Carb loading and all that?"

"I get to eat all the baked potatoes I want and my friends can't. Makes them so jealous."

"I'm jealous," Jill said.

"I'll bet you take vitamins and supplements?" I asked. "Right?"

"Absolutely. They really help with my energy and keep my weight under control. Hard to run over the hills if you're carrying extra pounds." She laughed again.

Life is a matter of timing. A minute here or a minute there can change everything. Had Valerie arrested a couple of minutes earlier, before her father raced into the emergency parking lot, she might have suffered severe and irreversible brain damage and I would be here looking at a brain-dead girl on a ventilator rather than talking with a pleasant and delightful young lady. Had she arrested five minutes earlier, she might not be here at all.

"Do you have any of them with you?" I asked.

She shook her head.

"Do you think those have anything to do with what happened?" Tony asked.

"I don't know."

"I can bring some in," Tony said. "I've got to go home, but I'll be back later. I can bring them then."

"That would be great. Can you give them to Ms. Casey when you do?"

Jill raised an eyebrow in my direction.

"Will do."

"Where do you get your vitamins?" I asked.

"She sees a nutritionist," Tony said. "For the past few weeks anyway. Seems to help, because her times are lower than they've ever been."

"What's his name?" I asked.

"Dr. Julian Morelli," Valerie said. "He's the best."

Chapter 27

I handed Valerie's chart to the charge nurse and we left the ICU. As the door hissed closed behind us, Jill asked, "Where's my coffee?"

"Maybe in the ER?"

She hesitated and then said, "Yep. I left it on the counter in the nurses' station."

"I think I can spring for another one."

"Cafeteria? Where I get it free?"

"Of course."

"Big spender."

Jill pushed open the stairwell door and I followed her down.

"What exactly am I supposed to do with these pills when Mr. Gilroy brings them in?" she asked over her shoulder.

"I was hoping the lab might be able to test them."

"You know our lab isn't equipped for that. I'd have to send them out to one that did chemical testing."

"I assumed that."

"I'm not sure I've ever done that before, but I am sure the board won't be thrilled with me spending money."

"How much could it be? A few hundred dollars?"

We exited the stairwell and entered the cafeteria. It was

quiet with only a few of the tables occupied. We each grabbed a cup of coffee and sat at a table.

"I'll just grab a few hundred off the money tree out back," Jill said.

"Don't you think this would come under the heading of patient care? Valerie had a cardiac arrest because her electrolytes were out of whack and she had amphetamines, digitalis, and thyroid hormone on board. I think we need to know where those came from."

"I'll take care of it."

"I might have some more for you to analyze, too."

"Oh?"

"Rose Maher and Amanda Brody? The patients I ran into while jogging yesterday? They're also taking Morelli's pills."

"What? You're thinking this guy is poisoning people?"

"I don't know. You have to admit that the lab findings on Valerie Gilroy are troubling. She's got all that crap in her system and the only thing she takes are a handful of pills from some dude whose name keeps popping up everywhere."

Jill cradled her coffee in both hands and took a sip. "This young girl and a couple of your patients isn't exactly 'everywhere.'"

"Nicole is also seeing him."

"Nicole? Odd-behavior Nicole?"

"My point exactly."

She stared into her coffee for a minute, then looked up at me and nodded. "Bring the pills in. I'll make sure they get tested."

"I knew you'd come through."

"That's me. Take one for the team."

"I owe you."

"Big-time."

I parked in front of Rose Maher's house, a rambling ranch-style with two guesthouses and sweeping ocean views.

Amanda Brody's sleek black Bentley convertible sat in the circular drive. I pulled my trusty Saab up beside it.

I'd called Rose before I left the hospital, telling her I wanted to come by for a chat. She said that she and Amanda had an appointment in forty-five minutes. I told her I'd be there in fifteen.

"What brings you by?" Rose asked as she led me out onto her rear patio.

Amanda was sitting at a table, partially shaded by a vine-covered pergola, drinking some thick brownish liquid through a straw.

I took an empty chair. "I wanted to talk to both of you about your new dietary program."

"You mean this?" Amanda lifted the glass toward me. "It's a protein drink. I have three a day."

"From Julian Morelli?"

"Of course. It has protein powder, two eggs, omega-3 oil, flaxseed, grape-seed oil, and a ton of vitamins." She extended the glass toward me. "Want a taste?"

"No, thanks."

"You don't know what you're missing."

"Have either of you experienced any unusual symptoms? Fatigue, shortness of breath, nausea, or palpitations? Maybe seeing a yellow hue to everything?"

Rose looked at me with narrowed eyes. "What's this about?"

"Just worried about your health."

Rose propped one foot on the chair next to her and retied the laces of her walking shoe. "Hank, I know you're not a big fan of natural-food products, but this stuff really does work." She waved a hand toward Amanda. "We've been dieting and working out together for years and we've never seen anything like this. We've lost weight and our energy levels are sky-high."

"That's true," Amanda said. "I haven't felt this good since I was twenty."

"Something about all this is bothering you," Rose said. "What's going on?"

"I just resuscitated a young woman, a runner, over at Hamptons Heritage Hospital. She had toxic levels of a couple of medications, amphetamines in her system, and her blood chemistries were all wrong."

"Is she okay?" Amanda asked.

"Fortunately, yes. But she was lucky."

"What does that have to do with us?" Rose asked.

"She was also taking Julian Morelli's vitamins."

"Sounds like she was taking some other stuff, too."

"Not according to her and her father."

Amanda drained the last of her protein drink, placed the empty glass on the table, and wiped her mouth with a napkin. "I don't understand. Are you trying to say that Julian gave her all that stuff?"

"I don't know, yet. We're analyzing the pills she took. Then we'll know."

"What do you want from us?" Rose asked.

"To stop taking this stuff until I know more."

"No way," Amanda said. "I've never taken anything that works like this. There's no way it could be bad."

"You might be right. But don't you think it would be safer to test it before taking it?"

They both gave me skeptical looks.

"Both of you watch your diet and exercise. Do all the right things. Why would you want to take something and not know what it is?"

"All the ingredients are natural," Amanda said.

"Arsenic is natural. Would you take that?"

"That's ridiculous. Of course we wouldn't. But these are just vitamins and herbs."

"Most poisons come from herbs. Foxglove, belladonna, narcotics, all come from the plant world."

"Julian Morelli wouldn't give us anything harmful. He's a nutritionist. He's an expert in this."

I could see this argument wasn't going very far, so I decided to take a more practical approach. "Why don't you give me a couple of your pills and let me draw some blood? Then we'll know what you're taking and whether it's doing any harm. Does that seem reasonable?"

Again they hesitated, glancing at each other, each apparently waiting for the other to say something.

"You don't really have anything to lose," I said.

They finally agreed.

The pills and the blood samples were in my pocket as I walked back out to my car. A polished silver 750Li BMW pulled up and parked next to my Saab—trusty, old, and a green color that should probably never have been put on a car. The fact that it wasn't worth the cost of a tune-up on either the Bentley or the Beemer it sat between crossed my mind.

Julian Morelli stepped from the BMW.

I had never met him, had never seen him before, but I knew it was him. Couldn't be anyone else. He was the proverbial tall, dark, and handsome. His deep tan was permanent, his black hair thick and wavy, and his teeth were blindingly white when he smiled.

I felt underdressed. I had on my usual jeans, untucked shirt, and tennis shoes. His suit, Italian, perfectly tailored, definitely overpriced, his open-collared black silk shirt, and his spit-shined shoes screamed Hamptons. His diamond pinkie ring caught the sunlight.

"So you're the famous Hank Lawson," he said. We shook hands. "HankMed. Right?" I nodded. "I've heard wonderful things about you."

"I pay people to say those things."

"You must pay them well." His smile wattage increased. "Everybody says you're the best concierge physician in the Hamptons." He nodded toward the house. "Were you seeing Rose and Amanda?"

"Yes, I was."

His face adopted a look of concern. Real or forced I wasn't sure.

"I hope everything is okay," Julian said.

"Just fine. This was more a social call than anything else."

He consulted his oversized, diamond-encrusted Breitling. "I have an appointment with them." Another blinding smile. "Come see my clinic sometime. I would love to show you what we're doing."

"That would be nice."

He nodded and headed toward the front door. Before he reached it, he stopped and turned. "Actually, we're having an open house tomorrow. To kick off our new 'Take Control' program. Why don't you come by?"

"I might do that. Thanks for the invitation."

Chapter 28

Before taking the pills and the blood vials to Jill, I swung by the Wentworth estate. Sam told me that Ellie had gone shopping with Jackie. I told him that I wanted to talk to Nicole anyway. He said he would see if she was there. He hadn't seen her for a couple of hours and she might have slipped out.

Sam picked up the phone from the table in the foyer and punched a couple of buttons, which I assumed was the extension to Nicole's room. He told whoever answered that I was there and then hung up.

"She's coming down," Sam said. "Would you care to wait in the parlor?"

"Sure."

Sam left and almost immediately Nicole came down the stairs. Ashley followed.

"Sam said you wanted to see me?" Nicole said.

"I'd actually like to talk with both of you."

"Sure," Ashley said as she flopped down in a chair. She wore jeans, no shoes, and an oversized sweatshirt. She tugged the cuffs down over her hands, so that only her fingers were visible.

Nicole, also barefoot, wore jeans, frayed at the cuffs, and a pink V-neck T-shirt. She sat on the sofa, curling her legs beneath her. "Talk about what?"

"Julian Morelli."

They exchanged a quick glance.

"What about Julian?" Nicole asked.

"There might be a problem with the vitamins he's giving you."

"Are you kidding?" Nicole said. She lifted the waistband of her jeans away from her abdomen. "Look at this. I've already lost six pounds and I feel great."

"More important," Ashley said, "you're going to look fabulous in that wedding dress."

One thing you could say about Julian Morelli was that he was one heck of a salesman. Valerie, Rose, Amanda, and now Nicole and Ashley bought into his program, no questions asked.

"Let me tell you a story," I said. "It's about a young girl who nearly died a few hours ago."

Now I had their attention. I told them Valerie's story. Not giving her name, of course. That her body chemistry was all sideways. That she was also taking vitamins dispensed by the one and only Julian Morelli. That young Valerie had brushed fingertips with the grim reaper.

"Her heart stopped?" Nicole asked.

I nodded. "Had she lived a mile or so further from the hospital, she might not be alive."

"You think Julian's vitamins like caused that?" Ashley asked.

"I don't know. We're running some tests. I'd suggest that in the meantime you stop taking the pills."

"I can't do that," Nicole said. "The wedding's a week away. After that I'll stop."

"That might not be wise."

"But you don't know for sure?" Nicole asked.

I didn't and I told her as much. Then I said, "I'd like to have the pills you're taking analyzed so we'll know exactly what they contain."

"No problem," Nicole said. Ashley nodded in agreement.

"I'd also like to draw blood from each of you."

"Why?"

"To see what's in your system. To see if you have any of the same abnormalities we saw in the young girl I told you about."

"I'm not big on needles," Nicole said. "I'll give you some pills but not a blood test."

"It could be important."

She thought about it for a minute and then said, "I'll make a deal with you. If the pills contain anything dangerous, I'll let you draw blood." Again, Ashley nodded in agreement.

Rather than arguing the point, I took a couple of pills from each of them and left.

"It truly pains me to say," Divya said, "but I'm impressed. You've done an excellent job on this."

"So you're ready to admit that I was right?" Evan asked.

Divya had spent most of the afternoon updating patient files and preparing for the visits she had scheduled for the next day. Then forty-five minutes ago Evan blew in and immediately began spreading photographs and sketches over the kitchen table. He had obviously been back to Fleming's Custom Shop and picked up some new drawings of his HankMed van. He had dragged Divya over to the table and gone over each in great detail.

"I'm not sure I'm quite ready to admit that you were right, but this is interesting," Divya said.

"It's more than interesting. It's the future. With this, HankMed will become more full-service and more famous."

She tapped a pencil on the tabletop and raised an eyebrow. "Famous? I'm not sure famous is what we're after."

Evan's cell phone buzzed. He looked at the screen and punched the button, apparently sending the call over to voice mail. "I'll get that later." He looked back at her and smiled. "Come on, you know I'm right. You know this would be an asset for HankMed. Just admit it."

"I'm not sure HankMed needs this and I definitely know we can't afford it, but it does have some intriguing features."

"Just say . . . 'Evan R. Lawson is right.' "

"I don't think so."

"Humor me. Just this once."

She tapped the pencil on the table again. "Okay. Evan R. Lawson is right." She raised an eyebrow. "Happy now?"

"Ecstatic."

He held up his cell phone and pushed a button. *Evan R. Lawson is right,* came from the speaker.

"You recorded me?"

Evan R. Lawson is right.

"Stop that."

Evan R. Lawson is right.

"You can be so infuriating."

"You're just now figuring that out?" I said as I came through the door.

They both looked up.

"What has he done now?" I asked.

Evan R. Lawson is right.

"That's what he's done," Divya said.

"That sounds a lot like your voice."

"He tricked me."

"No, I didn't," Evan said. "You said yourself you were impressed."

Ah, the sounds of Divya and Evan bickering. No place like home. I walked over and began shuffling through the pages on the kitchen table. "What are all these?"

"The new HankMed van."

"The one we can't afford?"

I pulled open the refrigerator, grabbed a small bottle of OJ, twisted the cap off, and took a couple of swallows.

"Just look at the new design before you get all negative," Evan said.

I sat down at the table. "I'm not negative. I just think it's an extravagance."

Evan picked up one of the sketches and handed it to me. "Look at this. Here beneath the floorboards there's a compartment for storing a treadmill. We can do stress testing right in the client's home." He handed me another of Rachel's renderings. "Here is a compartment for storing a portable X-ray machine. We won't have to call an outside service every time we need an X-ray."

I sifted through a few more of the pictures. "What is this?" I pointed to a rectangular box in the rear compartment.

"A storage locker. It'll hold our EKG machine, oxygen bottles, and a portable sonogram."

"A portable sonogram would be nice."

"See? I told you it was cool," Evan said.

I took another sip of OJ. "It might be cool, but it's also expensive."

"You keep saying that. But it'll pay for itself."

"It could also sink us, Mr. CFO," Divya said. "In case you haven't looked at the books lately, we're not exactly wallowing in cash."

"With this we'll get a lot more clients and that will bring in a lot more money," Evan said. "That's how it works."

"I know how it works." I looked at a couple of the photographs before tossing them aside. "On another note, I ran into Julian Morelli today."

"What's he like?" Divya asked.

"Smooth. Smarmy."

"I heard he's very handsome," she said.

"Not to me. But you can decide for yourself when you meet him tomorrow."

"Tomorrow? Where?"

"He invited us to his clinic for open house."

"That place is supposed to be incredible," Evan said.

"You knew about this?" I asked. "How come I've never heard of it?"

"Because you lead a sheltered existence, while I, Evan R. Lawson, CFO of HankMed, am a man about town."

"Do we have to listen to this?" Divya said.

"Afraid so," I said. "I've been listening to it all my life."

"Does it ever get easier?" Divya asked.

"I hate to disappoint you, but no, it doesn't."

Chapter 29

StellarCare, the Star in Healthcare.

That's what the sign over the entrance boldly stated.

I guess Julian Morelli wasn't the bashful type.

Even I had to admit the place was impressive. Four towering floors of glass and chrome, massive windows that overlooked the churning ocean, and beautiful people everywhere.

Divya, Evan, and I had barely gotten through the front door when we ran into Jill. She looked great. Tan slacks and a dark green silk shirt, glass of champagne in her hand.

Jill hooked arms with Divya. "Come on. I'll show you around."

They walked away, leaving Evan and me to fend for ourselves. We stood near a large window and munched on the chunks of lobster and sipped the champagne that was thrust our way.

"This place is great," Evan said.

When I didn't say anything, he went on. "We need to do this."

"This what?" I asked.

"Build a place like this."

"Why?"

"It's so freakin' cool." He watched a waitress flow by.

"Just look around. Have you ever seen so many beautiful people?"

"I hadn't noticed."

One of the beautiful people, a trim, tanned blonde, approached us.

"I'm Cindy McCann," she said. "One of the physical therapy techs here."

"Evan R. Lawson," Evan said. He shook her hand with a slight bow. "CFO of HankMed."

"HankMed?"

"My brother's concierge practice." Then as an afterthought he glanced at me. "This is my brother, Dr. Hank Lawson."

"Welcome to StellarCare," she said, her smile polished and perfect. Like her boss's. "What do you think of our new place?"

"Large and dramatic," I said.

"It is, isn't it? I love it." When I didn't respond, she went on. "Have you met Dr. Morelli yet?"

"We met yesterday."

"Isn't he wonderful?"

"I take it you enjoy working here?" I said.

"Are you kidding? This place is awesome. Julian is a pleasure to work for."

Right now Mr. Wonderful was across the room, mingling with his guests, laughing, shaking hands, and dispensing hugs, as if he were running for office. He wore a tux and looked as if he had jumped off the cover of *GQ*. I didn't like him. Particularly since at that very moment he had Jill and Divya cornered. He stood too close to Jill and too often flashed his polished and perfect smile. I wondered if he had had his teeth bleached.

"I'll bring him over," Cindy said.

"That's okay. We aren't staying much longer."

"We're not?" Evan asked. "Why would we leave here? This place has everything. Champagne, ocean views, great food." Evan lifted his glass of champagne. "And of course Cindy."

She laughed. "You're funny."

"That's just my B material. Wait until you know me. I get even funnier."

"You're funny all right," I said.

"I'll be right back." Cindy headed toward Julian.

Evan looked at me as if I were from another planet. "What's wrong with you?"

"What do you mean?"

"Look around." He waved an arm. "What do you see?"

"Glitz. Flash."

"This is the future."

"If you say so."

Cindy was whispering in Morelli's ear. He glanced our way and then he and Cindy moved toward us. Jill and Divya followed.

"Welcome," Julian said, hand outstretched. "Glad you could make it, Dr. Lawson."

We shook hands. "Call me Hank."

"Evan R. Lawson," Evan said. "CFO of HankMed."

"Yes, I know," Julian said.

"You do?"

Julian offered an easy, practiced laugh. "I make it a point to keep up with the medical community." He looked at me and winked. He actually winked. "So what do you think of our clinic?"

"Very impressive," I said. "What I've seen, anyway."

"Let me show you around."

"That won't be necess—" I started.

"We'd love to see it," Evan jumped in.

Jill excused herself, saying Julian had already given her the tour. Now I really didn't like him.

The tour took forty minutes. Evan hung on every word Julian uttered. Probably as much as he did with Nathan Zimmer.

Me, not so much.

The place was definitely top-drawer. No expense spared. The main floor, actually the second floor, held the reception area and a dozen exam and consultation rooms, each spacious and airy, most with one glass wall that offered full ocean views and custom drapes for privacy from the outside world when exams were in progress. The Fitness Floor, as the top floor was labeled, was completely glass-walled and had multiple weight stations, an aerobics/yoga area, and several rows of treadmills, stationary bikes, stairclimbers, and elliptical trainers. The third floor held the men's and women's locker rooms, Jacuzzis, and showers as well as the physical therapy department, which had more equipment than a Hollywood spa.

"You do physical therapy here?" I asked.

"It's part of our new Take Control program. Our clients are encouraged to take control of their own health care. Exercise, diet, weight loss, controlling things like high blood pressure, high cholesterol, and diabetes. Since many have aches and pains, arthritis, and even some with previous orthopedic procedures, we feel that an active PT program will keep them moving and keep their exercise going." Another high-wattage smile. He had definitely had his teeth whitened.

"It's very well equipped," I said.

"Our client list includes many generous donors. Every little bit helps."

Particularly if that little bit has a handful of zeros after it. I wondered how much of his income came from these donors and how much came from pushing pills. Of course PT can also be a very lucrative venture.

We descended the stairs to the first floor and entered an area designated as the Nutrition and Weight Loss Clinic. That's what it said on the double glass doors anyway. Inside were several consultation rooms, two conference rooms, and a large lecture hall.

"This is the heart and soul of our new Take Control program. We have plenty of room for personal consultations as well as patient and public educational lectures. We'll be bringing in leaders in the nutrition community to give talks and work with our patients one-on-one."

"Is weight loss a big part of your practice?" Divya asked.

He nodded. "So many of our patients need that and there is such a paucity of quality weight-loss programs."

He actually used the word *paucity*. It rolled off his tongue so easily. Princeton, I'd bet.

"So you fill that need?" I asked.

He nodded. "We not only help people lose that ten to fifteen pounds of winter weight before hitting the beach at spring break, but we're very proud of the help we offer those with serious weight problems. Those that need to lose fifty or more. We have several programs in Europe that have had outstanding results. We're simply copying that model here."

"You have facilities in Europe?" Divya asked.

"Two. One in Zurich, where StellarCare started, and another in Paris."

"I didn't realize that," I said. "I thought your business was local."

"I practiced for many years in the city. Then I learned about StellarCare a few years ago. I met the principals, we decided the Hamptons would be a good place for a new state-of-the-art clinic, and here we are."

"What do you make them do?" Evan asked. "To lose weight. Celery and water?"

Julian laughed. "It's a little more than that. We design a personal exercise program for each client and assign each a private trainer in our gym. We have intensive nutritional counseling that instructs them in food choices, healthy cooking, restaurant dining, and even grocery shopping. We teach them to take control of their own health. That's why we named the program Take Control."

He sounded like a brochure.

"Besides diet and exercise," I asked, "do you recommend vitamins and supplements? That sort of thing?"

"Absolutely. We use several types designed to correct metabolic abnormalities and promote weight loss."

"What exactly?" I asked.

He led us down a hallway and into a large room with several rows of shelves, each stuffed with an assortment of boxes and bottles.

"These are some of our patented vitamins and nutraceuticals."

Uh-oh. My antennae went off at his nutraceutical lingo.

"Do you use nutraceuticals in your practice, Hank?" Morelli asked.

"Flintstones chewables," I said. "I think the red Barneys and Bettys taste best."

He laughed and clapped his hands together. "That's funny."

He picked up a bottle of vitamins and handed it to me. The label read "Metabolic Boost" and the subtitle, "Weight Loss Vitamins." I read the ingredients label. Basically it was a Flintstones with a little extra calcium and zinc tossed in. I twisted off the cap and looked inside. Fat pasty gray capsules stared back.

"Let me see," Evan said. He snatched the bottle and dumped a pill into his palm. "You need better marketing, dude. These things are depressing. Maybe some bright reds or yellows."

Another high-voltage smile. If he revved up the volts much more, I was afraid his mouth might explode into flames.

"I'll pass that along," Julian said.

Evan handed the bottle to Divya. She also read the label.

"Who makes these for you?" she asked.

Julian gave her a patronizing smile. "That's proprietary. I'm sure you understand."

We then moved into another area. More alarm bells. The windowless room held three eight-foot-long cylindrical tubes. Hyperbaric oxygen chambers.

Scam.

The concept is simple. The patient goes in the chamber, which is then pressurized with one hundred percent oxygen, the oxygen supposedly curing whatever ails you. The bill is sent and life goes on.

The truth is that unless you have an evolving stroke, carbon monoxide poisoning, decompression sickness from a botched scuba trip, or one of several types of nasty infections like gas gangrene, there's no medical use for these. Scammers tout them to "cure" all sorts of things: macular degeneration, Lyme disease, multiple sclerosis, various cancers, chronic fatigue syndrome, arthritis, and even autism. Doesn't work, but it does make money.

Another old medical adage: Desperate people reach for desperate cures. People with serious, chronic, or terminal illnesses, like a drowning man, grab whatever life preserver is tossed their way. Whether it has holes in it or not. Weight loss works the same way. People who have tried everything and failed are always looking for the next big cure. The next magic bullet. Their desperation sets them up to be exploited. Salesmen like Julian Morelli feed on that desperation.

Then there are the complications of the high-dose, high-pressure oxygen these chambers deliver. Things like bleeding sinuses, ruptured eardrums, and even collapsed lungs. Bet those aren't in the brochure. Another problem? The damn thing might catch fire or explode. Pure oxygen under pressure can do that. Ask NASA. Gus Grissom, Ed White, and Roger Chaffee died when a fire ripped through a hyperbaric chamber called *Apollo I*.

But the oxygen buzz does make most people feel better and people will always pay for momentary pleasure. Old P. T. Barnum had it right. A sucker was born every minute.

"This is so cool," Evan said while running his hand over one of the chambers. "I want to try it."

What'd I tell you?

"Sure," Julian said. "Cindy will help you."

She lifted the lid and Evan crawled in, settling onto the

pad inside. Cindy closed the lid and spun a couple of knobs. I looked through the window. Evan gave me the thumbs-up.

While Evan soaked up oxygen, we settled in a conference room, where Divya peppered Julian with questions about what other programs he offered, how many employees he had, marketing, and whether he made house calls. She would've made a great lawyer.

Julian's answers were:

They had programs to help diabetics control their blood sugar, cardiac patients lower their cholesterol, and hypertensives reduce their salt intake.

They did orthopedic and stroke rehab.

They helped with hospice care and with grief counseling.

He did indeed see many of his clients in their homes. Discreetly, of course.

A total of eighteen people worked for StellarCare, including two PAs.

His marketing was far-reaching and he'd love to sit and go over it with her sometime.

Evan came in, Cindy in tow.

"That was great," he said. "A total buzz. We need one of those."

"I'll remember that for your next birthday," I said.

We went to Julian's office. It was the office equivalent of an infinity pool. Corner location. Two totally glass walls that met in an invisible seam. It looked as if you could fly right out over the beach.

"Not much privacy," Evan said.

Julian sat down behind his impressively large, chrome-legged, glass-topped desk and pressed a button on one corner. The windows progressively fogged until they were opaque.

"Whoa," Evan said. He moved to one glass wall and ran his hand over it as if he expected it to be wet or something. "Do that again."

Julian pressed the button and the window cleared.

"Can I?" Evan said as he walked over to the desk.

Julian waved a hand. "Of course." He stood and moved around the desk, propping one hip on the edge. "Please, sit."

Divya and I took the two chairs that faced him. Evan played with the button, the walls now fading to opaque again.

"So, tell me," Julian said, "what do you think of our little operation?"

"There's nothing little about it," I said. "You've put together an impressive clinic here."

It was, particularly in comparison with what Divya and I had to work with—the trunk of my Saab and the back of her SUV.

"I've heard good things about you, Hank. That you're a good doc and your clients really like you."

"We call them patients, but that's always good to hear."

"Maybe we can help each other."

"In what way?"

"I see many clients who need a good doctor. I'm sure you see those who need nutritional counseling, weight loss, and an overall wellness and prevention program. That's what we do here."

The windows cleared.

When I didn't respond, Julian continued. "Since we aren't really competitors, we could help each other. Complement each other's practices."

I wanted to say *not a chance*. I wanted to scream *charlatan* in his face. I wanted to tell him that I suspected that he was poisoning people with his herbs and spices. Instead I said, "We can explore that."

He clapped his hands together and then rubbed them back and forth. "That would be great. I think we could have a bright future together."

The windows became opaque again. About as opaque as any future Julian and I could have.

At least Evan was entertained.

Julian rubbed his chin as if in deep thought and then said, "How would you like to have an office here?"

"What do you mean?"

"I know you see your clients in their homes. I understand that. But aren't there times you wished you had an office? Where you could do more testing?"

He did have a point. There are times when an actual office would be nice. Expensive, but nice.

"HankMed could be a part of the StellarCare family," Julian said.

Family? Did Charlie Manson start this way?

The windows brightened again, the diffused sunlight settling over the left side of Julian's face, highlighting his features. As if he were a model prepped for a cover shoot.

"I'm not sure that fits with our practice, but I'm flattered that you would ask."

"Give it some thought," Julian said. "I believe that when you do, you'll see the wisdom of such a partnership."

Partnership? I didn't see that happening.

The windows fogged again. I wondered when Evan would get bored with his new toy. If past experience was any indication, it could be hours. Evan could focus on the most inane things sometimes.

"If we have an office here," Evan said, "I want one with windows like these.

My cell buzzed. I checked the screen. Jill. Text message. It said: *Need to talk. Labs back. Meet out front.*

Chapter 30

Evan, Divya, and I met Jill near the front entry and walked across the parking lot to Jill's Prius, passing half a dozen beautiful people on their way into Julian Morelli's palace.

"The lab results on Rose Maher and Amanda Brody are back," Jill said. "The tech said they weren't normal."

I felt a knot in my gut. I hate when that happens.

"He e-mailed the results," Jill continued.

She unlocked her car, lifted her shoulder bag from the front seat, and placed it on the hood. She slid her laptop out, rested it next to the bag, and began the booting process.

"Any idea what the results are?" I asked.

"He said they're similar to Valerie Gilroy's."

Jill opened the e-mail and then its attached file. I used one hand to shield the sun from my eyes while she scrolled through the pages of lab results.

Rose Maher had a potassium of 3.2, a magnesium of 1.1, a digitalis level of 2.2, elevated thyroid studies, and a low level of amphetamines in her blood. Amanda Brody's labs were similar except that her digitalis level was slightly higher at 2.8.

"They aren't quite as high as Valerie's were." I turned my gaze back toward the StellarCare clinic. "They haven't been taking Julian's little poison packets quite as long."

"You don't know that all this came from those pills," Jill said.

I gave her my best "get real" look. "Let's just say my index of suspicion is extremely high. All three are seeing this clown. All three have the same lab profile. The difference is that Valerie almost died. Rose and Amanda are headed that way."

"Does this mean I don't get an office with cool windows?" Evan asked.

"Sorry you're not getting a new toy," Divya said. "This is a serious problem. If Julian is handing out toxic drugs, we have to do something."

"Like what?" Jill asked. "We don't have any proof."

"When will the testing of the pills be completed?" I asked.

Jill adjusted her sunglasses. "I'm not sure. Could be as early as tomorrow."

"Let's hope. Then maybe we'll have the proof we need."

"What now?" Jill asked.

"Go have a talk with Rose and Amanda."

"I'll go with you," Divya said. "We can take my SUV."

I tossed my car keys to Evan. "Looks like you're on your own."

"I'll head over to my office," Jill said, "and call the chemistry lab to get an update on where they stand."

As I climbed into Divya's SUV, I heard Evan ask Jill, "Want to swing by and see a cool van first?" Not waiting for a reply, he went on. "It's not far. Just follow me."

Relentless. Focused. Annoying. My brother.

Rose Maher listened with mounting anxiety as I went over the results of her lab tests. Divya and I sat on her living room sofa, Rose in a deep wingback chair.

"I can't believe this," Rose said. "Why would Julian give me something like that?"

"The short answer?" I said. "Money."

Shaken, Rose stood and left the room for a couple minutes before returning with a paper bag. She handed it to me. "These are all the pills I have left. I want them out of my house."

I took the bag and gave it to Divya.

"Should I sue him?" Rose asked. "Couldn't what happened to that young girl you told me about have happened to me?"

"Possible. But now that you're no longer taking the pills, everything should return to normal. I'll recheck your blood in a few days to make sure."

"Is that enough time?"

"Probably. At least everything should be moving in the right direction."

"I'm so angry. With me for being so stupid. With him for . . ." She sat again, sighing heavily. "Unbelievable."

"Relax. Everything will be okay."

She looked at me for a beat and then shook her head. "I'm going to sue his ass off."

"That's up to you. We're testing some of the pills. If they're the source, we'll know soon."

"They are and you know it."

I nodded. "That's the one thing you, Amanda, and the young girl have in common."

"That would surely bolster my case," Rose said.

"Most definitely," Divya said.

Rose absently squared a stack of magazines on her coffee table and then stood. "I need to call Amanda and tell her about this."

"We're heading over there to talk to her right now," I said.

"I feel like such a fool." Tears collected in Rose's eyes. "I know better than this. I know there's no quick fix."

"Don't beat yourself up," Divya said. "You're like everyone else. Intellectually you know that something doesn't make sense, but at the same time you hope it works."

"That's the problem," Rose said. "It did work."

"Poisoning yourself isn't the safest of weight-loss programs," Divya said.

Rose sniffed back tears. "Thank you both for being so persistent. For taking care of me when I wasn't taking care of myself."

"That's what we're here for," I said.

First, do no harm.

One of the oldest rules in medicine. Dates back to Hippocrates, even Aristotle. The rule has been passed down through the centuries by the giants of medicine. Names such as Galen and Paracelsus, and on to the twentieth-century icons Sir William Osler, Proctor Harvey, and Tinsley Harrison. Like every medical student in the country, I had devoured *Harrison's Principles of Internal Medicine* while in school. Still crack it open on a regular basis.

First, do no harm.

The rule smacks of common sense and sounds like a very simple thing to do. Do not harm the patient while trying to heal him. It's unfortunately not as easy at it might sound. Doesn't surgery harm before it helps? Don't many medications have the potential to harm and even kill? Didn't physicians once do things that now seem silly and dangerous? Bloodletting, treating syphilis with arsenic, and using leeches to suck out vile humors each made sense at one time. Will our current use of coronary-bypass surgery seem insane and barbaric a hundred years from now?

First, do no harm.

Another modern dilemma is what we in medicine call "consuming the patient, making the diagnosis." Sounds sinister, doesn't it? It is, and it isn't. Sometimes making the proper diagnosis requires days and weeks of testing and the patient can die during this pretreatment testing phase. Also some of these tests possess inherent dangers. Angiograms, colonoscopies, exploratory laparotomies, and many other tests and treatments have significant, even deadly complications. It's the nature of modern medicine. Even well-intentioned and very competent physicians have traveled this road.

First, do no harm.

Then there are those who do things outside good medicine and common sense. Usually profit is the motive.

Rose got it. She understood that Julian was in the game for the money. She understood that he didn't grasp the "do no harm" principle but had a firm grasp on the bottom line.

Amanda was the exact opposite.

After Divya and I told her the results of her blood tests, she became defensive. She refused to believe that Julian Morelli would do anything to harm her.

"Look at me," she said. "I feel and look better than I have in twenty years. Do I look like I've been poisoned?"

"There are very few toxins that have any outward effects," I said. "They don't give you a skin rash or grow hair on your chest or anything like that. They work inside. They alter the body's biochemistry. Often they do a great deal of harm before the first symptom appears."

"But I feel great. I don't have any symptoms at all."

"Really?" Divya asked. "Hasn't your appetite dramatically decreased?" Amanda nodded. "Haven't you lost weight?" Another nod. "Didn't you say you are having trouble sleeping?"

"Those are minor aggravations. I have more energy. I'm getting more work done. My exercise capacity has increased dramatically. Aren't those all good things?"

"They would be if you were doing it solely with a better diet and a more aggressive exercise program," I said. "But not this way. Not with a handful of miracle pills."

"Hank, I like you and I trust you, but I just can't believe what you are telling me is the truth."

I looked at her with a raised eyebrow.

"I don't mean you're lying. Not that. What I mean is that you said yourself you haven't had these pills analyzed. So how do you know what is in them?"

"I know what the lab tests on you, Rose, and a very lucky young lady showed. There's little doubt in my mind that these abnormalities came from Julian Morelli's pills. All I'm asking is that while we're completing our testing, you stop taking them. Doesn't that make sense?"

She looked at me but said nothing, skepticism etched all over her face. I knew I wasn't getting anywhere.

"Humor me," I said.

Once we got back in the car, Divya said, "She's not going to stop, is she?"

"Doesn't sound that way to me. Let's hope she's lucky enough not to have any problems until we have the proof to convince her otherwise."

Divya cranked up her SUV and pulled from the curb. "So we are relying on luck?"

"Never underestimate the power of luck." I grabbed the dashboard as she tore through a turn. "Like you and your driving."

"What does my driving have to do with luck?"

"You're lucky you're still alive."

"You do know that you sound more like Evan every day?"

Chapter 31

As Divya and I headed back toward Shadow Pond to work on patient files, Divya got a call. From her mother. She dropped into her native language, but it was easy to tell this was an argument, not a polite conversation. Divya maneuvered the SUV through a series of breathtaking turns with one hand while holding her cell to her ear with the other. I started to ask if she wanted to pull over and let me drive, but I was afraid to distract her. The trees along the roadside looked unforgiving.

Maybe Evan was rubbing off on me. A scary thought.

Maybe fear is universal.

The human startle response is genetically ingrained. So is the fear of falling. Probably from when our ancestors slept in trees to avoid predators. Seemed to me that fear of crashing would be similarly ingrained.

Divya finally disconnected the call, tossed her cell phone into the center console, and white-knuckled the steering wheel. Her jaw set, eyes narrowed. I could almost see steam coming from her ears.

"What's that?" I asked.

"Nothing."

"Yeah, that's what it sounded like."

She laughed. Sort of. More a short exhalation. "My mother."

"Want to talk about it?"

"No."

I shut up and held on.

Here is what I know about Boris Kuester von Jurgens-Ratenicz.

It's easier to call him simply Boris.

He owns Shadow Pond and is our gracious host, letting us live in and work from his guesthouse.

He is crazy rich, shadowy, and I have no idea what he really does for a living. Something international and murky.

He is extremely private.

He has connections. To what, I don't know, but his web of influence seems to be wide and complex.

It was his connections that pushed me to knock on the door to Shadow Pond's main house. Boris's assistant Dieter answered. I told him I'd like to talk with Boris, only needed a minute or two. He led me to the library, where Boris sat, half-glasses on his nose, shuffling through a mess of papers on his desk. Dieter left, closing the door behind him.

"What can I do for you, Hank?" Boris asked as he stacked the pages and turned them facedown.

"I need to ask a favor."

He removed and folded his glasses, laying them on the desktop. "What is it?"

"Have you ever heard of StellarCare?"

"Julian Morelli's new clinic, no?"

I'm constantly amazed at what he knows. "That's right. It seems his outfit is connected to StellarCare in Zurich and Paris."

"Yes?"

"Do you know anything about the two European clinics?"

"I didn't even know they existed."

Guess he didn't know everything after all. "I'm concerned about what Julian might be doing at his clinic and hoped I could find out something about the parent company."

He folded one hand over the other on his desktop. "What things?"

"I'm not sure."

"Of course you are, or you wouldn't be asking for my help. No?"

"He might be giving his patients some dangerous drugs as part of his weight-loss program."

His forehead furrowed and he gave a single nod. "You think his clinic might not simply be a rogue operation? That these drugs might come from Europe?"

"Something like that."

"I'll look into it. Anything else?"

Just like that. *I'll look into it.* No further explanation needed. I felt like I was imposing. Like I should apologize for even asking for his help. But he didn't seem to mind. Just a matter of fact: *I'll look into it.*

"No. That's all."

Dieter reappeared. Not sure where he came from or how he knew the meeting was over, but there he was, escorting me out.

Chapter 32

Divya and I sat at the kitchen counter, watching Evan cook. He was messy but definitely knew what he was doing. He had learned a lot hanging around the kitchen when we were growing up, but that wasn't where he learned all the gourmet stuff. As with most things Evan, his cooking skills came about because of a girl. In New York. After he graduated from college and got a job. She was a secretary with an advertising firm two floors below Evan's office and was Evan's fascination of the moment. When he learned that she was taking lessons from a Cordon Bleu–trained chef, he of course joined the class. Good thing she wasn't into skydiving, since heights and Evan didn't mix well.

I think he confused the old saying that the way to a man's heart is through his stomach with one of his own making—the way into a woman's pants is through her stomach.

Either way, we were reaping the benefits of Evan's culinary education.

The menu was shrimp in a butter and white wine sauce over angel-hair pasta, caramelized brussels sprouts, sliced tomatoes with pine nuts and lemon-infused olive oil, and homemade French bread. Much better than the pizza I would have ordered.

Rich aromas filled the room. Hunger rumbled in my stomach. I glanced at my watch. Jill was twenty minutes late. I was getting ready to call her when she came through the back door.

"That smells wonderful," she said. She placed two bottles of wine on the counter. "Sorry I'm late. I got hung up at the hospital."

"No problem," Evan said. "You hungry?"

"Starving. What are you making?"

Evan went over the menu as he put half a stick of butter and some olive oil into a skillet and turned the gas flame on low. He retrieved a bowl of peeled and deveined shrimp from the fridge.

I opened one of the bottles and poured everybody a glass.

The brussels sprouts simmered in one skillet while the butter and olive oil bubbled in another. Evan dumped the shrimp into the butter, stirred them until they became pink, and then added a generous splash of white wine. As they simmered, he drained the pasta and placed it into a bowl, tossing it with a small amount of olive oil.

"I should open a restaurant," Evan said.

"That would be a marriage doomed to failure," Divya said.

"Who said anything about getting married?" Evan said.

"Owning a restaurant is a marriage. It's twenty-four/seven."

"But if you did, you could never eat at another restaurant," Jill said with a laugh.

"At least not a competitive one," Divya added.

Evan turned off the flame beneath the shrimp. "Maybe I should reconsider."

"Good idea," I said.

Evan dumped the shrimp and sauce over the pasta and tossed it. "Soup's on."

We sat at the table and ate in silence for a few minutes

before Divya said, "I think you've outdone yourself this time. This is excellent."

Evan extracted his cell phone from his pocket, punched a button, and held it up.

Evan R. Lawson is right.

"Is that you, Divya?" Jill asked.

"Yes, it is," Evan said. "I now have proof that she actually said I was right about something."

Divya stabbed a shrimp. "He tricked me." She popped the shrimp into her mouth.

Evan R. Lawson is right.

Divya pointed her fork at him. "I think that's quite enough."

Evan R. Lawson is right.

"I never get tired of hearing that," Evan said.

"Do you know what a subdural hematoma is?" Divya asked.

"It sounds awful."

"It is. But in your case, it might be an improvement."

Dessert was peaches and cream with chocolate-dipped macaroons. Afterward we gathered in front of the TV to watch a movie. Evan and Divya sniped from time to time; Jill stretched out on the sofa, her head in my lap, and dozed. I found the movie boring, so I thumbed through the latest edition of *The New England Journal of Medicine*. It was boring, too.

It was near eleven when Evan's cell phone chirped. He answered and mostly listened before saying, "We'll be right there." He snapped the phone shut.

"What is it?" I asked.

"That was Ashley. Nicole's missing again."

O'Brien's Pub was a faux-Irish bar and restaurant just off Main Street in the heart of East Hampton. It nestled among other trendy bars and restaurants as well as retail outlets with names such as Tiffany, Cole Haan, Polo, and J. Crew, and of course a Starbucks coffee shop.

We parked in the rear lot and entered through the back door, which placed us in the bar area. It was insane. Standing room only. The crowd was mainly twentysomethings, mainly beautiful, and certainly rich. Silk, diamonds, and plastic surgery ruled.

We found Ashley near the bar. The noise level approached my tolerance threshold and precluded conversation, so we escorted her outside to the parking lot.

"That's better," I said. "Tell us what happened."

"One minute she was here—the next she was like gone," Ashley said. "Just like the other night."

"What was she doing when you last saw her?" I asked.

"Sitting at the bar, talking with the bartender. Jake. We know him from school."

"Did you talk to him?"

"Yeah. He said she sat at the bar for like a half an hour and then she said she was going to mingle."

"He didn't see her leave the bar, I take it."

Ashley shook her head. "I asked. He said he didn't really notice. He was too busy."

"Anything odd about her behavior? Before she went missing?" Divya asked.

"She seemed a little quiet, but I just thought she was tired."

"Did she have much to drink?" Evan asked.

"A couple glasses of wine, but she wasn't drunk or anything." Ashley's cell phone buzzed. "Maybe that's her." She pulled out her phone, stared at the screen for a second, and then dropped it back into her purse. "Not her."

I guessed whoever it was would have to call back.

"Does she hang out at any of the other bars around here?" I asked.

Ashley tossed her hair over one shoulder. "Not really. I mean like we go to all of them at some time or another. We don't really have a favorite."

Déjà vu all over again.

Another midnight search through bars and restaurants. Nicole was becoming predictably unpredictable.

Might as well get to it.

We divided into teams. Divya and Jill headed up the block one way, while Ashley, Evan, and I headed the other.

It wasn't until we reached the fourth bar, a place called the Seafoam Tavern, that we got lucky. A waitress, a young redhead named Chloe, had seen Nicole half an hour earlier. She recognized her from the picture that Evan had on his cell phone. Chloe said that Nicole had been with a guy named Bobby Richter.

"Do you know him?" I asked. "This Bobby Richter guy?"

"Sure. He's one of our regulars."

Somebody waved her toward their table and she started to leave, but I grabbed her arm. "Just a couple questions?"

She looked around. "We're really busy and I need to get to work."

"Is this guy a good guy or what?"

"Absolutely. He's a cool dude. I've known him for years." Now her eyes narrowed. "Is something wrong?"

"Probably not. We're just trying to find Nicole."

"That's not her name," Chloe said. "The girl in the picture? I served her and Bobby some wine. He introduced us. She said her name was Tiffany."

"Are you sure we're talking about the same girl?"

"Let me look at her picture again."

Evan showed the picture again. She studied it, tilting her head slightly, forehead furrowed. Ashley pulled up another picture of Nicole on her phone.

"Does this help?"

"Yes. No doubt. That's the girl Bobby was with. She said her name was Tiffany. I'm certain of that." Again she looked around. "I've got to get back to work."

"One more question. Did you see them leave together?"

She shook her head. "After I served them, I never saw

them again." She looked around the room. "This place is pretty crazy, so they could've left at any time."

"Last question, I promise. Do you know how to reach Bobby?"

"I don't have a phone number, but I know where he lives. It's very close. Over off Dunemere Lane."

Chapter 33

I called Divya as we left the Seafoam Tavern. We met Jill
and her back at O'Brien's Pub, climbed into Divya's SUV,
and headed south on Main Street. Just beyond the John
Drew Theater at Guild Hall, we turned toward the ocean
on Dunemere Lane. Modest homes flanked the narrow
street. Modest by Hampton standards. We quickly found
Bobby Richter's place and turned into the driveway, parking near an outbuilding that could've been a garage or
maybe a storage unit. Hard to tell in the dark.

A front-porch light illuminated the entry area, the house
itself mostly dark. I could see a faint light through the front
window but no activity inside. I rang the buzzer. Nothing. I
rang it again and then heard footsteps. The door swung
open.

"Yes?"

The young man standing in the doorway appeared to be
twentysomething. He wore jeans, frayed around the cuffs,
no shoes, and an untucked blue shirt. He held a glass of
wine in his hand.

"Bobby Richter?" I asked.

He hesitated for a minute as his gaze traveled over each
of us. I could see the confusion in his eyes. Finally he looked
back at me. "Yes. Who are you?"

"I'm Hank. We're looking for a friend of ours. We believe she's here. Nicole Crompton."

He shook his head. "Don't know her."

"What about Tiffany?" I asked. "Anyone here by that name?"

Again he hesitated and looked me up and down. "Who are you?"

"A friend of Nicole's. Or Tiffany's. She could be using either name."

"I'm afraid I don't know what you're talking about."

He started to push the door closed. I stopped him.

"The girl we're looking for might be confused. She might be ill."

"What do you mean by ill?"

Before I could answer, Evan jumped in. "She has a brain disease. A contagious brain disease."

I turned and looked at him. Where did that come from?

"Contagious?" Bobby asked.

"Please ignore my brother," I said. "I'm Dr. Hank Lawson. Nicole, the girl we're looking for, might have a medical condition that causes confusion."

"She doesn't seem confused to me," Bobby said.

"So she's here?"

"I don't know anybody named Nicole, but I do have a friend here whose name is Tiffany."

"Can we talk to her?"

"Look, I'm feeling a little uncomfortable here. You people show up here late at night and start talking about contagious diseases and confused women. I think it might be best if you leave."

Again he started to push the door closed and again I stopped him.

"Bobby, the girl that you have here is not who you think she is. She's engaged to be married this weekend and she has some type of medical problem that causes confusion. I need to see her and talk to her."

"I don't see that happening."

"If you'd like, I can call the police," I said.

Concern crept into his face. His eyes narrowed and his lips tightened slightly. "Look, I haven't done anything wrong. This girl . . . she told me her name was Tiffany . . . seems fine to me."

"Just let us talk to her," I said. "We can resolve all this."

He nodded. "Just a sec."

He turned and walked across the living room and disappeared through a doorway, returning a minute later with Nicole in tow. She had a glass of wine in her hand and a smile on her face as she walked up to the front door.

"Nicole?" I asked.

She gave me a puzzled look. "Nicole? My name is Tiffany."

"Do you remember me?" I asked.

She took a step forward and looked at me closely and then shook her head. "No. Should I?"

"I'm Dr. Lawson. Your grandmother's doctor."

"My grandmother? I don't think I have a grandmother." Her brow creased and she seemed to be thinking of something. "At least I don't think I do."

"Why don't you come with us and let us take you home?"

Her brow creased further. "Home?"

"Your grandmother's house? Ellie Wentworth?"

Now Bobby looked concerned. He looked at Nicole. "You didn't tell me Eleanor Wentworth was your grandmother."

"I don't know anybody by that name," Nicole said. "I don't know who any of you are. I don't know why you're here."

"Nicole," Ashley said. "You know who I am, don't you?"

Nicole shook her head. "I've never seen you before. Who are you? Who are any of you?"

"You're having another one of your spells," Ashley said.

"I don't know what you're talking about. I'm fine. My

name is not Nicole. I do not know any of you and I don't know anyone named Wentworth."

I looked at Bobby. "See what I mean?"

"What I see is that she makes more sense than any of you do. She's a very pleasant young lady. We met tonight. We were having a glass of wine and then you guys come along with this outlandish story about her being sick and being someone other than who she is."

Hard to argue with that logic, since it made much more sense than the truth did. From Bobby Richter's perspective he was doing the right thing. Protecting Nicole, who was too confused to protect herself. Chloe was right. He was a good guy.

But he didn't truly understand the situation.

"We're telling you the truth," I said. "I'm a physician and I'm here to help Nicole. She is ill. She needs medical care. If you interfere with that, you could set yourself up for trouble."

"So, what? You think I should just let her walk out of here with you? Someone I don't know? Someone she doesn't know?"

"We could call her grandmother, if you want," Divya said. "That would resolve this."

"Or I could call the police," Bobby said.

"Yes, you could," I said. "But I don't think her grandmother would want that. I think she would prefer that this was handled discreetly."

"What about your ring?" Divya asked. "Your engagement ring? From Robert?"

Nicole looked at the four-carat rock. "This is my ring. I don't know anyone named Robert."

"Where did you get the ring?"

Nicole hesitated as if thinking. "I don't know."

"Driver's license." It was Evan. "Why don't we look at your driver's license?"

Sometimes my brother comes up with good ideas. Not

often, but sometimes. I was mad at myself for not thinking of it first.

"You don't believe me?" Nicole said. "You don't believe I know who I am?"

"What's the harm in showing us your driver's license?" I asked.

"If that's what it takes to get you people to leave." She turned and disappeared into the house.

"Look, Bobby," I said, "I know this sounds bizarre. Nicole is under a lot of pressure from her upcoming wedding and she's been having episodes of confusion and disorientation. I'm not sure what the cause is yet, but we need to get her safely home and then figure it out."

Nicole returned with her purse. She rummaged inside until she found her wallet and pulled it out, handing it to me. I opened it to reveal her New York State driver's license.

Her license photo looked nothing like mine. For sure nothing like Evan's. Mine made me look fourteen. School picture. Evan? Maybe some freak from one of those Halloween movies. Hair wind spiked, one eye closed, the other shifted far left, probably checking out some babe in the next line, mouth open. To cut the photographer some slack, catching Evan with his mouth closed was no easy task.

Nicole's photo was a different story. Cover of *Vogue* different. She even looked beautiful to the DMV camera. The name on the license: Nicole Anne Crompton. I turned the wallet around and showed it to Bobby.

"Satisfied?"

He handed the wallet back to Nicole. She studied it for a minute and then said, "This isn't mine."

"Really? Look at the photo."

"That's me, but I'm not this Nicole person."

I glanced at Bobby.

"I didn't do anything wrong," he said. "She told me her

name was Tiffany. Nothing happened. We're just having a glass of wine and talking."

"Relax," I said. "Everything's fine. We'll take Nicole back to her grandmother's place."

The expression on his face was a mixture of confusion and relief. I imagined anyone would be a bit confused by this entire scenario. A group of people show up on your doorstep and tell you that the girl you're with is not who you think she is and, in fact, isn't who she thinks she is. I didn't even understand what was going on, so I'm sure poor Bobby Richter didn't have a clue.

It took twenty minutes of arguing, cajoling, and pleading to get Nicole into the car. Even Bobby wavered, saying that if she didn't want to go, perhaps she should stay. There was no way that would happen. I wouldn't abandon a confused and disoriented young woman at the home of someone I didn't know, even if Bobby did seem like a decent enough guy, even if Chloe the waitress thought he was a "cool dude."

What won the day, or the night, was Nicole finally admitting that she was tired and needed to sleep. We convinced her she had a bed waiting at Westwood Manor.

Nicole sat in the backseat, right side, next to Ashley, and lolled her head against the window as we rode. Divya drove, Evan snagged shotgun, and I sat in the back, Jill in my lap. I watched Nicole closely. She seemed to be staring out the window but not really focusing on anything. Little was said during the entire trip.

Divya parked near the steps that led from Westwood Manor's circular parking area to the front entrance. We all piled out. Nicole took a few steps, hesitated, and seemed to study the mansion. I could see her eyes were wide with confusion, her hands and lips trembling, and an erratic tic worked the right side of her mouth. The entry lights reflected off moist eyes.

"Nicole?" I said. "You okay?"

"How did I get here?" She looked around the front garden and then back toward the mansion. "I don't remember...."

I gently grabbed her by the shoulders. "You had another one of your spells."

She sniffed back tears. "I don't know what you're talking about."

"Nicole, you've got to quit ignoring this," Ashley said. "There's something wrong and you've got to figure out what it is."

Nicole shrugged herself from my grasp and shook her head. "There's nothing wrong with me."

Ashley stepped forward and grabbed Nicole's arm. "Listen to me. There ... is ... something ... wrong ... with ... you." She emphasized each word. "I love you. I can't stand to see you like this."

"I'm fine. I just want to go to bed."

Now Ashley was crying. "You're not fine. There's something wrong. You have to let Hank find out what the problem is."

"I will not be poked on." She started up the stairs toward the front door. Over her shoulder she said, "I wish you people would just leave me alone."

Chapter 34

The next morning, I woke early. Not that I had slept all that well. Nicole kept marching through my head. In my dreams, I saw her as a frightened child, a wicked Salem witch, and even an amazingly beautiful psychotic zombie. Not sure where that last one came from.

Around six, I rolled out of bed and decided to hit the beach for a run. Evan was still holed up in his room. I didn't wake him to see if he wanted to go. He would've probably said no, but maybe not, and that was the problem. Evan had so many early-morning rituals it would've been at least half an hour before we got out the door. Better to let sleeping dogs lie.

I parked at the lot where Ocean Avenue met East Hampton Main Beach, retied my shoelaces, worked my way down to the water's edge where the sand was firm, and headed west.

I felt sluggish for the first mile, but then things loosened up and I fell into a rhythm. Like most runners, I find the monotonous pat, pat, pat of my footsteps soothing. Meditative. It doesn't take long for your mind to wander. Mine went back to Nicole.

I knew there was more going on in her head than simply drugs. Sure, Morelli's herbs and spices and the recreational chemicals she might be using could exacerbate her symptoms, but there was something else stirring inside. Whether it was physical, chemical, or psychiatric was the question. Her differential diagnosis included several not so pleasant possibilities: brain tumors, schizophrenia, seizure disorders, and various infections. The list went on.

I reached the halfway point and turned around, now facing the rising sun. In my sleep-deprived brain, it seemed harsher than usual.

The question I couldn't shake was what role Morelli's concoctions played in all this. Were they simply a red herring? If she was on the same stuff that Valerie Gilroy and Rose and Amanda had been given, it was entirely possible they could be the problem. Not the sole problem, since Nicole's odd behavior began long ago, but they could be unmasking or complicating some existing condition. Of course, I didn't yet know what Julian's pills contained, but I knew some of it. Thyroid, digitalis, and amphetamines for sure. Excess thyroid and almost any amount of amphetamine can uncover previously occult schizophrenia, can increase seizures, and can definitely make sane people seem squirrelly.

In Nicole's case, I just didn't know. Her refusal to allow even simple blood tests, much less a complete neuropsychiatric workup, left me with my hands tied. Frustrating, but that's the way it was.

I finished my run and swung by Main Street Bagels. I picked up fresh-from-the-oven bagels, cream cheese, lox, sliced tomatoes, and two cups of coffee before returning home. Evan was just rolling out of bed when I arrived.

"Cool," he said. "Breakfast." He then looked at me, seeing my sweat-stained shirt, and asked, "Where have you been?"

"Running on the beach."

He cracked the lid on one of the cups of coffee and took a sip. "Why didn't you wake me up?"

"Somehow I didn't think you wanted to go for a run this morning. Or any other morning, for that matter."

"That's true. Besides, I have to save myself for tennis later today."

I put the bagels in the toaster and arranged the tomatoes and lox on a plate. "Who are you playing with?"

"Ashley and a couple of her friends."

"Here?"

"Of course. Where else would I play?"

"I'm sure Boris won't mind you using his property to entertain your friends."

"I asked Dieter and he said it was fine."

The bagels popped up from the toaster. I placed them each on small plates, handing one to Evan. He slathered on the cream cheese.

"I'm surprised you asked," I said.

"What? You think I'm a Neanderthal?"

"Something like that."

"I'm classy." He took a bite of bagel. "I can give you some lessons in classy if you want."

"I'll pass."

"Suit yourself. Just trying to help your image."

I frowned at him while I built a bagel sandwich: cream cheese, a slab of lox, and several slices of tomato. I took a bite. Excellent.

"So what do you have planned today while I'm being classy?" Evan asked.

"Divya and I have a few follow-up appointments." I took another bite of bagel and spoke around it. "But first I'm going to run by the hospital and see if the lab results on Julian Morelli's wonder pills are back."

"You really think that's the problem?"

"Sure smells that way."

"He has a good reputation. His clients seem to love him."

"That doesn't mean he knows what he's doing."

Evan swiped a bit of cream cheese from his left cheek

and licked it off his finger. "How can that many people be wrong?"

"How can so many people watch *Dancing with the Stars*?"

"Good point."

That has always been one of the dichotomies of medicine. Often the doctors that are most loved by their patients are the ones that are the most incompetent. Maybe they're better salesmen than they are scientists. Maybe they cover their lack of competence with personality. Maybe they're simply following the tradition of snake oil salesmen, a breed that has been around for many years.

It was possible that I was wrong about Julian Morelli. That he was driven more by compassion than compensation. That his little pills had nothing to do with Valerie Gilroy's brush with death. I didn't believe it. Not for a minute. Finding the same out-of-whack chemistries in three different people, all of whom were taking drugs supplied by Julian, put him directly in the crosshairs. What were the odds that these three people could have ingested these toxins any other way? The answer to that was fairly simple. Virtually zero.

After we finished breakfast, Evan cleaned up while I showered. I put on a pair of jeans, tennis shoes, a black T-shirt, and an open light gray dress shirt, sleeves rolled up. Since it was now after eight, I called Ashley to check on Nicole.

"She's still asleep," Ashley said. "Probably won't be up for a while."

"What about last night? Anything unusual happen after we left?"

"She was like major angry with me for calling you guys. Said it wasn't anybody's business what she did."

"Sorry."

"Honestly, I think she was more scared than angry. Last night like really shook her up."

"Tell me."

"She doesn't remember leaving the bar, doesn't remember us bringing her home, nothing. Just she was like in the bar and then she was home. Nothing in between."

"Is that how it usually is when she has one of these?"

"More or less. This one might have been worse. I think she's more freaked than she's letting on."

"What about Bobby Richter? Does she remember him?"

"No. When I asked her about him, told her she had like picked him up at the Seafoam, she said she didn't know what I was talking about. Said she never picked up any guy."

"I'm not surprised she doesn't remember him."

I could hear her sigh on the other end of the phone. "I finally convinced her that I was telling the truth. Sort of. She still isn't sure. But the fact that she might have gone home with some random dude really like tweaked her. She's never done that before."

"Are you guys going anywhere today or just hanging around Ellie's?"

"I'm playing tennis with Evan later today, but other than that, I don't think there's anything planned until tonight. Unless Nicole wants to like go shopping or something, we'll probably be here. Why?"

"I'm going to swing by. I want to talk with her."

"She may not want to."

"I'm counting on you talking her into it."

"Me? Thanks a lot."

"Ashley, I'm worried about her. You're her best friend. I know you're worried, too. Do your best."

I parked near the emergency department at Hamptons Heritage Hospital, walked through the ER and down the hall to Jill's office. She wasn't there. Her secretary said she was in a budget meeting but should be back in half an hour. I decided to go see a couple of my patients.

Jesus Morales was still in the ICU. Most of his IV lines had been removed and he was sitting in a chair next to his bed. His nurse said he would be transferred to the surgical ward later in the day.

"Will I be okay without that thing they took out?" Jesus asked.

"Your spleen? You won't even know it's missing."

"Really?"

"Only reason it's there is so surgeons will have something to do."

He laughed. "When can I work?"

"Probably a few weeks, but you should ask your surgeon that one."

"*Cerveza*? Okay to have beer with my friends?"

"After you heal up? Absolutely."

Jesus was happy.

I found Valerie on the third-floor medical ward. Her father, Tony, dozed in the chair next to her bed, a newspaper crumpled in his lap. She smiled when I came in.

"Dr. Lawson, how are you doing today?" Valerie asked.

"The real question is, how are you doing?"

Tony stirred, his eyes blinking open and then focusing on me. He sat up, placing the newspaper on the bedside table.

"Couldn't be better," she said. "I'll probably get to go home today."

"Depending on this morning's lab results," Tony said.

I rested my hands on the bed rail and looked down at Valerie. "I want you to take it easy when you get home. Sort of get your legs beneath you again. No running for a few days."

"Why not? I feel great."

"You went through a very traumatic event," I said. "It might take another week for all those drugs to get completely out of your system. Don't rush it. A week away from running is not going to hurt you."

Tony stood. "Do you hear what he's saying?" He reached out and closed his fingers over his daughter's hand. "Listen to him."

"Okay, okay. If you guys are going to gang up on me, I don't really have a choice, do I?" She smiled.

I said good-bye and headed out the door. Tony followed, stopping me in the hallway.

"What can I do about this?" he asked. "About that Morelli guy? He gave her this stuff."

"I'm looking into it." A nurse walked by. I waited until she had passed. "Valerie might not be the only person harmed by this."

"Then we must do something. Tell someone."

I reached out and touched his arm. "Like I said, I'm looking into it. Give me a day or two and I'll let you know what I turn up."

He nodded. "Okay." He glanced toward his daughter's room. "You saved Valerie's life. I can't tell you what that means to me."

"I did what any other doctor would've done under the circumstances. I'm just glad I was there."

"You and I both know that's not true. Not every doctor would've reacted as quickly as you did." I started to say something, but he raised a hand to stop me. "I know and you know that's the truth." His gaze locked with mine. "She's so much like her mother. I see Verna—that was her name—in Valerie every day." His face screwed down tight as he fought to control his tears. He swiped the back of one hand across his eyes. "I'm sorry."

"No reason to be sorry. I think you've held up remarkably well considering the circumstances."

He sniffed and wiped his eyes again. "Would you be our doctor? Valerie and me? After she gets out of here?"

"I would love to. You have a very special daughter, and between the two of us, we'll take good care of her."

Tears welled in his eyes as we shook hands. He clasped

my hand in both of his and nodded. I told him I'd call and arrange to see Valerie again in a few days. He promised he'd keep her out of her running shoes.

"I'll hide them if I have to," he said.

"You might have to. I get the impression she's stubborn when it comes to that."

Tony nodded. "Like her mother."

Nathan Zimmer had been transferred from the CCU and was just down the hall from Valerie's room. When I walked in, he was sitting in bed, his laptop open on his lap. Todd sat in a chair near the window, talking on his cell phone. Papers were scattered over the bed as well as the bedside table.

"Can I come into your office?" I asked.

"Wall Street never sleeps," Nathan said. "Got to stay ahead of the curve." He nodded toward Todd. "At least they'll let us use cell phones now."

"What you have to do is stay aboveground. I'm not sure jumping into all this right after a heart attack is the best way to make that happen."

He cocked his head to one side and looked at me. "You honestly think that I could sit here and do nothing without climbing the walls? Or going postal on the nurses?"

He had a point.

Todd pressed his cell phone against his chest and said, "What's the decision? Are we going to pull the trigger on this deal?"

"We have to decide right now?" Nathan asked.

"He said the project was almost fully funded and he has half a dozen people waiting to get in the door. So yes, you have to decide right now."

Nathan rubbed his chin, his fingers rasping over stubble. "Okay. Tell him we'll take a million shares at ten and a quarter."

Todd nodded and raised the cell phone to his ear again.

"I'm glad to see you've got the world under control," I said to Nathan.

His fingers worked the keyboard. "Always."

I told him I'd drop by again in a couple of days. He didn't say anything, didn't look up, but tossed a quick wave as I left the room.

Free enterprise. Nothing quite like it.

Chapter 35

Before going back to Jill's office, I swung by the cafeteria and picked up two coffees. She probably already had some, but Jill never turned down a fresh cup. Most women might prefer flowers or chocolate, but with Jill it was coffee. Gourmet better than cafeteria, but so long as it was strong and hot, she was fine.

When I walked in, she was thumbing through some papers on her desk, a cup of coffee in her hand. She looked up, first at me and then at the coffee I held.

"I was just getting ready to head down for a refill."

What'd I tell you?

"How did your budget meeting go?" I handed her the coffee and sat down.

"The usual. They expect everything while paying nothing."

"Seems to be the way of the world."

She handed me the pages she had been looking through. "The lab results on those pills."

I shuffled through the reports. It's not easy to be both surprised and not surprised. I knew what the pills contained, just not exactly. Now that I saw, it was very disturbing: ephedrine, furosemide, desiccated thyroid, and digitalis leaf.

Who would manufacture something like this?

"Want to tell me what this all means?" Jill asked.

I handed the reports back to her. "It's easy to see what happened to Valerie Gilroy now."

"That bad?"

I massaged the kink that was settling in my neck. "It contains ephedrine. An amphetamine. It's found in one form or another in several over-the-counter cold remedies. It's also used to make crystal meth."

"You're kidding."

"I wish. This explains the energetic feeling and loss of appetite. Furosemide is a powerful diuretic that not only causes dehydration and water-weight loss but also washes potassium and magnesium out of the system."

"Explaining the low potassium and magnesium levels we found in all the blood tests?"

I nodded. "Then there's a little desiccated thyroid to rev up the metabolism and help with weight loss. Even more sinister is the digitalis leaf. Basically the foxglove plant ground up and stuck into the pill. Very hard to calculate an accurate dose this way."

"That's why the digitalis levels were so high?"

"Exactly. What you have here is the digitalis and amphetamine killing the appetite, the thyroid boosting metabolism, and the diuretics causing weight loss through dehydration. So people taking it feel hyped up, and they do indeed lose weight."

"That's what everybody says." She sipped her coffee. "Two of our surgical nurses are on the same program."

"Better tell them to stop or they'll end up like Valerie Gilroy. Or maybe not so lucky."

"It really is that dangerous?"

"Extremely. Low potassium and magnesium makes the heart jittery. Sets the stage for a handful of dangerous arrhythmias. Throw in digitalis toxicity and an amphetamine, both of which can produce deadly rhythms, and you have a combination that's a ticking time bomb."

"Why would he give them this?"

"Stupidity. Greed. Take your pick."

"Shouldn't he know this is dangerous?"

"File it under a little knowledge is a dangerous thing. He might only know that the side effects of these drugs produce what he wants . . . increased energy, decreased appetite, and weight loss. He's not medically trained and has never treated anyone with arrhythmias or dig toxicity or electrolyte imbalances. Doesn't truly understand the consequences of his actions."

"So you think this might be an innocent mistake?"

"No. There's nothing innocent about this."

"Hmmm." Jill tapped her pen on her desk. "Maybe he knows more than you give him credit for."

"How's that?" I asked.

"Apparently his program is three or four weeks on the pills and then a few weeks off. Wouldn't that allow the levels to rise enough to produce the effects and then fall, preventing them from getting too high?"

I thought about that for a beat and then nodded. "Which means he knows exactly what these drugs do and how they accumulate in the body."

"That would make sense." She dropped the pen on her desktop and folded her hands before her. "What are you going to do about it?"

"Have another talk with Nicole and Amanda, since they both refused to stop taking this crap. Armed with this information, hopefully they'll see the light."

"But Morelli is still out there pushing this stuff. What can we do about that?"

"Maybe if I confront him, let him know that I know what he's up to, he'll stop."

She looked at me for a minute as if considering what I'd said. "Somehow I don't read him that way. I think money is more important than safety, and I think if anything he'll try to hide what he's doing."

"But we have the proof now."

"Do we?" she asked. "Would any of this hold up in a court of law?"

I started to say of course it would, but then I realized that Jill was right. We didn't get any of the pills directly from Julian, so they could have been tampered with after they left his office. I didn't for a minute believe that was the case, but I could easily see that a defense attorney would argue that. Perhaps successfully.

"Maybe I'll have a chat with the president of the Suffolk County Medical Society."

"Dr. Bernard Bernstein? I don't think he'll be much help."

"Why not?"

"He and Julian Morelli are friends. Went to school together at Princeton and then Yale."

"How do you know that?"

"Dr. Bernstein was on staff here once. Before he semiretired and took his position as president of the society."

"Even so, with something like this, I don't see how he could turn a blind eye."

She shrugged as she studied me. "Are you sure this is a fight you want to take on?"

"Do I have a choice?"

She thought about that for a minute and then said, "Not really."

Was this a fight I wanted to jump into? No. Did I really have a choice? Not to my mind. Could this blow up in my face? Absolutely.

Then again, if it did, it did. I knew I couldn't stand by and watch Julian Morelli harm anyone else.

First, do no harm.

Did I have enough evidence to point the finger at him? There's no doubt that at least three people who were taking his magic pills had significantly and dangerously deranged blood chemistry. Young Valerie Gilroy almost lost her life. To me this was fairly strong evidence, but whether it would impress the medical society or a court of law was a different story.

I needed something else. I needed to determine where these pills were manufactured. Did Julian whip them up himself or did he buy them from some wholesaler? From the parent companies in Europe? I couldn't imagine any legitimate company, US or European, putting out a product like this? Digitalis leaf? That hadn't been used in medical practice for forty years. Amphetamines and thyroid extract? Insanity. Since it would be very unlikely that any legitimate manufacturer would create these little poison packets, they must come from StellarCare, the Star in Healthcare.

How was I going to uncover that? Only one answer came to mind. Divya. She could probably charm the information out of somebody at StellarCare.

I had left Jill's office and was now sitting in my car in the ER parking lot. I picked up my cell phone to call Divya but hesitated as I watched a car swerve into a nearby parking space. A man jumped out, circled the car, and then helped a very pregnant woman from the passenger's seat. The woman, dressed in a nightgown, one hand pressed over her abdomen, the other clutching the man's arm for balance, shuffled through the double pneumatic doors that led into the emergency room. I could tell by the man's wide-eyed expression that this was their first. They would remember this day forever.

I dialed Divya's number. She answered after the first ring.

"Where are you?" I asked.

"At your place. Trying to get some patient notes typed up, but it's not easy with Evan going on and on about the van."

"I need you to do something."

"Away from here?"

I laughed. "Yes."

"Gladly. What is it?"

"Do you think you could charm some information out of someone at StellarCare?"

"Charm?"

"Charm, trick, cajole. Whatever word you want to use."

"I'm flattered that you think I'm charming, but what exactly do you need?"

"I'm heading over to chat with the president of the Suffolk County Medical Society. I need you to uncover where Julian Morelli gets his pills. Does he buy them somewhere or manufacture them himself?"

"I see. You want me to do some undercover work?" She laughed. "Steal the secret codes?"

I heard Evan in the background ask, "Undercover work? Sounds like a case for Lawson, Evan R. Lawson."

"Do you see what I'm dealing with over here?" Divya said.

"Actually, you might want to take Evan with you."

"You can't be serious. How on earth would Evan be of benefit?"

Again, Evan chimed in. "Because I am a master spy. You need information? I'm on it."

"There is little doubt that you need to be on something," Divya said. "Perhaps some medication to help with your delusions."

"You two knock it off," I said. "Evan might be a good distraction if nothing else. He can create chaos without even trying. While he's doing that, you might be able to sort out the right person to give us the information we need."

She hesitated for a minute and then said, "I hate to admit it, but you might be correct." She sighed heavily. "I don't look forward to this, but we will see what we can discover."

"Where are we going?" I heard Evan ask in the background.

"Let me go brief Mr. Bond on our mission," Divya said. "I'll call when we know something."

Chapter 36

Divya and Evan approached the reception desk at Stellar-Care. A tanned, fit blonde smiled at them. Her name tag read BRITTANY.

"How can I help you?" Brittany asked.

"I am Divya Katdare from HankMed. I would like to—"

Evan cut her off by extending his hand and saying, "Evan R. Lawson, CFO of HankMed."

Brittany shook his hand. "You guys were at the open house the other day."

"That's right," Evan said. "I loved those oxygen chambers."

"Aren't they great? I use them all the time. A few minutes in there is better than a cup of coffee."

"Can I hop in one again?" Evan asked.

Brittany smiled. "Usually you have to make an appointment for the oxygen chambers, but since you're associated with a local medical practice, I think I can squeeze you in."

"Please do squeeze him in somewhere," Divya said, glaring at Evan. Then to Brittany she said, "Is one of your nutritionists available?"

"I think so. Let me go check." Brittany stood, circled her desk, and disappeared down a hallway to her left.

"What are you doing?" Divya asked.

"Nothing."

"Did you completely forget why we are here?"

Evan shook his head. "No. You're trying to get information. I'm trying to get oxygen."

"What happened to Lawson, Evan R. Lawson?"

"He thinks better with oxygen in his brain."

"I suspect your brain has plenty of oxygen," Divya said. "Air anyway."

Before Evan could respond, Brittany returned. Another blond woman was with her.

"Cindy?" Evan asked. "Good to see you again."

Cindy laughed. "I hear you need some more oxygen."

"Absolutely."

"Come on. I'll get you set up."

Divya watched as Cindy and Evan walked toward the stairs and then disappeared down them. At least he was out of her hair for a while.

"Tracy Byrnes can chat with you," Brittany said. "She's one of our best nutritionists."

"That would be excellent."

The phone rang. Brittany picked it up and listened for a second, before saying, "Let me look that up for you. Can you hold on just a sec?" She put the call on hold and then looked up at Divya. "I need to handle this. Tracy is down in her office. Next floor. If you take the stairs and then turn right, hers will be the second office on the left. Her name is on the door."

"Thank you," Divya said.

Tracy Byrnes was young and fit, like everyone else that worked at StellarCare. She was also pleasant and obviously bright. Divya went through her cover story. HankMed was interested in nutritional counseling and treatment for some of their patients. Many of them had heart disease, diabetes, obesity, and the usual lifestyle diseases and might benefit from StellarCare's programs.

"We would love to work with you and help your patients in any way we can," Tracy said.

"I was here at the open house the other day," Divya said. "This place is very impressive. And busy. I didn't really get a chance to see how your programs worked. I thought I would take this opportunity to do that."

"We try to give our clients comprehensive yet personal service. We tailor our treatments to the client's individual needs. Maybe better control of their cholesterol or blood sugar. Maybe weight loss and blood pressure control through diet and exercise. We even have a smoking-cessation program."

"Let's say I have someone who needs to lose fifty pounds. What type of program would you design for them?"

"It varies from person to person, but in general we would perform cardiac stress testing and extensive blood evaluations. Those that are referred by physicians, such as your patients, often have already had these tests. If so, we don't duplicate any of that." She smiled. "We try not to waste money here."

"Commendable. Especially in the current climate."

"We then place the client in an aggressive dietary program with control of calories, fats, sugars, and carbohydrates. We call it our Take Control program. We design an individual exercise regimen for each client. Some only need walking, while others need more extensive workouts."

"Sounds perfect," Divya said. "What about vitamins and supplements? I understand you use those also."

"Very much so. We have our own brand of vitamins and minerals as well as herbal medicines, many of which come from ancient Chinese traditions. Others are more modern."

"Such as?"

"Most people are deficient in vitamins and some of the minerals. Particularly things like magnesium, zinc, and chromium. We test for these and then prescribe supplements that fit the person's individual needs. We are all about treating patients as individuals."

"That's always the best medicine," Divya said. "Do you

use branded products or do you have someone that makes them for you?"

Tracy smiled. "All of our formulas are proprietary. I can only discuss them in general terms, but I can't talk about specifics."

Divya nodded. "I understand. I was simply wondering if you purchased them somewhere or produced them here at the clinic."

"I'm not at liberty to discuss that. I'm sure you understand."

"Of course."

"Is there anything else you'd like to know about us?"

Divya asked a few more generic questions and got equally generic answers. Finally, Tracy opened her desk drawer and pulled out a stack of cards. She handed them to Divya.

"If you have any patients you think we can help, give them my card and I'll personally take care of them." Tracy stood, indicating the meeting was over.

As Divya came back up the stairs, she saw Evan standing in the reception area talking with Cindy.

"Ready to go?" Divya asked.

"How did your meeting go?" Evan asked.

"Just fine." She smiled at Cindy. "I think we'll be able to work together."

"That's wonderful," Cindy said. She turned to Evan. "Be sure to tell your patients about our oxygen treatment."

"I will. And I'll come back again, too."

"Just let me know and I'll set it up." Cindy nodded to Divya and headed toward the stairs.

They walked outside. As they crossed the parking lot, Evan asked, "What'd you find out?"

"Only that the products they use are proprietary."

"Not where they are made?"

"Ms. Byrnes wouldn't talk about that."

They climbed in Divya's SUV and she cranked up the engine.

"So you didn't really find out anything?" Evan said.

"I discovered that they use noncommercial proprietary meds. I'm just not sure where they are manufactured."

Evan held up his cell phone. "I want you to say something."

"I don't think so."

"Come on. Just say, 'Evan R. Lawson is a superspy.' "

She looked at him. "Why would I do that?"

"Because I am." He held the phone close to her. "Go ahead. Say it."

"I'm not going to play your silly game."

"Okay, but you'll never know what I found out."

"What?"

"Say it."

"No."

"Have it your way."

"What do you know?"

Evan shook his head. "I only report to those who believe I'm a superspy."

"You're impossible."

"No. I'm a superspy."

Divya took in a deep breath and exhaled loudly. "Okay. You win."

Evan held up his phone. "Go ahead."

"Evan R. Lawson is a superspy. Now tell me what you found."

"Just a sec." He pressed a couple of buttons on his phone.

Evan R. Lawson is a superspy.

"Perfect," Evan said. He twisted in his seat to face her. "I know where they make their meds."

"Where?"

"Here," Evan said. "They make them at StellarCare."

"And you know that how?"

"Cindy told me."

"She just up and told you that?"

"I had to use my charm."

"Charm? I'm not sure that's one of your qualities."

"But I did find out what we came here for."

"How did you accomplish this amazing feat?"

"Small talk. Chitchat. I just brought up the fact that many of our patients could use a weight-loss program, and from that, we began talking about vitamins and minerals and all that stuff. When I asked her where these vitamins and minerals came from, she said Dr. Morelli designed them himself and that they mixed and packaged them in a clean room in the basement."

"This is hard for me to say," Divya said. "But I'm impressed."

Evan flipped open his cell and pressed a button.

Evan R. Lawson is right.

He pressed another button.

Evan R. Lawson is a superspy.

"Enough of that," Divya said. "Now buckle up." She settled the gearshift into reverse and backed from the parking space. "But good job anyway."

"Lawson, Evan R. Lawson, at your service."

"I'll call Hank and tell him what we found."

"We?"

Chapter 37

The Suffolk County Medical Society nestled just south of the Long Island Expressway near its intersection with Route 454, the Veterans Memorial Highway. I had taken Route 27 west out of the Hamptons and veered north on 454. As I blew past the Long Island MacArthur Airport, my cell phone buzzed. It was Divya.

"He makes this stuff at the clinic," she said.

"I'm not surprised. I can't imagine any legitimate manufacturer putting this combination together." I swerved to avoid getting clipped by two teenagers in a jacked-up pickup truck. Obviously not paying attention, probably texting, and driving much too fast. Not that I wasn't breaking the speed limit, just that they had shattered it. "Did you have any trouble getting the info?"

"Believe it or not, it was Evan."

"Really?"

"That's Evan R. Lawson, superspy," I heard Evan say. Then I heard Divya's voice, obviously recorded, say, *Evan R. Lawson is a superspy.*

"Don't tell me he tricked you again?"

"More like forced."

"Forced?"

"Boring story. I'll tell you later. The important thing is that we found out what we needed to know."

"We?" Evan said. "We didn't do anything. It was Lawson, Evan R. Lawson, that broke the code."

I heard Divya sigh loudly. "Can I shoot him?"

"Be my guest. But first tell me how he managed to do it."

"That girl he met at the open house? Cindy something? She took him down for another oxygen-chamber visit. While down there, charming her, as he put it, she told him they have a room where they put all their meds together."

"One thing you can say about Evan, he has the gift of gab."

"The problem is getting him to shut up," Divya said.

"I'm almost at the medical society's office. I'll give you a call when I leave."

I then dialed Amanda Brody's number. She needed to know what I had learned about the pills she was taking. Maybe then she would stop them. I got no answer, so I left a message, asking her to call.

Ten minutes later I parked near the entrance of the low-slung building and went inside. The receptionist told me that Dr. Bernstein was on the phone but should be off any minute. She offered coffee and soft drinks, but I declined. I sat on a sofa with cushions too firm to be comfortable and thumbed through a six-month-old issue of *Scientific American*.

"Any minute" turned out to be fifteen before she directed me into his office. Dr. Bernard Bernstein looked to be in his sixties with thinning gray hair that swept over the top of his head. He wore a brown suit, a white shirt, and a yellow tie. His desk was neat except for a loose stack of papers in front of him. He stood when I came in.

"Dr. Lawson, welcome."

"Thanks for seeing me."

We shook hands. He waved me to the single chair that

faced his desk, and dropped back into his high-backed ox-blood leather seat.

"I've been hearing good things about you. Seems you're developing quite a practice over in the Hamptons."

"I pay people to say nice things." I smiled. He almost did. "Things are going very well."

"That's wonderful. Maybe we can interest you in a membership to our society. We have excellent educational programs for our physicians. I think you'd enjoy being a member."

"I just might do that. Thank you."

He scratched one ear and studied me for a minute. "You were a little cryptic when you called, so what exactly can I do for you?"

"I didn't want to talk about this on the phone. It's delicate. I thought it might be better face-to-face."

He settled his elbows on the edge of his desk and tented his fingers before him. "Now I am intrigued."

"It's about Julian Morelli. I have some concerns about some of his treatments."

His eyes narrowed and his lips pursed slightly. "I can't imagine that. Julian has had a nutrition practice for many years and has a very loyal following."

"I know. I've visited his clinic and it's quite impressive."

"So what's the problem?"

I explained to him what had happened to Valerie Gilroy and her blood test results as well as those of Rose Maher and Amanda Brody. I didn't tell him about having the pills analyzed, since I wasn't sure what the legal ramifications of doing that might be.

He squared up the loose papers in front of him and aligned them with the edge of his desk. He nodded slowly and then his gaze came up to me. "You think that Julian Morelli is giving these ladies all of these medications?"

"Each of them have been taking supplements that they received from him. Each of them had similar laboratory findings. Dig, amphetamines, and thyroid for sure, and probably some type of diuretic. This seems like an odd, even a dangerous, combination. I think you can see my concern."

"I've known Julian Morelli for decades. We went to school together. College at Princeton and then he studied nutrition at Yale while I was there in medical school. I can tell you without a doubt he is one of the most competent and professional people I've ever known."

I was torn. Should I tell him about the chemical analysis of the pills? He apparently wasn't willing to accept what appeared to be obvious to me. I decided it might be better to see how far he would go to cover for Julian, if indeed that was his intention.

"Perhaps there's another explanation for how each of these women ended up with the same toxic substances in their blood," I said. "I just can't think of one."

"Dr. Lawson, I don't have to tell you that in medicine things are not always as they seem. These women might be getting pills from several doctors. Thyroid medication from one. Digitalis from another. Diuretics? People pass those to each other all the time. So there might be an innocent explanation for your findings."

"I thought about that. The problem I'm having is that two of the women are my patients, so I know what they are taking. Valerie Gilroy is a high schooler. Runs cross-country on the track team. Very much into diet and nutrition. The only medications she takes are the ones she received from Morelli."

He raised an eyebrow. "As far as you know. Right? Patients don't always tell us everything, do they?" He offered a paternal smile. "And teenage girls?" He opened his palms toward me. "They do some very strange things. Swap medications and drugs with classmates all the time." He closed his eyes and pinched the bridge of his nose for a minute before continuing. "It's a big problem. It's one that we here at the society are attempting to solve through a school-outreach program we're putting together. It might simply be that. She might have gotten these medications from her classmates."

"I agree that that's possible, but it doesn't feel that way."

"Feel that way?"

"Too many coincidences to ignore, I would think."

He pinned me with a hard stare. "I must admit I'm a little taken aback by this. You come here with allegations that are quite serious yet you have no real proof. What do you expect me to do?"

"I'm not sure you can do anything. This might be more a legal matter than a medical matter. I don't know. I just thought you might have a committee that looked into complaints of this nature."

"We do. We take every *legitimate* complaint against a physician or health care provider in this county very seriously."

He leaned on the word *legitimate*. Basically saying that my complaints had no legitimacy and that he wasn't going to do anything about it.

I also knew that I was wasting my time here. I stood.

"I just wanted to make you aware of my concerns. That's all."

Now he smiled as he walked me to the door, a hand on my shoulder. "I appreciate you coming in and bringing your concerns to my attention. Even though I doubt there is any merit to them, you can be assured that I will look into this matter."

As I walked across the parking lot to my car, I knew there wasn't a chance in hell that he was going to open any investigation on this. He was going to protect his buddy and brush me aside.

Should I have told him about the test results on the pills? Would it have made any difference? I doubted it. Would exposing the fact that we secretly analyzed a proprietary product blow up in my face, or more important, in Jill's face? Possibly. Though testing the pills seemed commonsensical to me, the law isn't always that practical. The truth was that we had no legal standing to perform such tests and doing so could bring down a ton of trouble. On one level it might even be considered corporate espionage.

Hmmm. Maybe I could blame it on Lawson, Evan R. Lawson.

Chapter 38

The traffic was light on both Route 454 and Route 27, so I made good time. I also made a few calls. The first to the Wentworth estate. I wanted to talk to Nicole about the poison pills she was taking. Sam answered and said she had gone shopping with Ashley and probably wouldn't be back for another hour or so. I asked how Ellie was doing.

"She looks splendid," Sam said. "She's out back overseeing the wedding preparations. She complains about the work her parties require, but she thrives on them. Sometimes I think that's when she's happiest."

"Don't let her overdo it."

"I just made a fresh pitcher of lemonade for her and the workers. I'll make sure she sits down and relaxes for a while. Maybe. Sometimes she can be most difficult."

I couldn't help laughing to myself as I disconnected the call. That was so Ellie. She was one of those who would never let age turn her to rust. I had no doubt that she would be busy with some project at the moment she took her last breath. We should all be that lucky.

Next I called Amanda Brody. Again. Still no answer. I left another message.

Last, I called Jill. She was in her office pushing paper around, as she called it.

"How'd it go?" she asked.

"Not well. He didn't seem very interested and is definitely going to protect Julian Morelli."

"I figured. They go way back. No way Bernstein would turn on him."

"I didn't tell him about the analysis of the pills."

"Why not?"

"I'm not sure what we did was entirely legal. Sending his products to a lab for testing without his blessing? I know the police or the medical examiner could do that, but I'm not sure we can."

"But that might have made a difference. If Bernstein had evidence that the pills Julian was pushing contained all these toxic chemicals, he might've seen things differently."

"Maybe," I said. "But I don't think so. I got the impression he didn't really care what I had to say."

I could hear her take a sip of coffee. "I'd bet he got on the phone to Julian before you left the building."

"I'd be surprised if he didn't."

"What do you think he'll do? Julian?"

"What would you do? I suspect he'll go through the roof." I sighed. "Too late to worry about that now."

"What's next?"

"I'm heading home to hook up with Divya and Evan. Another ESM, I'm sure."

"ESM?"

"Emergency staff meeting."

Jill laughed. "Better you than me."

"I'm sure it'll be about the van."

"He hasn't let that go yet?"

"You know Evan. Once he gets focused, it's hard to shake him loose."

"True." Another sip of coffee. "But what I was asking is, what are you going to do about Julian Morelli?"

"Try to warn Nicole and Amanda Brody. After that, I'm not sure."

"The police? Would they be helpful here?"

I was now only about ten miles from home, but the traffic on Route 27 had suddenly thickened and my speed was down to thirty miles an hour. I maneuvered around an eighteen-wheeler with a giant picture of a Hostess cupcake on the side. I just realized I was hungry.

"Maybe. I guess if we presented them with the evidence we have, they might open an investigation."

"Might be worth a shot."

"Might get me sued, too. Defamation or slander or something like that."

"Hmmm."

"Hmmm what?" I asked.

She sighed heavily. "With your history . . . I can just see Morelli dragging all that up. Turning the tables on you."

My history. Getting fired for letting a billionaire die. I couldn't defend myself then, so how would I be able to now? Morelli might use that against me. And if Morelli could cover his tracks, spin things back on me, I might even lose my license. False accusations, or those that couldn't be proved, same thing, could do that. What a mess. Damned if I did, damned if I didn't.

"You sure know how to brighten my day," I said.

"I'm sorry. I shouldn't have said anything."

"No. You're right. I have to at least consider that possibility."

"I've got a meeting to go to. You want to grab a drink later? Maybe dinner?"

"Maybe a drink and then straight to dessert?"

"Is this becoming an obscene call?"

"Absolutely."

She laughed. "We'll see."

"It sure would brighten my day."

She laughed again, told me she would call later, and hung up.

As I drove up the long driveway that led to Shadow Pond, I saw Boris's Bentley behind me. Dieter driving, Boris in back. Looked like he was on the phone.

I parked and climbed from my Saab. The Bentley slid to a stop next to me. Boris stepped out, closing his cell phone and dropping it into his jacket pocket.

"That matter you asked about," Boris said.

"StellarCare?"

"Exactly." He motioned to Dieter to go ahead inside. "They are well funded. Two Swiss venture capitalists with an interest in health care. They own several clinics and spas. Saint Moritz, Vienna, Cologne, Munich, Monte Carlo, and Oslo. Plans are in the works to open more in Hong Kong, Sydney, and Bali."

"StellarCares?"

"No. These are a combination of a medical clinic and resort spa. They call it Destination Healthcare."

"Like medical evaluations combined with spa facilities?" I asked.

"Exactly. StellarCare seems to be new for them. Only two years." His phone buzzed. He tugged it from his pocket and answered, telling whoever it was that he'd call right back. "For these facilities it seems they partnered with Dr. Wilhelm Dietrich. Ever heard of him?"

"No."

"Right now he's in Zurich. He's been there since StellarCare began. Before that, he moved around a great deal."

"Why?"

"Let's say his methods are odd. Unsound. He's been accused of many things over the years. Mainly medical malpractice."

I sighed. "This is bigger than I thought."

"I'm afraid you're correct. Dietrich's specialty is nutrition, herbal treatments, and the like."

"Any evidence that Julian gets his herbs from Dietrich?"

"I haven't looked into that. Would you like me to?"

I did, but I felt uncomfortable asking Boris for another favor. "You've been generous with your time already. Let me think about it."

He nodded. "It's no problem." He turned and walked into the house.

When I reached the guesthouse, I found that the ESM had been set up outside on the patio table, where Evan and Rachel Fleming sat. New drawings of the HankMed van littered the tabletop, and surrounded a bowl of popcorn.

I grabbed a handful of popcorn and sat down. Through the windows I saw Divya at her desk, laptop open, phone to her ear. How did she pull off avoiding this meeting?

The popcorn was still warm, a little salty, and definitely not as good as a Hostess Twinkie would have been. I should have hijacked the truck I had seen earlier.

"How's the hand doing?" I asked Rachel.

She held it up. "Better. Still a little sore, but I'll survive."

"If you keep your distance from Evan, that is," I said. "Let me see."

She extended her hand toward me. The fingers, still splinted and taped together, felt warm and had good capillary blood flow. Seemed to be healing well. Except for the two fingernails. They were black and ugly.

"You know those are going to fall off," I said.

"My fingers?"

I looked at her and realized she was kidding me. "Hopefully only the nails."

"Sure trashed my eighty-dollar manicure."

"When they regrow, maybe Evan will pay for a new one."

"It was an accident," Evan said. Then he looked at Rachel. "I guess a new manicure is the least I could do."

"So, what is all this?" I asked, already knowing the answer.

"The next iteration of our van," Evan said. "It's even cooler than it was. See? The TV screen is larger and it now has two laptop connections."

"I'm sure that makes it cheaper?" I said.

Rachel laughed. "Not cheaper. Just better."

I looked through the pages of drawings. Impressive. No doubt Rachel knew her business.

"What do you think?" she asked.

"I think it looks great. I wish we could afford it."

"Banks," Evan said. "Think banks."

I nodded. "I'll think about it."

"See," Evan said. "I knew he'd come around."

"I said I'd think about it. That's all." I grabbed another handful of popcorn.

"Either way," Rachel said. "my dad is impressed with your health plan." She looked at Evan. "Evan's a good salesman."

"Don't tell him that. He'll be insufferable."

She laughed. "Probably true."

"So now both of you are going to gang up on me?" Evan said.

Rachel glanced at her watch. "I have another appointment to get to." She squared a stack of papers, slid them into a folder, and handed it to Evan as she looked at me. "I'll leave these here for you to look at."

"Thanks," I said. "I promise I will. And I'll give your proposal some serious thought."

"Fair enough." She looked back at Evan. "When you get the contract drawn up for my dad, bring it by and I'll get it to him."

"Will do." Evan stood. "I'll walk you to your car."

I went inside.

"How'd you avoid Evan?" I asked Divya.

"Not avoid, merely delay. I told him I had a few important calls to make." She smiled. "I suggested popcorn."

"Good diversion."

"It worked."

"You wanted to wait until I got here. So you wouldn't have to deal with him alone."

She laughed. "True."

"Anything new?"

"I saw Oscar and Maria Mendez. They found an assisted-living arrangement. With Jill's help of course."

"Maria is okay with that?"

"Not really, but she sees the necessity. It was so sad. To see her sitting in her house, knowing she was going to have to give it up and move to a strange place."

"We'll need to keep a close eye on both her and Oscar. This move will be stressful."

"It won't happen for a week or so. I told Maria I would come by in a few days to check on them." She looked up at me. "How did your meeting go?"

I sat down and went through everything with her, including what Boris had uncovered.

"What now?"

"Jill thinks I should involve the police." I shrugged. "That might be the only option we have."

Chapter 39

Evan returned from seeing Rachel off. He flopped in a chair across from Divya.

"How's that?" he asked.

"How's what?" I said.

"Eight new patients."

"Eight?" Divya asked.

"Rachel, her father, and their six employees."

Divya nodded. "Very good, Evan R. Lawson, CFO."

Evan aimed his cell phone at her. *Evan R. Lawson is right.*

"Will you quit that?"

"I never tire of hearing it."

Divya took a deep breath and exhaled loudly. "You are so exasperating."

Evan R. Lawson is—the message was interrupted by the ring tone. Evan flinched as if unsure what had happened. Then he answered.

After he listened for a minute, he said, "I had fun too. You're a great tennis player." Again he listened. "Sure. Tomorrow should work. Maybe around noon?" More listening. "How was shopping?" A nod. "So you're headed back home?" A pause. "A half hour? I'll let him know." He disconnected the call.

"Let who know?" I asked, sure that the "who" was me and that I might not like it.

"That was Ashley," Evan said. "I called her earlier and told her that you wanted to talk with Nicole again. They were shopping, so she said she'd call when they finished. She'll be home in half an hour. You can call her then."

"Does Nicole know I'm going to call?"

"Not exactly."

"What does that mean?" Divya asked.

"Ashley's been trying to talk her into seeing Hank and getting those tests done, but Nicole has resisted."

"So this is an ambush?" Divya said.

"Sort of," Evan said.

Divya looked at me. "Well?"

"I think an ambush should be done face-to-face."

Divya closed her computer. "Do you think she'll be any more receptive now than she was the other day?"

I shrugged. "I don't know. But based on what we've uncovered, I think I have to tell her about the pills she's taking."

Divya nodded. "I agree."

"Whether she'll listen or not is another story."

When Divya, Evan, and I arrived at Westwood Manor forty-five minutes later, we walked into a fashion show. Nicole modeling her purchases.

Sam escorted us into the great room, where the entire family had gathered. Ellie sat on the sofa, beaming as she watched Nicole spin around in a sleek black cocktail dress. Her mother, Jackie, sat in a wingback chair, Mark standing behind her.

Ellie waved us in. "What a pleasant surprise. Please, come and enjoy the show."

Nicole turned toward us and gave a mock curtsy. "What do you think?"

"I think you look stunning," I said. "Every girl needs a little black dress."

"It's too short," Mark said. "And way too low-cut."

It was. On both counts. On Nicole it looked outstanding.

Nicole laughed. "You always say that."

"Try this one," Ashley said, holding out a pewter-colored evening gown.

Nicole took the dress and on bare feet hurried down the hall to change. Ashley followed.

"What brings you here?" Ellie asked.

This wasn't exactly how I envisioned things going. I wanted to talk to Nicole alone and then if necessary enlist Ellie's help. The hope was that once I told Nicole about Julian's poison pills, she would stop taking them. This little impromptu fashion show had mucked up that plan.

"I came to talk with Nicole."

"About what?" Jackie asked, undisguised hostility in her voice.

"Julian Morelli."

"Why?"

"Perhaps I should talk with Nicole privately."

"You will not," Jackie said.

I couldn't think of a graceful way to solve this. To isolate Nicole for a one-on-one chat. Better to just jump in and see what happened. If I could somehow recruit Ellie or, less likely, Jackie and Mark as allies, I might be able to make headway with Nicole. I wasn't optimistic, since if Ashley couldn't break down her resistance to doing the right thing, what chance did I have?

"I've learned a few troubling things about the pills he's handing out," I said.

"I thought we made it clear that you are to have nothing to do with Nicole," Mark said. "I don't think you should be digging around in things that are of no concern to you."

"I dug around, as you say, not just for Nicole. A couple of my patients are taking the same stuff."

"Then perhaps you should be seeing them rather than Nicole," Jackie said.

"I did. And now I'm here."

Mark and Jackie responded with steely stares.

This wasn't going well. I decided that trying to win over Mark and Jackie wasn't going to happen. Their hackles were up, their minds closed, and I was the enemy. I looked at Ellie. "Nicole could be in danger."

"Aren't you being a little melodramatic?" Jackie said.

"Not at all. If you'll simply listen to what I have to say, you'll see my concern."

"Your concerns, as you say, are of no concern to us," Mark said. "I don't know how much clearer I can make it. Let's try this. If you interfere with our daughter in any way, I'll come after you with everything I've got."

"Mark," Ellie said, "why don't you listen to what he has to say?"

Nicole reappeared. The dress was magnificent. It shimmered in the lights, its hem and her bare feet whispering across the carpet.

"Isn't this gorgeous?" Nicole asked.

"You're going to look so hot at the reception," Ashley said. "I am going to be so jealous."

Nicole stopped short, apparently now aware that there was tension in the room.

"What's the matter?" She looked from face to face.

"Nothing," Mark said. "Dr. Lawson was just telling us he had an emergency and had to leave."

The phrase "in for a penny, in for a pound" crossed my mind.

"Actually, I'm not leaving," I said. "I'm going to tell you what I know and then you can decide what you want to do with it." I looked at Ellie. "If you love your granddaughter, listen very carefully to everything I say." Then to Nicole. "You, too."

"Listen, you . . . ," Mark said.

Ellie waved him into silence. "Mark, be quiet."

Showtime.

"I was over in the Hamptons Heritage emergency room

the other day. A young girl was brought in by her father. She suffered a cardiac arrest in the backseat of the car." I now had their full attention. "She was a few years younger than Nicole. We resuscitated her and fortunately she's doing fine now. But had she arrived at the hospital just a few minutes later, she would be either dead or brain damaged."

"That's all very interesting, but what does this have to do with Nicole?" Jackie said. She seemed to spit the words out.

"The young lady was taking the same vitamins and herbs that Nicole is taking. Drugs given to her by Julian Morelli."

Mark scoffed. "You think a few vitamins and herbs caused that poor girl's problems?" He shook his head. "Must be the first time in history that vitamins did someone harm."

"The pills that Morelli is handing out are not harmless. They contain some very toxic drugs. I have proof. The girl I told you about not only had very elevated levels of things like digitalis, thyroid hormone, and even amphetamines— she also had severely depleted potassium and magnesium levels due to the powerful diuretic he puts in these little time bombs."

"But they work," Nicole said. "I know a lot of people that have seen him for years and nothing bad ever happened." She looked at Ashley. "Isn't that right?"

"I've been seeing him off and on for years," Ashley said. "He's a miracle worker."

"Actually, he's very dangerous," I said.

"I'm not going to stand here and listen to this," Nicole said. She looked at Ashley. "Let's go."

Nicole and Ashley collected several dresses and half a dozen yet-to-be-opened boxes and headed toward the stairs that led to her second-floor bedroom.

"That's about enough, Dr. Lawson," Mark said. "I think you should leave."

From the corner of my eye I saw Evan melt into the background and then slip up the stairs after the two girls.

"Not just yet," I said. "You can ignore it all you want, but the facts are that Nicole has exhibited some very bizarre behavior lately. I've witnessed it twice, Divya once."

Divya nodded. "That's true. The other night she met some guy in a bar and went off with him. To his home."

Mark and Jackie stared at her.

"I don't think so," Jackie said.

"We tracked her down," I said. "We went to this guy's house and brought her here. She didn't know who she was and didn't remember anything that happened." I looked Jackie in the eye. "Does that sound normal to you?"

"What it sounds like is that you and your assistant here"—Jackie waved a dismissive hand toward Divya— "are trying to trash the reputation of your competition. You saw things that you misinterpreted and now you're making a big deal out of it."

"It's not just us. Jill Casey, the administrator at Hamptons Heritage, witnessed this behavior, too."

"Is this the Jill Casey that's your girlfriend? I wouldn't exactly call her an unbiased witness."

She was unbelievable. She absolutely refused to hear anything that didn't fit her perfect little picture of her perfect little family.

"I could call the guy. Of course he knows Nicole as Tiffany. That's who she thought she was. Even when she looked at her own driver's license, she refused to believe she was Nicole."

"That's ridiculous," Mark said.

"No, it's bothersome," Divya said. "It's a sign of a potentially serious problem."

"What about Ashley?" I asked. "She's seen this behavior for years."

"What behavior?" Jackie asked. "Nicole's a normal, bright, intelligent young woman."

"Yes, she's all that," I said. "She also has a problem. She

has episodes where she doesn't know who she is or where she is. I don't know why, but I do know she needs to be fully evaluated."

Concern now etched Ellie's face. "Evaluated for what kind of things?"

"Things like drugs, brain infections and tumors, a seizure disorder of some type, even several psychiatric conditions."

Jackie's knuckles whitened as she gripped the arms of the chair. Her face tightened and her jaw pulsed. Her words hissed between clenched teeth. "My daughter is not a drug user. My daughter is not a psycho. My daughter is fine and healthy and happy and I don't want to hear any more about it."

The door to Nicole's bedroom was cracked open an inch or so. Evan knocked gently. Ashley pulled the door open.

"Can I come in for a minute?" Evan asked.

"Sure."

Nicole perched on the edge of her bed, tears welling in her eyes. Several thick pillows and a dozen stuffed animals were piled near the headboard. Remnants of Nicole's youth.

Evan sat down next to her. "Are you okay?"

Nicole sniffed. "I hate it when people argue. It's such a waste of energy. It's so negative."

"Hank's right," Evan said. "Deep down inside you know that."

"I don't know any such thing."

"The other night? Remember how scared you were?" He glanced over at Ashley. "We were all scared."

Nicole wound a tissue tightly around her index finger and sniffed back tears. "You don't have to be, because I'm fine."

"Really? Do you remember everything that happened that night? And all the other times this has happened?"

Nicole stared at the floor but said nothing.

"Look, I'm squirrelly," Evan said. "Ask anyone. I say and do things that are odd all the time." Nicole looked at him. "Been that way all my life. But never have I not known where I was or who I was. Never."

Nicole dabbed a tear away with the tissue.

"The other night you didn't have a clue. Doesn't that scare you?"

Her gaze dropped to the floor again. "I just had too much to drink."

"That's not true," Ashley said. "I've been like totally worried about you for a couple of years. You have these random episodes. When you aren't yourself. It's not always after you've been drinking."

Nicole swallowed hard. Her voice was soft when she said, "It's no big deal. It's just something that happens."

"It's something that needs to be checked out," Evan said. "My brother is pretty smart. If he thinks something's wrong, he's usually right."

"Usually, but not always?" Nicole said. "He's being major-league dramatic here."

Evan sighed. "Why would you want to ignore this?"

"I told you, it's no big deal."

"Then where's the harm in making sure?"

Nicole stood, walked to the window, pulled the curtain back, and looked out. She didn't say anything for a minute and then turned back toward Evan. "I'm getting married in four days. I don't have time to worry about this stuff." She picked up one of the dresses off the bed and held it up. "Don't you just love this one?" She plastered it against her body and turned to look at herself gilded in the full-length mirror on the wall. "I think you should go back downstairs so Ashley and I can finish getting these put away."

Evan realized this was going nowhere. He left. Before reaching the stairs, Sam intercepted him.

"Mr. Lawson? A word?"

"Sure."

Sam guided him into the library. Book-filled, floor-to-ceiling shelves covered each wall. A fireplace and two thick leather reading chairs occupied one end, a long table with several glass-encased, very old and very expensive-looking books the other.

"I'm sorry you have to see the family this way. Jackie wasn't always like this. Just since she married Mark. Fortunately Nicole is more like her grandmother." He glanced toward the door as if making sure no one was eavesdropping. "Tell Dr. Lawson not to give up. Tell him that he is on the correct track. There is something wrong with Nicole. I don't know what it is, but she's had these episodes for years."

"Hank is stubborn, so I don't see him giving up on this."

Sam nodded. "Nicole is very special to me. I would hate to see her mother's anger and narcissism get in the way." He hesitated, his gaze to the floor, unfocused, as if in thought. Then he said, "Nicole was always a playful and inquisitive child and now she has grown into a beautiful and intelligent young woman. It would literally kill me if anything happened to her."

Chapter 40

"There have never been any psychiatric problems in the history of our family," Jackie said. "And it's not going to start with Nicole."

The thought that the family psychiatric problems just might begin and end with Jackie crossed my mind. "All I'm saying is have her seen by a physician. It doesn't have to be me, but it has to be someone. And it should be soon."

Evan came back into the room. He gave me a slight shake of his head, indicating that he had made no progress with Nicole. I had the same feeling about the family. I racked my brain for something clever to say. Something that would turn the tide. I had nothing.

My cell phone rang.

"Excuse me just a second." I flipped open the phone and I walked into the entry area.

The call was from Jill. Apparently a middle-aged woman, also a client of the great Julian Morelli, had appeared in the emergency room with dehydration and vomiting. She had similar blood chemistry to Valerie, Rose, and Amanda. Looked like she was going to be okay, but she thought I should know.

"Any progress with Nicole?" Jill asked.

"If you mean with getting Nicole to do the right thing,

the answer is no. If you mean really pissing off her parents, then mission accomplished."

"Anything I can do to help?"

"Keep your fingers crossed and think pleasant thoughts."

I walked back into the great room in time to hear Jackie say, "I know you like him. But he's not even a real doctor. He just pushes pills to rich old women like you."

"I'm not senile, Jackie," Ellie said. "At least not yet. I've seen exactly what he is talking about. Nicole does have episodes where she seems confused and out of it."

Jackie looked up at me. "Happy now?"

"That phone call," I said. "It was from Jill Casey. Another woman just came into the emergency room with very toxic levels of chemicals in her blood. She was also seeing Julian Morelli."

"Is this what concierge medicine is all about?" Jackie said. "Tearing down the competition? If you were a real doctor, if you could make it in the real world, you wouldn't have to feed on the rich."

"You wait just a minute," Ellie said. "Hank is my doctor. He is my only doctor. He takes very good care of me for one simple reason. He cares. I think you should listen to him and get off your high horse."

"Just stop it. I want you all to stop this."

All heads turned toward the doorway where Nicole stood. Ashley stood behind her.

"Why are you arguing about this?" Nicole said.

"The arguments are over, honey," Jackie said. "Dr. Lawson is leaving."

Divya stepped forward, glaring at Jackie. "There is nothing more dangerous than someone who refuses to listen to reason. Dr. Lawson has explained the situation, yet you refuse to hear. You're putting your daughter's life at risk because you're worried about appearances. I've seen this before. This neighborhood is full of it. If you love your daughter, if you really care about her, you will hear everything that Dr. Lawson has said and you will act on it."

Way to go, Divya. I wished I had said that.

"And what are you?" Jackie said. "A physician assistant? Assistant? Not even to a real doctor. To one who left his practice in disgrace. One who killed a man." She looked at me. "We know about you. We did our homework."

"Mrs. Crompton, I'm not here to defend myself," I said. "Not that I really need defending. My only concern is that Nicole gets the help that she needs. You are actively interfering with that." I turned toward Nicole. "You're an adult. You're over eighteen. You can make your own decisions and right now you need to make the right one."

Nicole started crying. "Why is all this happening to me? Why are you arguing about me? I'm fine. I'm getting married in a few days. I don't have time for this."

Jackie exploded out of her chair and rushed to Nicole, pulling the crying girl to her. Her eyes flashed when she looked at me. "Get out. Get out now."

I knew I had gone too far. Pushed too hard. It was time to leave. I nodded to Divya and Evan. As I started toward the door, I stopped and looked at Nicole. Something was odd.

Her facial expression was blank, her gaze locked on something in the distance, unfocused. Her chin rose slightly and her eyes rolled upward, revealing only the whites.

Then it started.

A full-blown seizure.

Nicole's body jerked. Jackie recoiled in horror. Nicole fell, but I stepped forward and caught her, easing her to the floor. Her body began jerking in the rhythmic tonic-clonic motions of a grand mal seizure. Her bladder emptied, staining the front of her dress.

"Oh my God," Jackie screamed.

Mark rushed to her side and looked down at his daughter. "What the hell is going on?"

"She's having a seizure."

Divya grabbed her medical bag, which she had left near the front door. She handed me an oral airway. I slid it into place. Divya drew up five milligrams of diazepam and gave me the syringe.

"What's that?" Jackie asked.

"A drug to help stop the seizure," I said.

"Should we get her to a hospital first?"

"Not until we get this seizure under control. She could die from asphyxia or she could aspirate anything that's in her stomach. We have to stop this now."

"How do I know what you're doing is correct?" Jackie said.

Divya glared at her. "Dr. Lawson has handled many seizures in his career. Just relax and let us take care of this."

I pushed Nicole's dress up, exposing her left thigh. I jabbed the needle into the lateral portion of her quadriceps and injected the drug.

We then started an IV and begin running fluids wide open. The seizure activity continued, so Divya drew up two hundred milligrams of phenobarbital. I gave it as a slow injection over two minutes through the IV line. It seemed like an eternity, but by the time I finished, the seizure had broken.

Nicole began to moan, her head rolling from side to side, her arms and legs moving without purpose. She was in the postictal state: that time after a seizure when the brain works to reestablish its interconnections. A seizure disrupts normal brain transmissions and it takes several minutes to sort this out.

I removed the oral airway, its job done.

"What's wrong with her?" Jackie said.

"She's in what we call the postictal state. It's the confusion and disorientation that follows the seizure. She'll be fine in a minute."

Sam walked into the room. "Dr. Lawson, I called the paramedics. They should be here momentarily."

Nicole's eyes fluttered and finally she began to focus on the people around her, her confusion obvious.

"What happened?" she asked. Her voice was weak and slightly slurred.

"You're okay," I said. "You had a seizure. It's over now."

She attempted to sit up, but I pushed her back flat on the carpet.

"Just lie here for a minute. The paramedics are coming and will get you over to the hospital."

"The hospital? Why do I have to go to the hospital?"

"To find out why this happened and make sure it doesn't happen again."

•

Chapter 41

While mother Jackie and father Mark seemed more upset that their perfect day had been interrupted than they seemed concerned, Nicole was scared. A more appropriate reaction under the circumstances. Seizures in adults are always serious business. Children often have benign seizures, usually associated with high fevers from ear infections or some other febrile process, but in adults they virtually always mean something more sinister.

Earlier, while the paramedics loaded Nicole into their van, I told them I would ride in the back and keep an eye on her. They readily agreed. Jackie argued that if anyone rode with her daughter, it should be her, but when I asked her exactly what she would do if Nicole had another seizure, she took a step back and reconsidered.

The ride to the hospital gave me a chance to ask Nicole about her medical history. Something she had refused until now. Turns out there was little to tell. She'd been healthy and athletic her entire life. No real family health problems either. She had done a brief stint in drug rehab, but she said she didn't really need it, just went to pacify her mother. Five years earlier, she had been tossed from the saddle by a rambunctious horse and apparently struck her head, losing consciousness for a couple of minutes. This little bit of his-

tory was important because one of the causes of adult seizures is a scar from previous head trauma. An MRI would
easily answer that question.

Now Jackie and Mark were out in the radiology department waiting room, both chatting on cell phones,
while I stood in the control room of the MRI lab. Nicole
lay on the exam table beyond the shielded wall and window, eyes wide, lips trembling, and a death grip on the
edge of the scanner table. The headphones that would
pipe in music during the procedure were clamped on her
head.

The technician started to press the button that would
slide Nicole into the doughnut of the MRI machine. I
reached out and touched his arm.

"Hold on just a sec," I said. "Let me have a minute with
her."

I pushed through the door that connected the control
room to the MRI lab. I lifted the headphones away. "You
okay?" I asked.

"Scared to death. What if I have some terrible brain disease? Or a tumor? What if I can't get married?"

"Take a deep breath and relax. Don't let your imagina-
tion run wild."

"Hard not to. After what happened. I mean, I wet my
pants. What's that all about?"

I smiled and took her hand. "That's not uncommon with
seizures."

She sighed. "It's embarrassing."

"Maybe. But I don't think that's what anyone will remember about what happened today."

"Is this going to hurt?"

"No. It'll be a little noisy, but you won't feel anything."

She nodded.

"I'll be right over there in the control room. Watching
everything that happens."

"Can't you stay in here with me?"

"This is a single-passenger vehicle."

She laughed. "I'm sorry for being such a ninny. I'm not usually this way."

"Probably not since the last time you wet your pants," I said.

She laughed again. "You're funny. Anybody ever tell you that?"

"As the great Samuel Johnson once said, a physician's job is to amuse the patient while nature makes her well."

Her face relaxed, as did her grip on the table's edge. "Let's get this over with."

I reseated the headphones and left the room. The technician went about his job and forty minutes later the MRI was complete. It would take a half hour for the radiologist to review all the images, so I went out to the waiting room and told Jackie and Mark that the test was complete and that Nicole was doing well. The tech and I then wheeled Nicole back to the emergency department. Her parents followed.

I then walked back to the radiology department and found Dr. Glenn Alford, the chief of radiology, studying the images. He turned and looked at me over half-glasses as I entered. Behind him the images of Nicole's MRI were displayed on tandem computer screens.

"Hank," he said. "Is this your patient?"

"I'm not sure."

He raised an eyebrow.

"Let's just say her parents and I don't see eye to eye." I nodded toward the images. "See anything?"

"Not yet but I'm just getting started. Pull up a stool."

MRI images have always fascinated me. They are a look inside the body like nothing else can provide. They show things that even a surgeon would never see. The clarity of the images exposes even the tiniest defects in organs such as the brain.

I spent the next twenty minutes going over each image with Glenn until he finally removed his glasses and placed them on the table beside him.

"This is about as healthy as a brain can be," he said. "At least structurally. I don't see anything. Definitely no tumors, scars, or evidence of infection."

"That helps a lot. Thanks."

"I'll dictate the formal report and it should be on her chart shortly."

By the time I returned to the emergency room, neurologist Dr. Martin Gresham was examining Nicole. Mark and Jackie stood against one wall and looked up as I came in.

"The MRI is normal," I said.

Dr. Gresham nodded. "As is her neurologic examination."

"What does that mean?" Jackie asked.

Gresham turned toward them. "It means that she doesn't have a tumor or infection or anything like that. Which means she could have some form of epilepsy or it could be some chemical abnormality."

Jill stepped into the room. She handed me a lab report. "All the labs aren't back yet, but this is all we have so far."

I scanned the results. They weren't surprising: low potassium and magnesium, elevated thyroid, and a digoxin level of 2.1. Not as high as in the others, but high enough. The drug screen hadn't yet been completed, but I knew it would show amphetamines.

I handed the sheet to Gresham and he, too, studied it. I saw his jaw tighten and his brow furrow. He gave me a quizzical look. "This doesn't make any sense."

"Actually it does," I said.

"What is it?" Nicole asked.

I walked over to her. "It's exactly what we saw in the other patients I told you about." I glanced up at Jackie and Mark. "Those pills you've been taking cranked up your thyroid, messed up your electrolytes, and did all the nasty things that I saw in that other young lady." I looked back down at Nicole. "You're very lucky."

Gresham looked at me. "Want to tell me what's going on?"

I did.

Gresham didn't hide his shock well. "You're telling me that this Morelli guy is handing out pills that contain all this?"

"Exactly. Julian Morelli is quite a salesman. Not much of a nutritionist but one hell of a salesman."

"Code blue. Rolling in the front door right now," I heard nurse Susan Foster say as she rushed by.

Chapter 42

I rushed from the cubicle as the paramedics blew through the front double doors and into the nearest of the two major treatment rooms. I caught a glimpse of a woman with dark hair.

Jill and I both hurried down the hall and into the treatment area. The woman was Amanda Brody. She was awake and moving her extremities but appeared to be disoriented and confused, eyes glazed. She didn't seem to recognize me.

"What happened?" I asked one of the medics.

"Collapsed at home," he said. "We found her unresponsive and in V-tach. She converted with a single shock. We gave her a hundred of lido. She was stable on the way over but just now jumped back into V-tach. BP is seventy palpable."

I looked at the portable monitor and saw that she was indeed in V-tach. Rate around 180.

"Let's shock her," I said.

Nurse Susan Foster began switching the EKG lead wires over to the wall monitor while another nurse pressed defibrillator monitor pads into place.

I shook Amanda's shoulder. "Amanda? Can you hear me?"

She didn't respond. Her blood pressure was too low to supply blood and oxygen to her brain.

"Three hundred watts?" Susan asked.

"That'll work," I said.

She spun the defibrillator dial to three hundred and pressed the charge button. The unit emitted a soft whine as it transferred current into its capacitor. She smeared electrode gel on the two paddles and rubbed them together. She glanced up at me as if to ask if I wanted to do the honors. I nodded for her to go ahead. She pressed the paddles to Amanda's chest.

"Clear," she said.

She discharged the defibrillator. The audible thump of the discharge was followed by a slight jerk and arcing of Amanda's body. She let out an audible moan. The monitor showed she was back in a normal and steady rhythm.

"Amanda?"

She looked up at me. "Hank? What happened?" Her wide-eyed gaze shifted right and left. "Where am I?"

"In the ER. Your heart was acting up. Right now it looks like we got it back to normal."

"What's going on here?"

I turned to see Andrew Weinberg, the ER doc.

"This is Amanda Brody," I said. "Episode of V-tach at home and another just now."

"And another." Weinberg nodded toward the monitor.

I turned. Amanda was back in V-tach.

Weinberg moved forward. She was his patient now, so I backed away and stood near the foot of the bed.

Over the next thirty minutes, Amanda received three more electrical shocks, two doses of lidocaine, intravenous potassium and magnesium, a chest X-ray, an EKG, and a boatload of lab work. Finally, her rhythm stabilized.

Susan Foster showed up with some of the lab work. "There's an epidemic of this stuff today. Her potassium and magnesium are low, thyroid levels over-the-top, and look at this." She handed me a lab slip.

Amanda's digoxin level was 6.4. Deadly high. Explained the arrhythmia. I handed the results to Weinberg. He read over them.

"This is like that other girl," he said. "Nicole Crompton."

"Both were taking the same weight-loss pills," I said.

"Which means she'll have amphetamines in the mix."

"I'd be surprised if she didn't."

"What do you think about giving her Fab fragments?" Weinberg asked.

"With a level that high, I think that's the right choice."

Besides all the nasty things that excess digitalis can do, things like nausea and vomiting and deadly cardiac arrhythmias, it's a bitch to get rid of. The body dumps it through the kidneys, but that takes days and Amanda would be in jeopardy as long as her digitalis level remained high. Fab fragments are digoxin-specific antibodies that immediately bind to and inactivate the drug.

By the time the Fab fragments were given, the drug screen returned. Amphetamines, type not yet known. That would take further testing. I already knew what those results would show. She would have the same ephedrine-like chemical that was found in the pills Julian had dispensed

While I was going over everything we had uncovered with Amanda and explaining to her just how lucky she was, Jill stuck her head in the cubicle.

"Her husband's here. Should I bring him back?"

I nodded.

She returned a minute later with Amanda's husband, Daniel. He rushed to her side.

"What happened?"

"You better ask Hank," Amanda said. "I don't remember much."

I walked him through everything that had happened and the results of Amanda's blood tests.

Daniel took it all in soberly, but I knew inside he was seething. Daniel had a temper. Daniel would not sit quietly and let something like this pass. Daniel was connected politically and had a portfolio thick enough to buy the hospital. Maybe three or four hospitals.

He kissed Amanda on the cheek. "I need to talk with Hank for a minute."

"Are you going to talk about me?"

"No. Julian Morelli."

Daniel, Jill, and I walked outside the cubicle. Daniel looked up and down the hallway. The emergency room was busy, nurses moving quickly from one treatment room to another, a lab tech carrying a basket of blood samples down the hall, a woman shouldering a red-faced, crying baby, patting its back, doing her best to comfort the infant, her own anxiety etched on her face.

"Is there somewhere we can talk?"

"My office," Jill said.

Once there, Jill sat behind her desk, I took a chair, and Daniel settled on the sofa along the left-hand wall.

"I just want to make sure I understand all of this correctly," Daniel said. "The pills my wife has been taking— the ones she got from Julian Morelli—might contain all these dangerous chemicals? Is that correct?"

I nodded.

"And there is absolutely no medical reason that she should be taking any of them?"

"Each of the drugs in those pills have medical uses," I said. "Except maybe the amphetamines. But Amanda didn't need any of them. The digitalis leaf? That's an old preparation that hasn't been used in this country for many decades. It is literally crushed-up leaves of the foxglove plant, which means it's impossible to accurately control the dose."

Daniel sighed and his jaw set. "This combination almost killed her?"

"About as close as you can get," I said. "She's lucky that your housekeeper saw her collapse. Had she been in the bathroom or alone in her bedroom or somewhere where no one would've seen her, she very easily could've died."

"And there are others? Not just Amanda?"

"Three that I know of. Other docs in the neighborhood might have seen some cases we don't know about."

"Who are these other people?"

"I can only tell you that Amanda's friend Rose was one. She stopped the pills a couple of days ago."

"She knew these things were toxic and she didn't tell Amanda?"

"That's not what happened. I saw another young lady who was taking these pills. She also came close to dying. Closer than Amanda, but that's splitting hairs. I had a talk with both Amanda and Rose because I knew they were taking supplements from Morelli. Rose agreed to stop, but Amanda was, shall we say, reluctant."

He shook his head. "Vanity. That's always been one of Amanda's problems. Don't get me wrong. I love her, but sometimes she can be trying. Always on some crazy diet or taking handfuls of God knows what from whatever health-food store is the go-to place. For that month anyway." He looked down at the floor, shaking his head slowly from side to side.

"Don't be too hard on her," I said. "Vanity is a common disease around here."

He looked up at me, his face tight. "I told her that these over-the-counter concoctions were dangerous, but she wouldn't listen to me."

"I bet she will now," Jill said.

"Is the hospital going to do anything about this guy?"

Jill glanced at me.

"Jill and I are trying to figure out what to do," I said. "We had the pills analyzed. On the sly. There is no doubt that they contain each of the drugs in question here. I've even visited the county medical society."

"And?"

"Didn't get very far. It seems that the president and Morelli are good friends."

He took a deep breath and let it out slowly, glancing toward the door, at the floor, and then back to me. "I know who can solve this."

"Who?" Jill asked.

"Dr. James Hawkins. The county medical examiner. Julian Morelli might have his friends, but I have mine, too. I've known Jim Hawkins for years."

Chapter 43

It's not everyone who can summon the county medical examiner with a simple phone call, but Daniel Brody wasn't just anyone. He made a phone call and forty-five minutes later Dr. James Hawkins appeared at Hamptons Heritage. Daniel, Jill, and I met him in the front lobby and then walked down to Jill's office.

Hawkins was younger than I expected. He looked to be no more than forty or so. His thick, tightly curled black hair clung to his scalp like a skullcap, and his blue-gray eyes were bright and inquisitive behind tortoise horn-rim glasses.

"Thanks for coming," I said.

"Daniel said you had a situation here that extended beyond Amanda. Something about toxic medications?"

I nodded. "I assume you know Julian Morelli?"

"Sure. Does this relate to him in some way?"

I glanced at Daniel.

"I didn't want to tell Jim too much," Daniel said, "since I'm not sure I understand the entire situation. I thought I'd let you tell the story."

"This started a few days ago. At least I stumbled on it a few days ago. A young lady, a teenager, high school track star, suffered a cardiac arrest. Right outside the emergency room here. She was resuscitated successfully. Her lab work showed markedly elevated thyroid and digitalis levels as well as very low potassium and magnesium levels. There was also an ephedrine-like amphetamine found. According to her father, and her, she had been taking some energy and weight-loss pills from Morelli."

Hawkins's eyes narrowed and his jaw tensed. "A dangerous combination."

"I knew that Amanda and her friend Rose Maher were also taking the same concoction. So I had their blood tested. Both showed a similar pattern, though not quite as dramatic." I glanced at Daniel. "Rose stopped the medication, but Amanda decided to continue it."

"And it damn near killed her," Daniel said.

"Jill and I collected some of the pills from the young girl and from Rose and Amanda and sent them to a lab for analysis."

"And?" Hawkins asked.

"Exactly what you'd expect. Furosemide, desiccated thyroid, digitalis leaf, and the amphetamine."

"Dig leaf?" Hawkins asked. The surprise on his face was evident. "I haven't seen that in years." He scratched an ear. "I've certainly never seen a combination like this."

"Me either. But it worked and that's why he has such a loyal following."

"There's a sucker born every minute," Hawkins said. He looked over at Daniel and gave an apologetic shrug. "Sorry."

"No apology necessary. Getting this clown off the street is."

"The digitalis and amphetamines kill the appetite," Hawkins said. "The thyroid and amphetamine rev up the metabolism and energy level." He shook his head. "If it wasn't so goddamn sinister, it would be clever." His brow furrowed as if a thought had suddenly popped up. "Where does he get these pills from?"

"We think he makes them at his clinic. StellarCare."

"Figures. Can't see any legitimate manufacturer putting this one together."

"So where do we go from here?" I asked.

"Do you still have all the blood samples you obtained?" Jill jumped in. "They're stored in the lab."

"I'll need to take them and some of the pills to my lab for retesting. See if we can duplicate your findings. Also, I need to talk with everyone concerned. The young lady you mentioned. Amanda and Rose."

"There's one more," I said.

Both Hawkins and Daniel looked at me.

"Nicole Crompton. The granddaughter of Ellie Wentworth. She suffered a seizure earlier today and has been taking the same drugs. Her blood showed similar results, just not quite as high as the others."

Hawkins nodded. "She here in the hospital?"

"Yes. Dr. Martin Gresham is evaluating her."

"I know Marty," Hawkins said. "I'll need to talk to him and to young Nicole."

"I'm heading upstairs to see her," I said. "If you want, I'll introduce you."

"I'll round up the blood samples and the pills we've collected," Jill said.

Hawkins stood. "Let's get to work."

Nicole was sitting up in bed, cushioned by several pillows. She seemed to have recovered well and was her usual beautiful self. Both her parents were there and Ellie had arrived. I introduced Dr. Hawkins to them.

"She's supposed to get married in a few days," Jackie said. "Then something like this happens."

"This isn't Nicole's fault," I said.

"I know that. But do you really believe those vitamins she was taking are responsible for what happened?"

"Of course they are," Ellie said. "Julian Morelli and his poisons are the problem."

"We can't prove that yet, but I believe Ellie's right," I said. "We're still waiting for Dr. Gresham to complete his evaluation, but it's likely that these so-called vitamins triggered Nicole's seizures. Even if it turns out that she has some other reason to have seizures, the amphetamines and the disturbances we found in her electrolytes could certainly precipitate what happened today."

"It's just hard for me to believe that some vitamins and herbs could do that," Jackie said. "I mean they're supposed to be natural ingredients."

"Natural isn't always good," I said. "Health-food stores and people like Julian Morelli have made millions from the word *natural*. It sounds so right, so natural, when in fact it means that it hasn't been tested or blessed by the FDA."

"They aren't exactly competent, from what I've read," Jackie said.

I smiled. "They do make mistakes, but what they mostly do is prevent things like this from being sold. They would never approve this combination of chemicals."

"Do you agree, Dr. Hawkins?" Mark asked.

"I do. From what Dr. Lawson has told me, these pills contain some very toxic substances and in a very odd combination. My lab will analyze them over the next couple of days. If what appears to be in them is indeed present, this could easily have triggered what happened to Nicole."

"I told you about the young girl who nearly died the other day," I said. "Another woman came to the ER today under very similar circumstances. She nearly died, too. She had the same blood abnormalities that we found in Nicole."

"So I think you can see why we have to get to the bottom of this," Hawkins said. "And we must do it quickly."

"I'm going to leave you with Dr. Hawkins," I said. "I'll come back by and see how you're doing tomorrow, Nicole."

I excused myself and left the room. Before I took too

many steps, someone grabbed my arm. I turned around. It was Jackie.

"I owe you an apology. I was wrong. I had no idea that Julian Morelli could be poisoning my daughter."

"I'm just glad everything worked out."

"Did it? We still don't know what caused her seizure. Whether it was these pills or not."

"But we do know that she doesn't have anything sinister like a brain tumor or an infection. Let's let Dr. Gresham finish his workup and see what we're dealing with. Then we'll know how to make Nicole better."

She nodded. "Thank you for everything."

That went well. Everybody was now on the same page. Jackie even trusted me. A little bit anyway. And now with the medical examiner involved, we could get to the bottom of Julian Morelli's entire scheme.

I was feeling happy and satisfied with myself until I walked into Jill's office.

"I'll sue your ass off. Just you wait and see."

It was Julian Morelli. He stood looking down at Jill across her desk, his fists balled at his sides.

"You violated my privacy," Julian said. His voice was high-pitched and strained. "My patients' privacy. You've damaged my reputation and slandered my name. You'll pay for that."

I rapped my knuckles on the doorframe. "Excuse me."

Julian whirled in my direction, his face a red mask of anger, his neck veins thick ropes. "You." He jabbed a finger at me. "You did this."

"Actually, Julian, you did it to yourself."

"Who the hell do you think you are? You go down to the medical society and trash my name. You have no right to do that."

"You have no right to poison people with your concoctions."

He took a step in my direction. I honestly thought he

was going to attack me. I set my feet to respond but inside prayed he would back off. He did. Sort of. After two steps he stopped and glared at me.

"I know about you. I know about you being fired. I'll make sure that you never practice medicine in the Hamptons again."

I noticed now that Jill had the phone to her ear. She said something that I couldn't understand and then hung up.

"Security is on the way," she said.

Now Julian turned back toward her. "You called security on me? You're the one that's causing the problems, not me. I'm just here to defend myself."

"You'll get your chance," I said. "In court."

When he turned his gaze back to me, it was cold and hard. "You're damn right I'll have my day in court. When I sue you back to the Stone Age."

"I assume you know Dr. James Hawkins?" I asked.

"The medical examiner? What does he have to do with this?"

I noticed his anger ebbed a bit, now edged with a hint of concern. He knew what was coming.

"He's upstairs talking with Nicole Crompton right now. Then he's going to talk with Amanda Brody, Rose Maher, and Valerie Gilroy. He's also going to analyze the blood obtained from all of these people as well as the pills you gave them. That's what he has to do with this."

I heard the door swing back open behind me. Two security guards came in.

"Ms. Casey?" one of them asked. "Is there a problem here?"

"I think you should escort Dr. Morelli out of the hospital."

As the two guards moved forward, Julian raised both hands and said, "Okay. I'm leaving." As he walked by me, he muttered, "You haven't heard the last of this."

Neither had he.

Chapter 44

"It's my fault," Ashley said. "I'm the one who hooked Nicole up with him."

"You were simply trying to help her," I said. "How could you know what Julian Morelli was up to?"

Ashley, Jill, Divya, and I were sitting at the patio table outside our place at Shadow Pond. I had a beer, everyone else wine. Earlier in the day, Boris had sent over two bottles of what appeared to be very expensive French wine. Dieter had delivered it to Evan while we were at the hospital. There was no note and no reason given, so I just figured it was Boris being Boris.

Evan had decided to barbecue and right now he stood in a cloud of smoke, finishing up the tri-tip he had marinated all afternoon. Nearby he had a bowl of shrimp that would soon join the beef on the grill.

"How could he do that?" Ashley asked. "Give us pills that were harmful?"

"Greed is a very powerful motivator," Divya said. "You've been to his clinic, haven't you?"

"Sure. Several times."

"I love those oxygen chambers," Evan said.

"Me, too," Ashley said. "They're my favorite thing there."

"I think we should buy one," Evan said. "We could put it in the spare room."

"That would be so cool," Ashley said.

"I wonder if they make them for two people?"

"Why?" I asked. "So you could blow up someone besides yourself?"

"A double chamber could be fun," Jill said.

I scooped up some guacamole on a chip and popped it in my mouth. Speaking around it, I said, "Don't encourage him."

She shrugged. "I'm just saying, it could be interesting."

"Back to my original question," I said to Ashley. "You've been to the clinic. What does it look like to you?"

"Amazing," Ashley said. "It's so big and modern. It looks like an exclusive dance club, or something like that."

"That's my point," I said. "Like it's geared more toward entertainment than health care. Style over substance doesn't fly well in medicine. Julian is more interested in appearances than he is in your health."

Ashley had a chip in her hand. She tapped it against her lower lip a couple of times before biting off a tiny corner. "I guess I see what you're saying."

"Most nutritionists work to improve their patients' dietary and exercise habits. And like Julian, most use supplements of some kind. Vitamins and minerals. Maybe potassium and magnesium in those who exercise and sweat a lot. But some, like Julian, step way out of bounds and do some crazy things."

"I still don't see how he could do this," Ashley said. "Wouldn't he know that something like this could happen?"

One would think so. Unfortunately what seems obvious to some people is not so clear to someone else, particularly when that someone else is profit driven.

"The problem is that he might not know the difference. He's not a medical doctor. He's a nutritionist. He might understand proteins and carbs and fats and things like that, but he has no real experience in medical treatment. You know the old adage that a little knowledge is a dangerous thing?" Ashley nodded. "That's part of what's going on here."

Ashley forked her fingers through her hair. "He always seemed so smart. I thought he knew everything."

"Maybe he does," I said. "Maybe he just doesn't care so long as the money keeps rolling in."

"That'd be my guess," Jill said. "I've had no medical training and I know that digitalis and thyroid and amphetamines are a dangerous mixture. I would think anyone would know that."

"Who's hungry?" Evan asked.

"Starving," Divya said. "I did six follow-up visits today and didn't have time for lunch."

Evan placed a platter in the center of the table. Two dozen perfectly charred shrimp surrounded a pile of thinly sliced tri-tip. He disappeared into the kitchen and returned with a bowl of potato salad and a plate piled with marinated green beans.

Everyone served themselves and then ate in silence for a while. I switched to wine and refilled everyone's glasses. That emptied the first bottle, so I opened the second one.

"What do you think will happen now?" Jill asked.

"I don't think it will go well for Julian," I said. "Once Dr. Hawkins completes his testing."

"Then what?" Ashley said. "Will Julian be arrested?"

"I wouldn't be surprised if he was charged with assault by poisoning. He'll need a good defense attorney to avoid jail."

Ashley swirled the wine in her glass and stared at it for a minute. "Is Nicole going to be all right? I mean like this didn't do any permanent harm, did it?"

"I think Nicole will be fine," I said. "I'll see her tomorrow and talk with Dr. Gresham. We'll see what he uncovers and then take care of it."

"If Jackie will let you," Ashley said.

"I think she's beginning to understand that we're only interested in Nicole doing well."

"But is she?"

I stopped my tri-tip-laden fork just short of my mouth and looked at her. "Why would you think that?"

"That didn't come out like I meant. Jackie loves Nicole. There's no doubt about that. She just has odd ways of showing it." She bit off a piece of shrimp. "I mean like she buys her everything, and gives her everything she wants. But sometimes it seems to me that she's like not very interested in Nicole. Does that make sense?"

"You mean she doesn't get involved in Nicole's activities?" Jill asked.

"She's definitely not interested in those kinds of things. The swim meets and volleyball tournaments and other sports stuff that Nicole did in high school. She and Mark like never showed up for anything. I know that hurt Nicole's feelings, but that's just the way they are."

"Some parents are too busy," Jill said.

Ashley munched on a green bean. "Maybe. But sporting and school events aren't what I meant. I think they don't respect Nicole. Like they don't listen to anything she says and her opinions mean very little." Her eyes glistened with moisture. "That's just not right. Parents should listen."

Yes, they should. As disturbing as what Ashley said sounded, that was exactly my impression. I didn't really know them and so couldn't make a reliable judgment, but one thing about practicing medicine is that you see people of all types. I had seen couples like the Cromptons before. Okay parents in that they provided the basic needs, but extremely self-centered and inattentive to their children's true needs. This dynamic could produce some really screwed-up teenagers. To me, Nicole seemed well grounded and firmly centered. Maybe my view of her was skewed by the things

I had heard from Ellie. No doubt the two had a special bond. I imagined that Nicole's stability mostly came from Ellie. Nicole was more like her than she was her own mother.

Some things skip a generation.

Chapter 45

The next morning, Divya and I made several house calls before we headed to the hospital. The first was to Ellie to make sure she was tolerating the stress of Nicole's illness and the continued wedding preparations.

"I'm doing fine," Ellie said. "I'm just worried about Nicole. Is she going to be okay?"

"She's going to be fine," I said. "We have a couple of stops to make and then we'll head over to the hospital to check on her."

"Robert drove in from the city last night. He's at the hospital now."

"I'll give you a call after I talk with Dr. Gresham."

Ellie walked over to the window and looked out. "We almost have everything finished for the wedding." She turned and looked at me. "If Nicole is able to attend her own wedding, that is."

"She will."

"Promise?"

"Promise what?" Jackie walked into the room.

"I was just asking Hank if Nicole will be able to show up for her wedding."

Jackie settled onto the sofa. "I went by early this morning. She was sitting up and eating breakfast. You couldn't even tell anything had happened."

"That's always a good sign," Divya said.

"To answer your question," I said, "yes, Nicole will be here. Even if I have to roll her down the aisle in a hospital bed."

Even Jackie laughed at that one and then said, "She would be mortified."

"But she would be in white," Divya said. "Though hospital white probably isn't what she had in mind."

We left Westwood Manor and swung by to see Oscar and Maria Mendez. Oscar was back to earth. His brand of the earth anyway. Maria seemed comfortable with the move to assisted living, almost as if she were looking forward to it.

I knew that Maria had shouldered the responsibility of caring for Oscar and their home for many years. That weight can wear you down over time, and though Maria had marched on like a good soldier, the time had come for her to lighten her load. She had apparently reconciled herself to that fact.

Our last house call was to Nathan Zimmer. He and Todd were on the back patio, each with a laptop, each with a cell phone jammed to one ear. Once Nathan finished his call, he dropped the phone on the tabletop and looked up.

"Did you come by to check on me? To make sure I wasn't smoking?"

"Absolutely," I said.

Nathan laughed. "I feel great. I haven't touched a cigarette. I've been taking my medicines religiously. I've even been going to bed early."

Todd closed his phone and dropped it in his pocket. "That's all true. He's been a very good patient. Believe it or not."

"Remember," Divya said, "not smoking is forever."

"Forever forever?" Nathan asked.

Divya laughed. "Forever and ever."

Nathan's phone buzzed. He answered.

Back to work.

We said our good-byes. Nathan waved as we left.

A half hour later we walked into Nicole's room. She was lying in bed, watching TV. Robert reclined in the chair next to her, reading a book. One of the *Monk* series by Lee Goldberg.

"Dr. Lawson, Divya," Robert said as he closed the book, laid it on the bedside table, and stood.

"Ellie told us that you had driven out last night," I said.

He reached over and took Nicole's hand. "As soon as I heard what happened."

"What did happen?" Nicole asked. "I had more tests last night, but I haven't heard the results yet. They put all those wires and glue stuff in my hair. Took me half an hour to wash it out this morning."

"An EEG," Divya said. "That's short for an electroencephalograph. It measures the brain's electrical activity."

"I'll be surprised if it finds any," Nicole said. "Only someone brain-dead would fall for Julian Morelli's BS."

I laughed. "Don't be so hard on yourself. He's a slick salesman."

"What's going to happen to him?"

"They should shoot him," Robert said.

"I doubt they will do that," Divya said. "The medical examiner is involved, so I don't think things will go well for him."

I heard the door behind me open and turned to see Dr. Martin Gresham come in. He had a smile on his face.

"Here's your doctor now," I said.

"I've got good news." Gresham walked to the bedside. "We have a diagnosis."

"What's wrong with me?" Nicole asked.

"Don't panic when I tell you this, because it's not as bad as it sounds."

Nicole glanced at Robert. He squeezed her hand. She

looked back at Gresham and said, "You're not making me any calmer."

He smiled down at her and patted her shoulder. "You have a form of epilepsy. It's the type we call temporal lobe epilepsy."

I saw Robert's eyes widen; Nicole's followed suit.

"It's a seizure disorder involving one of the smaller lobes of the brain," Gresham said. "It's not common, but it's easily treated in most cases."

"So I'll have to take medications for it?" Nicole asked.

"I'm afraid so. But they will keep the seizures under control."

"For how long?"

"Maybe forever. There's ongoing research into various surgical procedures and even brain pacemakers to correct this problem. But for now, the answer is medications."

"That doesn't sound very exciting."

Gresham nodded. "I know that at your young age the need to take medicines for the rest of your life seems daunting. But you'll get used to it. It'll just become part of your daily routine."

"What about my wedding this weekend? Will I be able to go?"

"I don't see any reason why not. I'll start you on the medication today, and if you're doing fine tomorrow morning, I'll let you get out of here." His beeper buzzed. He glanced at it and then said, "I'm afraid I have to run down to surgery." He glanced at me. "They're doing a mapping procedure on one of my patients and I need to be there." He then said to Nicole, "I'll come by this evening and we'll talk more." He left.

"Medicine for the rest of my life?" Nicole shook her head. "Why does this have to happen to me? And why now?"

I walked around to the left side of her bed. "Because you're lucky." I smiled. "Diabetics give themselves injections every day. At least yours are pills."

"Oh lucky me."

"Many people your age deal with much worse problems and they go on like nothing's wrong," Divya said. "You will, too."

"What is this thing that I have? It sounds awful."

I grabbed an empty chair from the corner, scooted up next to her bed, and sat down. I could see the fear in her face, her eyes more black than blue. She asked Robert for a tissue. He pulled one from the box on the bedside table and handed it to her. She dabbed her eyes.

"A seizure is where the electrical activity in the brain goes all haywire," I said. "It's like one of those plasma globes. You know how when you touch a finger to the glass and those electrical pulses dance all around?"

She nodded. "Robert has one on his desk in his office."

"That's what happens in the brain during a seizure. The electricity gets all wild and crazy. In a generalized seizure, like you had the other night, this happens all over the brain. Everything malfunctions. That's why you passed out. That's why you had those jerking motions. That's why you lost control of your bladder."

"Is that going to happen again?"

"Not once you get on the right medicines."

"That's a relief. That was embarrassing."

"The type of seizure you had we call grand mal because it involves the entire brain. Other seizures are localized and only affect part of the brain. A seizure that occurs in the area that controls the left arm will make it jerk while the rest of the body remains normal. The person usually doesn't pass out or any of the other things."

She rolled her eyes. "Like wetting your pants." She looked at Robert. "I'm glad you weren't there."

"I can handle it."

She smiled and squeezed his hand.

"Do you understand what I've said so far?" I asked.

"I think so. The brain can have a seizure in just one part or it can involve the entire brain. And whatever part of the brain acts up will determine what happens to the body. Is that right?"

"I couldn't've said it better. Sometimes a local seizure can spread across the brain and become a generalized seizure. That's what happened to you."

"Sort of breaks containment?" Robert asked.

"Exactly," Divya said.

"The temporal lobe seizures you have are a special type of localized seizure."

"I knew you were special," Robert said.

"Maybe special needs," Nicole laughed.

"The temporal lobes lie on either side of the brain just above and behind the ears. About here." I touched the side of her head. "These areas don't move arms or legs or any other part of the body, so a seizure in these areas doesn't cause any abnormal movements. Instead the temporal lobes control emotions, memories, and certain feelings. A seizure in this area can make you feel happy, or sad, or giddy. You might have a déjà vu or an out-of-body experience. Alterations in taste or sound or one of the other senses can occur. They can also trigger fugue states. That's what's been happening to you."

"I thought a fugue was a type of music?" Robert said.

"It is," Divya said. "This is a little different."

"When someone has a fugue episode, their personality changes," I said. "They become someone else. Might not know who they are or recognize people they know. They appear completely normal but often do things that they wouldn't normally do and not remember any of it. It's as if those few minutes or few hours of their life isn't recorded on their brain's hard drive."

"That's exactly how I felt every time one of these happened."

"It can be scary," I said.

"Tell me about it," Nicole said. "One time I apparently walked out in the middle of a seminar. This was a year or so ago. I remember sitting in the conference room but not leaving. The next thing I knew, I was on the subway down in the financial district." She shook her head. "Totally freaked me out."

"That's what happened the other night," Divya said. "When you left the restaurant and we had to come find you."

"What?" Robert asked. "You didn't tell me about that."

"I will. Later."

"So that's basically what the problem is," I said. "With proper medication, the seizures will stop, and these episodes will disappear."

Nicole dropped her head back against the pillow and looked up at the ceiling. I could see the tears welling in her eyes. "I'm such a freak."

Robert bent over and kissed her cheek. "But you're my freak."

She laughed and threw one arm around him, pulling him down until their cheeks were mashed together. "I love you so much."

"You're not a freak," I said. "This type of seizure is not common, but it's not rare either. In many cases it probably goes unrecognized."

"So there are other freaks like me," Nicole said. She laughed as she dabbed tears from her eyes again.

"You're in good company. You know who Agatha Christie was, don't you?"

"Sure. I read her books when I was in high school."

"I don't know whether she had this form of epilepsy or not, but she did apparently have fugue states. I remember reading that she once disappeared for eleven days before showing up at a hotel. She had no memory of what had happened."

"Eleven days? That makes my few hours here and there seem small."

"That's the attitude I want you to take. This is simply an aggravation and not something that will alter your life unless you let it. Take your medicines and everything will be okay."

"I won't be Jekyll and Hyde anymore?"

"Wouldn't it be more like Jacqueline and Heidi?" I asked.

Nicole laughed. "I don't want to be them either."

Chapter 46

The Suffolk County medical examiner's office sat just north of I-495 in Smithtown, a nine iron from the medical society's office. It was just after noon when Divya, Jill, and I were ushered into Dr. James Hawkins's office by his secretary. He had called earlier and asked if we would come by.

After we were seated, he handed me a piece of paper. Lab results on his testing of the pills Julian Morelli had been spreading around the county.

"Ms. Casey, our lab confirmed everything your lab found. An ephedrine-like amphetamine, furosemide, desiccated thyroid, and digitalis leaf."

"That's a relief," Jill said. "Last night I tossed and turned, worrying that the lab might be wrong."

Jill stayed over last night. I didn't remember her tossing and turning. I gave her a look. She got it. Fought the smile I saw nipping at the corner of her mouth.

"You've got nothing to worry about on that front," Hawkins said.

"Morelli threatened to file a lawsuit," Jill said. "This might change his mind."

"We'll get to Dr. Morelli in a minute." Hawkins settled his glasses in place and shuffled through some papers until he found the one he was looking for. "We also repeated the

blood tests you had done. Again confirming your findings."
He handed me the lab report.

I looked it over before passing it to Divya. "This looks
like strong evidence. Is it enough?"

Hawkins nodded. "More than enough. These findings
suggest we have a true public health issue here." He slipped
off his glasses and pinched the bridge of his nose for a second. "I spoke with Bernard Bernstein a little while ago.
President of the county medical society."

"I bet that went well," I said.

He gave me a quizzical look.

"Before you got involved," I said, "I brought this up
with Dr. Bernstein. I thought he might help, but he wasn't
very receptive. I know that he and Julian Morelli are
friends."

Hawkins nodded and a slight smile appeared. "Maybe
not anymore."

"Really?" Jill asked.

"He started down that path with me, too. Until I presented him with all the evidence you've just seen. He back-
pedaled."

"So he's jumping off the Julian Morelli bandwagon?" I
asked.

"He didn't really have much choice."

"What's your next step?"

"A warrant for Morelli's arrest was signed an hour ago.
A search warrant and a cease-and-desist order for Stellar-
Care, too. The police should be making the arrest and shut-
ting the place down about now."

"That quickly," Divya asked. "I'm impressed."

"This is a public health issue," Hawkins said. "We don't
know how many people out there are taking these drugs.
Once we dig through StellarCare's records, we can identify
and warn them."

I wondered exactly how many people Julian had given
these little poison packets to. Twenty? A hundred? Several
hundred? The worst-case scenario was frightening.

"We've sent the word out," Jill said. "We passed along the information we had to every emergency room on Long Island. Gave them a heads-up on our findings so they will do the proper testing if any similar patients show up in their facilities."

"Excellent," Hawkins said. "Forewarned is forearmed."

Evan lay inside the oxygen chamber, eyes closed, listening to the piped-in music. Cindy had put him in there just five minutes earlier and already he felt both relaxed and energized. He wondered if he was becoming addicted to oxygen. Could that happen? Was there an Oxygen Anonymous?

He remembered reading somewhere about oxygen bars being big on the West Coast a few years earlier. At the time, he had thought it was silly. Something that could happen only in California. Why would anyone pay to sit in a bar and breathe oxygen? To him it was like paying for gourmet water. Water is water. Oxygen is oxygen. There's plenty of both free for the taking.

He still didn't understand the water part, but paying for oxygen made perfect sense now. He wondered what the home version of one of these would cost.

The cushion was soft, the music soothing, and the oxygen-rich air cool against his face. He felt as if he were floating on air and didn't realize that he had dozed off. Until a sharp knock on the side of the cylinder yanked him awake.

Cindy's face appeared in the window above him. Behind her was another face. A stern face. One that didn't look happy. When Cindy cracked open the chamber and lifted the lid, he saw that the other face belonged to a uniformed police officer.

Evan rolled out of the chamber and stood. "Evan R. Lawson. CFO of HankMed." He extended his hand toward the officer.

The officer, whose name tag indicated he was Paul Mc-Clusky, stared at him blankly, saying nothing.

"What's the matter?" Evan asked.

"We're shutting the place down," McClusky said. "You'll have to vacate the premises immediately."

"Am I in trouble? Is it illegal to buy oxygen?"

Cindy laughed. "Come on." She grabbed his arm and begin pulling him toward the door. "Let's get out of here. They're locking everything down."

"Does this have to do with those pills Julian has been handing out?"

"I don't know," Cindy said. She looked at McClusky. "Is that what's going on?"

"All I know is that this place is shut down. Gather all your personal belongings and clear the building. There'll be officers outside who'll ask you some questions and get your contact information."

As Evan and Cindy descended the steps into the parking lot, a handcuffed Julian Morelli climbed into the backseat of a patrol car. Morelli, face chiseled stone, lips tight, glared at Evan.

"Wow," Cindy said. "This isn't what I expected when I came to work today." She sighed. "Guess I'll have to find another job."

"Make it one where they have those cool oxygen chambers."

"For sure."

"And maybe those way cool windows."

"Absolutely," Cindy said. "Don't you just love those?"

Chapter 47

As weddings go, Nicole's was over-the-top. Three hundred people, most with eight- or nine-figure net worths, filled a portion of the garden, facing the white-lattice gazebo, now draped with flowers of virtually every color. A string quartet provided the music. Once the guests were ushered into place, the quartet fell into Mendelssohn's "Wedding March."

Divya, Jill, and I sat near the back along the aisle, Evan and Paige in the row in front of us. Paige had flown back from California the day before. Said she couldn't miss the wedding. Evan said it was him she couldn't miss. My brother. Mr. Humility.

Nicole entered through an arch of flowers, one arm hooked around her father's elbow. She looked stunning. A magazine cover. Her ivory silk and lace gown trailed behind as she walked down the gold-carpeted aisle Ellie had had constructed. Her blond hair, pulled back into some kind of twist except for the tendrils that framed her beaming face, reflected the late-afternoon sun.

The gathering shifted in their seats as one and watched as she glided past. I didn't see a dry eye.

Ahead, in the gazebo, Robert adopted the nervous stance of every groom I had ever seen. Face fixed in an expression just short of panic, shoulders erect, and hands clasped in front of his crotch, as if protecting himself. He looked like a tux-clad statue. I wasn't even sure he was breathing.

At the end of the aisle, Nicole and Mark climbed the three steps to the gazebo. Mark kissed her cheek and descended to his front-row seat between Jackie and Ellie. Nicole and Robert faced the preacher.

The ceremony was short. Robert and Nicole each recited vows they had written themselves. After the pronouncement and the obligatory kiss, they walked back up the aisle while the crowd clapped and cheered.

The receiving line was followed by the cutting of the cakes, one a four-tiered wedding cake and the other a two-layered chocolate groom's cake. Champagne was plentiful.

After fulfilling those duties, the newlyweds disappeared upstairs to change for the party. They returned twenty minutes later. Robert wore a navy blue suit and white shirt, no tie. Nicole wore the pewter silk dress she had modeled on the day of her seizure. That seemed months ago, not just a few days. Her hair was now down and she looked stunning. As usual.

Jill and I stood with Ellie near one end of the patio, sipping champagne and enjoying the sunset. It was spectacular, as if Ellie had ordered it up just for the occasion. She probably had. I believed there was nothing she couldn't do.

"Isn't this wonderful?" Ellie asked. "Look at all these young people having fun."

The string quartet had moved inside and now a four-piece band occupied the gazebo. The newly constructed dance floor was filled. The young and wealthy were in party mode. Evan and Paige, too. They had staked out a spot in the middle of the crowd, dancing, Evan's arm around her waist, her hand on his shoulder, head back, laughing, probably at something Evan had said. My brother the charmer.

"Ellie, you might have outdone yourself this time," Jill said.

"Oh, it was nothing. Just a matter of sending out a few invitations and calling the caterers." She laughed.

"If that's all there was to it," I said, "anybody could throw a party. But this"—I waved a hand over the dance floor below—"only you could've done."

"You're just saying that."

"I'm saying it because it's true." I raised my glass of champagne in salute. "Congratulations."

Someone tapped my shoulder and I turned to see Nicole and Robert standing there.

"Here's the beautiful bride now," I said. "It was a lovely wedding."

"All because of Grandma," Nicole said. "She always makes these things look so easy."

Ellie actually blushed. Not something I'd seen before.

Nicole touched my arm. "Can we talk with you for a minute?"

"Is something wrong?"

She laughed. "No. Everything's fine."

I followed Nicole and Robert across the patio to a quiet corner. They stood, arms interlocked, the setting sun glowing off Nicole's perfect face.

"What is it?" I asked.

"We wanted to thank you. We didn't want to do it in front of anybody and cause you any embarrassment."

"You don't need to thank me."

"Yes, we do." Robert slid his arm around Nicole and pulled her tightly against him. "This day might not have happened without you. I might have lost her."

I couldn't think of anything clever to say, so I said nothing.

"You were a bulldog," Nicole said. "When no one would listen to you. Not me. Not my mother or father. Not anyone."

"Ellie did. She knew something was wrong."

Nicole glanced across the patio toward her grandmother. She smiled as tears welled in her eyes. "She is so special."

"Yes, she is," I said. "So are you."

"You won't get an argument here," Robert said.

"I understand you're going to Bermuda for your honeymoon?" I said. "When do you leave?"

"We're going to spend the night here. At the mansion. Then tomorrow we fly to the island."

"I'm happy for both of you."

A waiter appeared with a tray of champagne flutes. We each exchanged the ones we held for fresh ones.

Nicole waved at someone down on the dance floor and then said to me, "We just wanted to thank you for everything you did."

"As I said, no thanks are necessary. Go and mingle with your friends. And have a great honeymoon."

Nicole and Robert descended the steps and melted into the crowd. As I walked back across the patio toward where Jill and Ellie stood, Sam appeared through the window, motioning me toward him. I opened the door and stepped inside. "What is it?"

"I'm afraid something's happened, sir."

Why was I not surprised?

But Sam's wide, beaming smile gave me pause. For once, I suspected, all was as it should be.

Chapter 48

Two weeks later, on Saturday afternoon, I took a long, relaxing run on the beach. I then swung by The Bagel Shack and had a bagel and a cup of strong coffee before heading back to Shadow Pond to work on some charts with Divya.

When I came up the long drive I saw Divya leaning against the back of her SUV in the parking area. She wasn't alone. Evan, Paige, Jill, and Rachel Fleming were there. So was a gleaming black van. I parked and climbed out of my Saab.

"What's going on?" I asked.

Evan opened his arms wide. "The new HankMed Healthmobile. It's got everything. Portable X-ray, echocardiogram, EKG, and a huge plasma-screen TV."

"I thought I told you that we couldn't afford this."

"You don't have to," Evan said. "It's free."

Rachel laughed. "Not exactly free, but close."

"How close?"

"Evan worked out a barter situation with my dad."

"He did?" This was going to be good.

"We do all their employee physicals and health care and they let us use the van," Evan said.

"And after five years, you'll own it," Rachel said.

"That's it? We take care of your crew and you'll give us this van?"

"Thanks to Evan."

My brother the negotiator.

"I'm impressed."

Evan beamed.

"Wait until you see what's in this thing," Evan said.

"Show me."